FAITH

FAITH

Robert De Cristo fano

iUniverse, Inc.
New York Lincoln Shanghai

FAITH

iUniverse books may be ordered through booksellers or by contacting:

iUniverse
2021 Pine Lake Road, Suite 100
Lincoln, NE 68512
www.iuniverse.com
1-800-Authors (1-800-288-4677)

ISBN-13: 978-0-595-33785-9 (pbk)
ISBN-13: 978-0-595-67008-6 (cloth)
ISBN-13: 978-0-595-78576-6 (ebk)
ISBN-10: 0-595-33785-6 (pbk)
ISBN-10: 0-595-67008-3 (cloth)
ISBN-10: 0-595-78576-X (ebk)

Printed in the United States of America

This novel is dedicated to my family and friends:

To my late father Elviro,

My mother Cesarina Masucci De Cristofano,

and to Teresa and Frank, Anna and Anthony, Gina and Larry, and to the next generation, Rina-ann, Frank, Anthony, Jennifer, Lauren, Ashley, Taylor and Skyler...

There are so many people who have touched my life in many special and incredible ways, and I am forever grateful to all of you.

I especially thank God and His entire family for...everything.

CHAPTER 1

"You promised me forever, once," she whispered.

"Forever," he replied.

At that very moment the fading evening Sun disappeared into the darkness of gray surrounding it, quickly, like a tossed pebble disappears into a deep ocean. A fierce wind swept down from the heavens, and it was unforgiving. Sheets of cold rain pounded the Earth with an unrelenting force, and everyone scattered in search of shelter. Centuries earlier learned men would have speculated that the gods themselves were angry had they witnessed such a hurricane of sheer force so brutal as this. Nature's wrath was upon the city, and it was terrifying. Strangers lurked behind their windows in the apartments nearby, mesmerized by the scene unfolding before them. In an instant nature had transformed the beauty of a day into the savagery of the night.

Two people, a man and a woman, could barely be seen running hand in hand across the soaked pavement toward a nearby urban church. Its rooftop crucifix was radiant amidst the shadows of the dark clouds, as if the Sun itself lay hidden within it. Its luminance seemed to beckon these two strangers—now alone on the cold, wet streets—before it. Its radiance seemed to forge a path for these two lives to follow, a path that would forever change the course of events for so many on this stormy late afternoon, a storm no one had forecast but everyone would remember.

The couple fought to climb the stairs to the church and struggled to open the front door against the howling wind. Once inside, dripping wet and panting for air, they quickly sat in a pew near the rear, relieved to be safe and out of the storm. A Christian service was underway when they entered, but everyone present seemed drawn to turn around and stare at these two young, wet, uninvited strangers. Even the minister atop the altar stopped and smiled at them, a smile of recognition, as if they were old friends, and he was welcoming them back home, as if they were the answers to his prayers; but they were only strangers seeking shelter from a storm, total strangers to them all.

Beautiful faces of every urban color faced these two for a few moments of sheer curiosity, before they all seemed to turn again in union to face their preacher. Every age group was present, and all seemed mesmerized by the tall figure before them upon the altar. The reverend was a strikingly tall figure dressed in elaborate robes; his dark skin and short curled black hair framed a rather large but warm and inviting face, which glistened with sweat in the reflected light. The wrinkles upon his brow, and surrounding his smiling lips, revealed his age but his sympathetic eyes were as innocent as a child's. Lit candles were aglow on the altar surrounding him, such a peaceful sight in the midst of such a menacing storm. His deep but earnest voice broke the silence created by the entrance of the man and the woman.

"After the gospel," he began, "My good brothers and sisters, sons and daughters, is a good time for reflection. A time," he paused, before continuing in a full and bellowing voice, "to recognize what the gospel is saying to us all today. It is a time for man to interpret the words of God and to make them his own, for the words of the gospel are often not heard; they are often forgotten, ignored, and distorted. Words read for centuries, now taken for granted."

The congregation applauded, interrupting their preacher, whose face beamed forth a happiness not seen by them in months.

"The words of the gospel," he continued in a commanding voice, "are like the rain outside. For some of us it falls upon the concrete and flows quickly into the sewers, for others it falls upon clay and sand and most of it washes away, but we must all struggle to be the fertile soil where the rain of the gospel gives life to the word and nourishes us. Sadly, the worst of these possibilities I have not yet mentioned. You see, the rain—like the gospel—is good. Without it, life as we know it would no longer exist, but when used for evil, when the very words of God and His prophets are distorted, this very rain can destroy everything and everyone in its path. From good can emerge the worst evil. We must all pray for guidance and for peace."

"Hallelujah!" the congregation chanted as they rose to their feet, some with eyes moist with fear and understanding.

The minister searched the congregation before him for the one he had been dreaming about, for the one that would touch men's souls with his words like so few before him. He searched throughout this small, rundown, urban church's faithful this day, a hundred or so present in a city of millions, for the one he would choose to deliver the homily, for the one he was waiting for. These hundred or so faithful before him sat in alternating worry and wonder, fearing one of them would be picked, and fail miserably, as had happened many times before. Unbeknownst to them, this minister was searching about the congregation for one very special person this time, one he knew to be present, *finally*, he thought. Their dress had a certain splendor this evening—more, it seemed, than most. The crucifix behind the altar seemed to cast a larger shadow. No one seemed to notice the rain pelting at the windows. An eerie silence ensued despite the outside chaos, a deafening calm.

The minister began again to speak in a loud voice calling out to only one of them not yet chosen. You could hear the anticipation in his voice. "He is here tonight, you see, but for the grace of God almighty, to speak to all of us here present about the words of today's gospel. He is a stranger amongst us who holds within his heart some of God's glory."

The congregation had heard similar words before but never so eloquent and so direct and so forthright, and never before with such conviction. Something was indeed different tonight amidst the raging storm. The minister's tone expressed a renewed hope not heard in a long while.

With that the reverend pointed toward and beckoned to a young man seated at the very rear of the church, a young man who only moments earlier had entered. He sat there unaware, holding hands with a young woman beside him, both still wet from the storm.

"Young man, in the rear, come up and speak," the reverend called out gesturing toward him with his hands. Everyone turned their heads toward him, young and old, in anticipation and relief. In the very last row he sat so pale, and so apparently unaware still of his appointment. He sat there in wet clothes, which appeared worn and common. One could see that he was newly a man, just older than a boy. He was so totally unaware that he was the object of this search. He had no idea that he was chosen.

"It is you," his beautiful companion was finally able to utter to him.

"What?" he quickly acknowledged, as he gazed toward her.

"He is calling out to you, Gian," she continued. "He is talking to you." This young woman at his side began to encourage him to go forth. Her body thin, her face pale, her large eyes were a hue of blue and green and brown, her chestnut hair glistened from the rain, which had washed it. She was indeed his friend for everyone could feel the concern in her voice, and could sense the fear in her eyes as she encouraged him to stand up in the pew. In a glance he appeared rather tall, almost majestic, and in another weak and frail. A mane of black hair wet from the storm shone as he searched about the church in wonder, before he finally seemed to understand what was being asked of him.

The young woman at his side was average in height, clothed in faded jeans and a top with a small leather jacket. The young man wore a long sleeved t-shirt, a deeper shade of blue than his eyes and dark blue jeans.

"Come on, Gian, we will both go up there, okay? I'll go with you," her face now aglow with the beauty of her youth, the innocence of early life.

"Come up, my young man, and bring your companion," the minister again beckoned from the altar. Apparently, sensing the stranger's anxiety, he called out again in a friendlier tone, "I have chosen you to speak to us today. Come up as we welcome you into our religious family. Come up, do not be afraid, for we are all children of God; we are all a reflection of His love."

Slowly, these two emerged from their pew at the rear of the church into the center aisle leading to the altar. The faces of the congregation were focused upon them, most encouraging, friendly and smiling. Some were bewildered by their reluctance, dismayed by their appearance, and a few angry at these two who were chosen before them, two wet, obviously frightened novices approaching the altar like two calves to slaughter. The young woman seemed to carry the courage for the both of them. Without her support, the young man probably would not have been able to make the short journey to the altar, his face pale, perspired and anxious. As they approached the altar, the sounds of the storm outside intensified. The minister quickly rushed up to greet the couple and at the moment that his extended hand grasped hold of the hand of his chosen speaker, the lights of the church began to flicker on and off for a few moments, as the congregation gasped almost in unison behind them. Once atop the altar these three faced the religious before them, and the lights steadied almost on cue.

"My brother and sister in God, welcome to our small house of worship. My name is Reverend Martin. Please everyone, now stand and welcome our new friends." With that, the entire congregation stood and politely applauded for a few moments.

The young woman, sensing that her role had changed, sat in a chair near both men standing on the altar, close enough to encourage and support her friend if the need arose.

"Do not be afraid, young man, for you have been chosen by God to be here amongst us today. You have been chosen to speak to us about the subject of today's gospel, the Holy Spirit. The gospel revealed to us all today another glorious manifestation of our God, that of the wondrous Holy Spirit. Please, my dear brother, please share with us all tonight what the Holy Spirit means to you and to us all, here gathered in His name, in His honor."

The reverend paused awaiting a response from his chosen speaker. At first there was none. "Do not be afraid to speak, for God will guide you," the minister repeated.

"I do not know where to begin, or what to say," a weak voice uttered in response barely audible above the screams of the wind outside.

The congregation before them seemed to grow impatient as their collective mutterings and movements increased. Their minister had indeed attempted this before, and each and every time it had ended in failure, utter failure. They all sensed failure again as the intensity of the rain outside increased around them.

"You will find the words, my son. God is with you. I can sense it," the still-believing minister spoke before departing for his elaborate chair atop the altar. Once seated, he again reiterated, "You know the words, my son."

A terrified young man now stood alone upon the altar, a microphone nearby awaiting his spoken words, but he remained silent. This rather tall figure of a man searched the faces of the faithful before him. His nervous eyes finally met those of his trusted friend seated to his right, and there he found the encouragement and the strength and the love that he needed to continue. His entire demeanor seemed to change as he positioned himself closer to the microphone and slowly turned to face the religious, seated there in front of him.

"The Holy Spirit is light!" he proclaimed to those in attendance before pausing again for a period of time to collect his thoughts, but to those before him it seemed like hours. The minister himself appeared anxious as beads of perspiration appeared on his brow. His church's attendance had dwindled in number every week, and failure seemed imminent. His belief in this man and in some inherent gift that he might possess did allow, though, for some hope to remain alive within him.

"The Holy Spirit is light!" this young man continued as the crowd before him hushed and his eyes met theirs with a renewed conviction. "It is a light like no other, so brilliant that it defies description, so warm that it embraces our souls with love." He paused again as he searched the crowd before him, hoping that he could fill them with his passion, his longing for the real truth. He hoped that they could sense his transformation, for indeed one had taken place and he could not explain it.

"Everyone here today knows what it feels like to be left in the darkness, even the children amongst us. Think about the days when the clouds seem to stretch out forever, when the darkness surrounds us and we feel lost and confused, alone and abandoned. There is a darkness in our very souls at times. For some it rarely leaves, a sadness, a longing, a sorrow, a pain deep within us. For some of us, this darkness is filled with the nightmares of our existence, the neglect, the abuse, the prejudice, and the hate, the overwhelming sorrow of the loss of a loved one somewhere in the darkness. For others it is guilt, the unrelenting guilt of a wrongdoing that has inflicted pain upon everyone we love. Could I have made a difference to my friend or to my child or to my brother or sister so that they would not have taken their own lives? Why would I hurt the ones who love me? If only I could go back to that night when I drank too much and drove, killing the innocent and whatever hope I had for peace during my life-time. If only I had held my child's hand that day before she disappeared."

As Gian gazed into each of the congregants' individual faces before him, he seemed to connect with them on another plane of truth, and most were stunned. Some seemed to look away, and others cried.

"If only my daddy would stop hurting me. If only my mommy would stop using drugs. If only my son had not run away, just maybe he wouldn't be in jail today. If only he had left me alone when I was too young to fight back. You see, my brothers and sisters, we are all living in a time of darkness. We are all tired and confused, angry and upset, lost and abandoned."

The speaker paused and total silence ensued, as all were enthralled by the words of a stranger amongst them, a stranger who could read their hearts and touch their souls.

"In the dark we are all children who have lost our way. In the dark lives prej-udice and pain, jealousy and anger, resentment and rage. In the darkness mur-der is committed and wars are fought, and sometimes the innocent are slaughtered in the name of God. In the darkness our very children are dying of starvation, of neglect, of abuse, and of violence. In this darkness we cannot see our neighbors; we do not see our friends. All hope is lost, all trust forgotten, all good is evil, and all that was love is buried so deep that most can no longer find it, recognize it, or accept it. And then, suddenly came light."

This young man paused before those now filled with his passion, and dur-ing this time all eyes remained focused on this stranger before them, this stranger whose words seemed to touch each one of them.

"The apostles felt it so many years ago on that glorious day. Many who have passed and returned have seen it, felt it, and most cannot describe it for this light of God is more powerful than all evil, more brilliant than our Sun. It is more forgiving, more compassionate, more loving than anyone of us could imagine it to be. It is a light that the very young sleep in, a light that so many of us have forgotten." The young speaker paused again as he closed his eyes before continuing in a quieter tone. "It is time for all of us gathered here today to experience just a fraction of the glory of this incredible power of the light of hope and of love and of salvation."

A quiet pause ensued.

"All of us must now join hands with those around you. We must all be connected as we unite as one, together as one family of God, for together we are more powerful in the eyes of our Father. Come, we all must join hands."

This young man beckoned the good reverend and his female companion to join him on the altar, and he held each of their hands, and others present came forward to create a circle of one family in God.

"Close your eyes and begin to sense its presence, begin to feel its warmth," he continued, as everyone present appeared to obey. "Travel with me in search of true life." A silence ensued as each participant stood with clasped hands, joined in unison with their neighbor, their faces forward, their eyes closed, even the sounds of the raging storm overhead lessened.

"Can you all begin to see it now? Can you feel it?" this young man exclaimed like an excited child. "Like the Sun warms the Earth on a beautiful spring day, let it warm your soul with its glory." This youthful leader paused momentarily and when he continued, his voice seemed different, no longer his own.

"A light so bright that all of the colors of this world fade, all the differences disappear. Within it, all pain disappears, all violence ceases, all wars end, all hate and prejudice is forgotten and sins are forgiven. Within it, all of our sorrow and all of our doubts cease. It is a light so pure that everyone bathed in it, is at peace, at long last home again. It is a light so strong that everyone of every faith who believes can see it, can feel it, can allow it to enter. A light so forgiving that all those truly repentant are forgiven. It unites us all in its warmth. All of darkness seems to fade in its presence."

The congregation stood, each still in each other's hand, and with eyes closed, smiled, most with tears streaming down their faces as a quiet ensued, an all-encompassing quiet, an all-forgiving quiet.

"Its strength, its power," a voice continued, "can overcome all hurt, all anger, all pain. It can stop the abuse and heal the abused. Everyone who allows it to enter will feel it strengthen their soul and renew their spirit. Everyone will become the innocent children of all creation united again at long last with their creator." The speaker now mused in silence, and silence surrounded them all.

"We are God's children here today," the young man continued as his own voice returned, "united in his warmth and loving embrace. Reach out and touch the soul of God as so few living have done before. In this light, warm your souls, cleanse your spirit, renew your faith. In this light begin life anew in the memory of its love forever."

In a more somber tone our speaker continued as the light seemed to fade. "If you believe it has found you and you feel at last at home, at last we are all home again. Every child is born of this light; we long for it all of our lives; we search for it everywhere. Please nurture it, remember it, please believe in it always!"

With those words this incredible journey ended. You could see the tears, and hear the sobs and feel the joy. Everyone opened their eyes to the blinding rays of sunlight that streamed in through every window, every door was open, revealing to all that the storm was over, and the setting Sun was glorious in the sky above, a rainbow of color surrounding its glory.

The minister fell to his knees in prayer and in thanks for at long last his prayers had been answered, his dreams fulfilled. His long search was finally over. He was totally unaware as almost everyone was, that his glorious speaker now lay unconscious by his side, with his beautiful friend holding his head in her arms and pleading for him to open his eyes. Afraid, for he had fallen so suddenly, and suddenly she felt so totally alone.

"Gian, Gian, please open your eyes, please Gian, please," she was finally able to beg. The reverend, hearing her faint cries, suddenly became aware of the fate that had befallen his chosen speaker. He knelt down beside them and helped to support the young man's head with one hand, and with his other he held the frightened girl's hand. She was indeed so beautiful then, and so very young, her multicolored eyes shone through the tears. The three of them lay in a bold stream of light emanating from the setting Sun before them.

"Oh, father," she sobbed, "Is he all right? Is he going to be all right?"

"My dear child, of course he is," the good reverend assured her, "For today marks the beginning of his miracle."

With those words this fallen hero opened his eyes, so deep, so blue were they in this light that all light around them seemed to fade in their presence. Struggling up, suddenly, he appeared pale, weak, and confused.

"I have to go now, Faith," he begged his friend. "Please we have to go," he reiterated again as he turned toward a back door.

"We must go now, please my dear Faith, please," he continued as he grabbed hold of his friend's arm and guided her toward the exit. Faith could not respond. She had never seen Gian like this before. The two of them approached the exit as the good reverend followed close behind, aware that he was powerless to stop them. Before they departed, they briefly paused to gaze out at the congregation before them, for it had grown in number, as many had joined them from the street outside, and all were marveling in their shared experience.

The good minister spoke quietly near Gian's ear. "My son, I knew that one day you would come, for I have heard you in my dreams, longed for you in my soul, and I also know that you must leave, but our paths will cross again, and until then, may God keep you safe, my son. May He keep you safe as you begin your journey."

The two strangers departed through the open rear door, as the good father fell to his knees behind them and yelled out, "Thank you!" for he knew that this day marked a new beginning for them all, for us all.

CHAPTER 2

The sky quickly darkened as these two lonely figures traversed the narrow, dimly lit city streets toward home. Everything appeared exceptionally still that evening, eerily quiet. No one spoke. Perhaps neither of them could speak, since so much had changed in just one evening.

Sometimes words aren't necessary; sometimes they can't be found. Sometimes there is only silence, a strange stillness. Footsteps, only familiar footsteps could be heard embarking this night it seemed on a new path, even though these two had traversed these same streets before, probably hundreds of times. A part of Gian instinctively knew his way home, that evening, that part of us that takes over in times of stress and guides us—a part of our minds that shifts into auto mode in our most disturbing moments. Gian was a young man of few words anyway, so Faith understood the quiet; she almost expected it.

Gian sought the solace of his past to help him now, but the past he recalled was anything but peaceful, and the solace he sought he could not find. He had moved to this big city four years earlier on a cross-country bus. All of his belongings were contained within two carry-ons; all of his dreams were in his head. He was alone, so totally alone, and he hoped that a new city would bring renewed hope and a chance, just a chance for a better life. He did not realize it then—but soon thereafter he did—that no matter how far he traveled, his past was always there, forever an integral part of his psyche.

His mother, Sarah Terzo, a majestic figure of a woman with a strong soul and an incredible work ethic, raised Gian. He was an only child, abandoned by his father when he was about five years old. Initially, his mom lied to him, repeatedly reassuring him that his father had left only to find a better job so that they could have a better life, and once he was established somewhere, "he will come for us, and we will all be together again. His father never called, though; he never wrote; he never returned, and as the years passed, his mother rarely spoke of him again. A part of her died in his absence.

Sarah supported them both by cleaning houses, hundreds of them it seemed to Gian, who sometimes accompanied her on his days off from school. She rarely took a day off, working almost every day, even most holidays. When Gian was sick, she relied on the kindness of her neighbors to help, and they always did, for Sarah was always there for them in their time of need. She was a deeply religious woman, active in her church and local charities in her rare free time. She had many friends and admirers. She was a survivor, a good woman, a gentle soul. She was strong of spirit, and when she smiled it was contagious. She taught her son well by setting a good example for him in every aspect of their life together.

She managed to send her only child to a private religious school until he graduated high school, and helped him win a scholarship to a prestigious northeastern university, which he attended for over three years. Gian was indeed a top scholar, an avid and voracious learner. His mother was his guide, his strength and his inspiration, and he loved her so.

One horrible day when he was only twenty-one years old, a knock on his dorm room door would change the course of his life forever. A policeman kindly explained to him that his mother was dead. She had been murdered. They both went inside as the officer explained how his mother had entered one of the homes she cleaned with a passkey and interrupted a burglary in progress. She walked in on a pair of teenagers. His mother had apparently startled the two as she entered, and one of the burglars panicked and shot her. The neighbors heard the shot and called 9-1-1, and the two criminals were apprehended at the scene, both under the influence of drugs, but it was too late for Sarah. Four lives ended on that day, two teenagers who had embarked on a road of darkness were now forever lost in it, and one innocent victim and her son. Gian at first did not comprehend what the officer was saying, and finally when he did, he was devastated. In an instant, his entire world darkened, and he could no longer see.

Gian would never be the same again. He immediately left school, never to return. Once back at home, he realized he did not even have enough money to properly bury his mom. Soon though, he was overwhelmed by the love and support of many of her friends from work, from church, and from the neighborhood. Thanks to them all, he buried his mom with dignity and honor. Hundreds attended the funeral to bid a fond farewell to their friend. The morning Sun was glorious that day as the birds sang in the heavens, joyous it seemed that another angel had indeed returned home, but for Gian, it was the darkest day of his young life.

For a year, Gian lived in his childhood home, surrounded by his mother's friends and her belongings, desperate to hold on to her memory, for he was still too lost to find his way. He prayed every day for guidance, and understanding. He also volunteered some of his time after work, at a local center for underprivileged youth hoping to make a difference, for he knew that his mother would have wanted him to. One day he awoke and, somehow, he knew it was time to leave. He gave notice to his landlord, sold all of his furniture and belongings, and boarded a bus to the big city in search of his future. While eating lunch at the very first diner he saw as he exited the bus on that very first day, he met Monsignor Lilli of Gerard's Place. The monsignor approached him as he ate, apparently sensing this young man's plight. Monsignor Lilli was the pastor of a church and nearby homeless shelter.

"St. Gerard's," he explained, "was a small Catholic church, one with a very active homeless shelter entitled Gerard's Place."

This man of God apparently sensed something special about this young man before him, during this their very first encounter, for they became friends that afternoon, and by the end of the lunch, he offered Gian a job as caretaker of Gerard's Place. He explained that a studio apartment in the rear of the shelter had a separate entrance, and was vacant, for the former caretaker had been fired the week before. Gian immediately accepted, and the two walked toward home. A chance encounter would prove a life-changing event for these two new friends, neither one of them could have possibly understood by just how much their lives were about to change.

Monsignor Lilli was a good man, a simple man of faith, and Gian quickly became his obedient disciple and trusted friend. In his early seventies, this silver haired, small framed, rather thin man quickly became for Gian the father figure he so desperately needed. The monsignor continued to teach Gian the lessons his mom began years earlier. He taught him about caring for the less fortunate, and encouraged him to complete his education at a nearby university. In him Gian seemed to find a trusted friend and advisor. There was indeed a spiritual connection between these two, from their very first encounter, and for over two years their bond became as tight as a father's to a newly found son. When Monsignor Lilli was chosen to become Bishop, Gian couldn't have been happier, but a part of him felt like everyone he loved eventually left, and an inner sadness returned.

Their friendship remained strong despite the distance, but in his stead, Father Thom from a neighboring parish had become the pastor of Gerard's Place. Father Thom developed an immediate dislike for Gian, as soon as it became apparent to him how close this young man and the new bishop were. Father Thom, a man in his mid-fifties, average in height but rather large in width, with a balding mess of salt and pepper hair about his head, was a poor substitute for the former pastor. It soon became clear to everyone at Gerard's Place that Gian retained his position there only at the insistence of his good friend, Bishop Lilli. Gian was treated as a janitor for the first time since his arrival, and his duties in service to the needy were drastically curtailed.

Father Thom was indeed a weak leader, given to occasional excesses of alcohol and temperament. He tried to fill his predecessor's shoes and soon came to realize he could not, and Gian seemed to be a constant reminder of his failure. Gian remained at Gerard's Place despite all of this, for this place had become his home, its inhabitants his family, and he felt an obligation to his dear friend, the new bishop.

Gian had come full circle in his mind that dark night as he approached Gerard's Place, with Faith by his side. Faith lived directly across the street in a modest home with a small porch at its entrance off the pavement. It was here that these two had met years earlier, right here in the street before them, and it was there that these two stood alone on this unusual night. The couple now walked toward the entrance of Faith's home, and as they approached they could hear the elevated but familiar voices of Faith's parents ahead of them.

They each climbed up the few stone steps onto the small porch, as they had done so many times before. It was there that these two had spent many nights during their three-year relationship. Father Thom did not allow visitors in Gian's studio apartment, and Faith hated being alone. Faith's home had become their sanctuary.

"Come in, Gian," Faith declared, breaking their silence as she opened the front door to reveal the living room. Her mother and father were seated in their respective worn recliners as they entered, puffing furiously away on their cigarettes with a six-pack of beer cans strewn about the end tables nearby. It was a familiar scene. The television was on, but neither of them appeared to notice it. Faith's parents struggled to support and care for their only child as best they could; they each worked hard to maintain their small home.

"Faith! Gian!" Faith's father immediately shouted upon their arrival. "We're glad you're home. We were worried, you know," he continued in a slightly slurred speech, "what with the storm and all." Dressed only in a worn t-shirt, shorts, and a robe, he appeared older than a man in his early fifties, a bit more gray, a bit more worn.

"Gian, hi," Faith's mom now added in a puff of smoke as she withdrew her cigarette from her mouth to speak, her stained teeth obvious to all. Although pleasant, her face was prematurely wrinkled, and her hair appeared dull and lifeless in a bun upon her head. Her eyes seemed a perfect match for Faith's, and in them you could still sense the love she felt for her daughter and her daughter's boyfriend. Her housedress was worn and stained about her body, with old slippers on her feet, and her hands trembled as she took another long drag on her cigarette.

No one asked if they were hungry. No one commented on how wet they still were as these two departed the room and entered Faith's bedroom behind them, like they had done hundreds of times before. This house, although worn and scarcely decorated, was indeed a home to them both. Flawed as it was, it was here, and only here, that these two rather poor young adults were able to spend some quality time together alone, and with their friends. This small house always felt like a home to all who entered; Faith saw to that.

Faith's room was remarkably extraordinary in a less-than-ordinary house. She had painted it herself, quite often, and always in another glorious color. Strewn around the room were all of her special mementos, each in their own sacred place. On the walls were paintings of beautiful landscapes and sunsets and flowers. Across one wall was a rather large bookcase filled with music. Faith loved music in all of its manifestations. She managed to take piano, guitar, and violin lessons years earlier with money she earned from a paper route; the entire neighborhood seemed to know her name. Eventually it became too dangerous for her to work any longer in the wee morning hours of a depressed neighborhood.

Faith had just turned twenty-two years old, but she appeared slightly older, and had always been wiser than her years. She was the picture of eternal beauty, her loving hazel eyes, her chiseled brow, her soft, radiant hair were just some of her most endearing qualities. Seemingly everyone loved to be in her presence, for she always made them feel more alive, and more appreciative of the miracles of life, for she seemed to embody them all.

Faith was also fiercely independent. Her parents loved her and worked to support her, but she lost them to beer and television and cigarettes almost every night and weekend. She was an only child who had very few true and trusted friends. It was so hard for her to explain her parents' behavior; she was embarrassed for them. Her light frame and average height hid an enormous soul. She was a creative force as a child and an even greater one as a young adult. Gian felt so fortunate to know her, to have her as a friend, and to love her as his girlfriend.

Faith strolled into her bedroom and immediately took off her damp shoes. Gian sat in a great old reclining chair near the bed and lay back in momentary peace. Faith quickly placed a few choice CDs into her stereo and as they began to play she left the room and entered an adjoining bathroom to change out of her damp clothes. In her absence, Gian noticed two sheets of paper lying on the floor in front of him. He reached down to pick them up, and immediately began to read.

> If I could have…
> Sometimes it all seems overwhelming.
> You grasp for change too late.
> You wait for when
> A dream is no longer yours to take
> Sometimes you feel so alone
> Trapped in this world of cold stone
> A single fragile bird in flight
> Struggling to escape the darkness
> You fly
> Into the endless beautiful
> Blue sky
> Above all the tears you soar
> Endlessly searching for more
> You see
> If I could have
> All the stars of the sky
> Shining brilliantly forever
> All the warmth of the Sun
> Every day in my life
> If I could find true happiness
> Every minute of every hour
> Then I'd have to have you
> For if wishes come true

In a beautiful world
I would wish all of this for us
If I could
I would wish all of this for us
A love without end
A life without pain
A world without sorrow
A rainbow without rain
You see
If I could have
All the stars of the sky
Shining brilliantly forever
All the warmth of the Sun
Every day in my life
If I could find true happiness
Every minute of every hour
Then I'd have to have you
In my life
For my lifetime
To make my every dream
Come true
If only I could have
If only I could
Have you
Only you
Forever
Together us two
Forever and always
If only I could have
If only I could have
You

Apparently overwhelmed, Gian just sat there in awe of Faith's incredible talent, and for the very first time in awe of her love for him. Suddenly Faith reentered the room and immediately recognized the sheets of paper Gian held before him in his hands. She stood silently there in the shadows, her eyes filling with tears, and Gian could not take his eyes off of her. He could not move. He could not speak. She quietly approached him, and lifted the song-poem out of his hands. It was then that Gian arose from his chair to meet her. Their eyes met in a different light before he reached out to embrace her. Her body smelled of the most fragrant flowers. He never wanted to let go of her at that moment. He never wanted to let go of this feeling. He wanted this embrace to last a life-time. But he knew it couldn't, for no matter how much he wished for forever, he knew in his heart that his wish was just that.

He let go enough to face her in this dimly lit room, to kiss her gently on her incredible lips. He let go enough to wipe the tears from her cheeks. For he knew all too well why she was crying, and yet he still didn't know what to say to her. Words always seemed to fail him at times like these, and to Faith they came so easily.

"If I could have you forever," he finally was able to speak, so softly, he wondered if she even heard.

"I'm frightened, Gian," she responded as she perched her head on his shoulder. "I am so frightened."

"Don't be afraid, my Faith," he responded into her ear, as they stood there together in the shadows of their special place.

"Hold on to me, forever," Faith whispered.

"I will," he responded.

Gian leaned back to face her, her angelic face met his, and he kissed her again for what seemed like forever, before they finally lay down upon her bed, and in Gian's embrace, Faith fell asleep so completely.

Gian could not sleep, for he knew that even though so little seemed different this night on this bed, so much had changed, and Faith knew it too. Faith, though, was always the stronger of the two, for she had faced adversity from her earliest days. She had become an adult while still a child, and her inner strength was immeasurable.

Sometime later Gian quietly arose and turned off the light and left for home. This evening had changed them both. Something was very different. Nothing seemed the same. This night somehow everything had changed. Somehow nothing would ever be the same again.

CHAPTER 3

Bernadette was as fragile as a delicate flower. She was a mystery to all who lived and worked at Gerard's Place. She mostly kept to herself. She rarely spoke to anyone, except Father Thom, and in the past to Monsignor Lilli. Father Thom rarely found time for any one, so it amazed everyone that he kept trying to reach Bernadette.

Bernadette was a rather large black woman with piercing eyes and a full mouth and nose. Her hair was straight and always in a bun atop her head. She dressed well, for a woman living in poverty. She was exceptionally organized and clean, and kept Gerard's Place the same way. When she smiled, and she rarely did, she brightened the room with contagious contentment. She was quite a beautiful woman despite her sad eyes and lack of conversation. She was one of the few residents of the shelter who found it hard to leave. She seemed to be disturbed by the presence of strangers, and most of the residents were just that.

She had arrived at Gerard's Place about three years earlier. Monsignor Lilli immediately recognized her humble and good heart, and he opened his home to her. Many believed that he was the only one who knew Bernadette at all.

Bernadette's day began very early. She spent most of the morning in the church. She would arrive before the earliest mass and help the nuns prepare. She kept the church meticulously clean, and always had time before mass to sit in a pew before the statue of Mary and pray. One solitary figure in a pew before mass was always that of Bernadette.

In the afternoon she would feed the birds on the sidewalks leading up to the church. She was so good to them that they would fly to eat from her hands or rest upon her shoulder. There she seemed most alive, and most needed.

She almost always ate alone at night, and generally went to bed early. She was rarely mean to anyone, and she rarely lost her temper. At Gerard's Place she was just another homeless visitor who had wandered in one night, and unlike most, found herself a home.

This morning was different, though. When Gian arrived at Gerard's Place to begin work, everyone was talking about it. Bernadette had not gone to church. Father Thom was in her room talking to her for almost an hour. Everyone was concerned. No one could hear anything emanating from her room until she screamed out in a voice none of us had ever heard before. It was the voice of panic.

"Don't touch me! Don't touch me!" All hear her yell. "No one can touch me!" She repeated over and over again. Father Thom finally opened the door, visibly shaken, tears in his eyes. No one had ever seen him like this before. He looked at Gian, and then at everyone outside of her room, and mumbled, "I went to take her hand, because she seemed so upset. I tried to talk to her, to find out what was wrong. I was worried when I heard she didn't go to mass this morning. I only tried to help," he whispered as he left.

The door was open and Bernadette lay on her bed crying. Gian had never really spoken to her much before, but today he felt he had to. Something had changed. He silently entered her room and sat quietly in an old chair near her. Her room was small but very well organized and meticulously clean. She lay there, as a frightened child would, clinging furiously to the golden crucifix that she wore around her neck, tears flowing from her pained eyes. The figure on the cross was worn almost unrecognizable as her fingers rubbed it furiously. Bernadette startled as Father Thom abruptly reentered her room and began to shout directly at Gian.

"You're just a custodian here, not a clergyman, or psychologist, or even her friend. You must leave at once," he demanded. Gian quickly rose to leave when Bernadette surprised them both by whispering for Gian to stay over and over again. Father Thom departed, startled by her request, and apparently shocked by the events of this most unusual morning, but not before leering at Gian as he closed the door behind him.

Sitting back down, Gian couldn't help but stare at his fragile acquaintance. He couldn't help but feel for her. He wanted to reach out and tell her everything was going to be okay. She seemed as frightened as a newly hatched young bird who had fallen out of her nest, afraid that if a stranger touched her, her mother would never take her back home again.

"Bernadette," he began quietly. "Sometimes it helps to talk, sometimes it is all we can do."

In response she focused her attention on him and let go of her crucifix. She uttered not even a sound.

"Bernadette, don't you see," he began again. "I am really a nobody here. Just a nobody, struggling to find my way in this world just like you. A nobody can't hurt you. A nobody could never hurt anyone."

"Nobodies aren't real," Bernadette interrupted.

"You're wrong, Bernadette, they are. You can see them all around you every day but you don't notice them, that's why they're nobodies."

"You're not a nobody," she interrupted again.

"Oh, but I am, Bernadette. I live here just like you. I work here every day, but the somebodies never notice me. Please believe me, Bernadette, when I tell you that I am here to help. I am here to listen, just listen. Sometimes it helps just to talk about it. A secret has more power when it lies dormant deep inside. Please, let me help you. Remember that a nobody can never harm you, and one is here with you now. If you tell me, Bernadette, nobody will hear, I promise, no one will ever know."

With those words, Bernadette sat up upon her bed and gazed into Gian' eyes as innocently as a small child would, and after a few moments began in a childlike voice. "Are we really alone here, really safe?" she questioned.

"Yes," he responded.

"Are you sure no one can hurt me?"

"Yes," he responded again.

"Are you sure no one can hear me?"

"Yes."

"Are you sure no one, no one at all, will hear me?"

"No one is here, Bernadette, to hurt you," he responded again.

Tears welled up in her eyes at that moment, tears of relief, as her pained facial expression lessened and her gaze became friendly and loving. It was as if a huge burden had been lifted, and she was suddenly free.

"My father died on the streets just outside of my house, you see, when I was just six years old, just six. I heard the shots and was scared. I didn't know what happened. I didn't know what to do." She paused and gazed downward. "Since I was just six years old," she began again, "just six, it seemed like every day since I was six, every day you see," she repeated so suddenly confused, her recollections flawed.

"Remember, my friend," Gian began, "I am here to help you. Remember that you are not alone any more for I am finally here," he whispered to his frightened young companion.

Bernadette looked up again and when her eyes met his, she could see her tears in them and she knew that they were one, one in spirit in that moment, one in pain.

"My mother was murdered too, Bernadette," he spoke and then couldn't continue. He didn't need to, for he had said enough already.

"My mother loved him so," she began again. "He was a great dad, a wonderful man. My mother had "no one now," she used to say. She quickly forgot all about me on that day when I was just six years old. I lost my family, you see," she sobbed quietly, "I lost my family."

"Remember, Bernadette, that you are no longer alone there," Gian reminded her. "You are not alone here. You will never be alone again."

"My mother died that day too, lost to drugs and boyfriends after that. I died that day. My childhood died when I was just six years old, killed by a drive-by shooting. It lay there on that sidewalk with the body of my father, bleeding out onto that cold pavement was my future. I can remember my mother screaming and the neighbors, too. I tried to wake him up. I tried to wake my father up. I cried for him to wake up. Soon after that I stopped going to school. No one noticed. No one even cared. Soon after that I didn't even talk for months at a time."

Silence had fallen, and the room that confined them both seemed to disappear. The rays of sunlight seemed to stop at the windowpane and dare not enter.

"You see," she mumbled with tears flowing down her cheeks, her body trembling as if she would die if she completed her next sentence. "No one has the right to hurt children, no one. No one has the right to touch them. No one had the right to touch me," she paused as she sobbed. "They didn't have the right to touch my daddy. I can't forget them touching me. Daddy, please help me to forget, please help me." She sobbed softly. Gian wanted to reach out and hold her, and tell her that everything would be all right, but he was too late, too many years too late.

Able to find the words, Bernadette continued. "Ever since I was old enough, I ran away after that. I ran away from my mother. I ran away from her house. I ran away from my life. I ran away from her boyfriends, her booze, and her drugs. But try as I could, I could not really run away. I could never really run far enough away." Her voice drifted somewhat as she spoke those last words, her eyes seemed so distant. You could feel the anguish in her words, see the pain in her soul as she sat there silently before she continued. "I can never run away from that, I can't. I thought I could forget and begin again, but I cannot. I thought I could forget their faces," she sobbed a little now, "That I could forget their touch. I thought that I could run away and find a place where I could finally forget, and then…and then, I realized that no place like that existed."

She paused again for a few moments, as if searching, searching for answers she could never find. "I pray every day to forget how my life died on that very day with my daddy. Oh those many years ago when I held onto my father and cried for him to wake up." Bernadette began to cry and Gian cried too. "I cry for every child that experienced such sorrow. I cry for every child that lost a parent too soon. I cry for every child that was hurt in a way that no one should be." They both cried, for it seemed like the only thing that they could do.

"I'm twenty-one years old now, grown up, you see, and I'm tired of running," she was able to say despite the tears, the sobs diminishing.

"Bernadette!" Gian cried out but his voice was so very different. It wasn't his voice. It wasn't his voice at all. His body seemed to tremble ever so slightly at that point, he couldn't control himself. "Bernadette," he continued in a voice so unfamiliar, "Bernadette, my beautiful little girl. Daddy's here, my beautiful, daddy's here."

With those words Gian glanced over to the place where Bernadette sat, and before him he saw a beautiful little girl dressed in a delicate red dress. Her eyes seemed to glow when she looked over toward him, and she smiled in a way that her whole face smiled with her. She was still wearing that incredible gold crucifix on a gold chain around her neck, only now it was brilliant and new. He stood up and immediately this little girl stood up too and ran into his arms. They hugged so tight for so long that neither one of them realized that Father Thom had reentered the room. Neither one of them wanted to let go; they embraced through the tears, through time and through place. They were both somewhere else, someplace else. They could each feel this intense love pass through them.

"Dear Bernadette," Gian continued in a voice only Bernadette seemed to recognize, a deep voice so unlike his own. "I am so very proud of you."

"Daddy, oh daddy!" Bernadette cried out as she held on even tighter, so afraid to let go.

"Your daddy will always be here for you, my little girl. I will always be right here. You will never be alone again. I love you my little Bernadette. I will always love you!"

The room about them seemed to change in that moment. The rays of sunlight reentered and illuminated everything in their path, and everything seemed renewed in their glow. It was a cleansing light, a purifying one, which now seemed to purify even the wounds of one's injured soul. It seemed to mark a new beginning, as if the Sun had appeared to mark a new day, after many years of rain.

Father Thom just stood motionless in the doorway, transfixed by the scene unfolding before him. He could not fully comprehend what was taking place but he knew he was witnessing a transformation. Bernadette never allowed herself to be touched by another; she never embraced anyone, ever. Everyone at Gerard's Place knew this and yet here she was in Gian's embrace, unafraid. It was enough to take a person's breath away.

"Gian, Bernadette," Father Thom was finally able to declare in an elevated voice, in this moment he appeared overwhelmed and confused, jealous and dismayed. "What is going on here?"

Suddenly Bernadette let go of Gian, and all at once Gian felt like himself again. He could not explain nor understand what had just taken place. He probably never would. Some things cannot be explained, as he had learned during his own chaotic life. There had been so many times in his young life, so many unexplainable events that had altered the course of his life that one more seemed almost routine.

Gian could finally see Bernadette clearly before him at this point, stunned and teary eyed she was. Glancing over at Father Thom, her composure suddenly changed, and she abruptly turned, apparently eager to leave the room. She bent forward and leaned near Gian's ear and whispered, "thank you," quietly, almost inaudibly. Holding back tears, she continued in a louder but still quiet tone, "Thank you, Gian, and thank God for you." With those words, she arose from her bed and, glaring over at Father Thom only for an instant, departed. Father quickly followed but not before scolding Gian, "Don't you leave this room before I have a chance to speak to you, young man."

Gian barely acknowledged his command, much less his departure. He sat down, bewildered at first, trying to make sense of chaos. "Did Bernadette see her father, feel her father, hear her father?" he thought. How was that possible? What was happening? The events of the past couple of days were frankly beginning to frighten him. Fatigue set in, as he lay back on the bed, and once his weary head hit the pillow, he began to wish that the chaos of the past couple of days would disappear and that his old, safe world would return. A part of him knew that this was impossible, that indeed his life had been changed forever by the events of the past two days, and he knew somehow that this was only the beginning. He was somewhat lost without his Faith by his side, somewhat frightened.

Father Thom abruptly reentered the room, and sensing Gian's fatigue as his body lay across a stranger's bed, he stood still for a moment just a few feet from him. He glanced down at him and all he could utter was a few direct commands.

"Gian, I do not know what happened here today, and frankly, I do not want to know. But remember this, your job here is well defined and if you stray from it again, well, I don't care what anyone else thinks, you will be finding yourself another one."

He must have fallen asleep at that moment, for a short while later when he awoke, Father Thom was gone, and suddenly he felt more alone than when his father had left, more alone than when he had arrived in this new city, more alone than when his mother had died. He felt more alone than ever before. He quickly arose from the bed and left Bernadette's room. The house was eerily quiet as he completed his chores; his thoughts were only of Faith. Bernadette was nowhere to be found and strangely, he knew that she was all right, that she was finally okay. He needed to find Faith, though. He knew that he had to find her.

As the Sun set at the end of this strange day, it painted in its passing a brilliant rainbow of color in the sky. The rainbow was fleeting, but all who were fortunate enough to have witnessed it could not help but admire its breathtaking beauty. As Gian gazed out through the back window, a sole love bird flew past and came to rest on the statue of St. Gerard in the courtyard. Soon another one joined it and together they took off in flight, disappearing into the glory of that early evening sky and its unheralded bursts of color. His thoughts quickly turned to Faith as he hurried out of Gerard's Place to find her at last, his work completed for the day. He had to find Faith. He had to, for he had so much to tell her, so much to share, and he needed her. He needed her desperately, so much that his soul ached.

CHAPTER 4

Gian rushed out of Gerard's Place that evening and could clearly see Faith sitting on her porch in the twilight. A familiar face in a familiar place was just what he desperately needed in such an unfamiliar time. He couldn't cross the street fast enough, and when he arrived at the top of her stairs, he stood still. Faith immediately sensed something was wrong and quickly stood up. Gian quietly approached and gathered her in his longing embrace, just feeling her warm body next to his was enough to reassure him for a time. After a few moments, Faith stepped back and queried him in a concerned voice, "Gian, is something wrong?," her brow wrinkled with consternation as she stood there before him. Gian could see in her hazel eyes a hint of fear. He appreciated her beautiful hair as it tumbled across her shoulders. Her body was clad in a long-sleeve violet sheer top and black denim jeans, and at first he couldn't respond. He continued to stare at her, not knowing exactly what to say. He didn't want to worry her; she was worried enough already. Finally, he blurted out a few misplaced words.

"I had to see you just in time."

"What?" Faith responded confused.

"Oh, I mean, well, I had to see you, Faith."

"But you always come over after work, Gian."

"Yeah, I know, well…this is different!"

"Different?" Faith quietly asked.

"Everything's different," he declared.

"What do you mean, Gian? Is something wrong? Did something happen?"

"Did I ever tell you," he paused, apparently rethinking what he was about to say. "Did I ever tell you how beautiful you are?"

"What?," Faith was even more concerned, for Gian rarely spoke like this.

"I needed to see you, Faith, to hold you in my arms and tell you how much you mean to me, how much I care for you, and, and, how very much I, I…"

"Gian, you're worrying me. Please tell me what it is, what are you worried about? Please tell me, did something else happen?"

Gian paused and just stood there staring into her concerned eyes before he answered.

"I think everything will always be all right as long as I have you," he said as he reached forward to caress her hair, and then they embraced, their bodies so close that their two hearts seemed to beat as one. "As long as I have you in my life," he whispered into her ear. It was unusually quiet that evening. It was almost a perfect evening until a stampede of footsteps was heard behind them and a familiar voice now pierced their dream.

"Oh no, what is this?" a voice demanded behind them. "Did I miss something? I mean, is it the end of the world or something?" he shouted sarcastically.

They turned to face Faith's brother, Pablo, standing there in the twilight, demanding an answer. Actually, Pablo was not Faith's biological brother. He was her adopted brother. Faith had claimed Pablo as her own kid brother about ten years earlier when he moved in next door with his dad. They had been almost inseparable ever since. Faith called it an adoption of the heart much stronger than blood, and anyone who knew them knew this to be true.

Pablo was only sixteen years old. He was of average height and weight, but unlike his name implied, he had brilliant blonde hair and shocking green eyes with an extremely fair complexion. He told everyone that he looked more like his Swedish mom than his dad. No one except Faith believed him. Pablo did not even have a picture of his mom to prove his point, and he tended to exaggerate the truth a lot. Pablo's dad worked two jobs to support the family and was rarely home, so Faith just took him in and cared for him in his absence. Pablo's mom had left mysteriously years earlier and the rest of his family was scarce. These two young souls, each parentless in their own way, had forged a union that no mere mortal could break, although Pablo did not make it an easy one. Trouble always seemed to follow him, or so he said. Anyone that knew him, if asked, would say that most of his trouble was of his own doing. Pablo rarely smiled, but he frequently made others smile. He had an incredible sense of humor and a knack for storytelling, despite himself. Gian had grown rather fond of him over the years, it was impossible not to.

"Well, if you two aren't going to talk, as usual, I guess I will," he stated mat-ter-of-factly as he sat down on one of the porch chairs. "Come on, you two, sit. You are never going to believe what happened to me today." Pablo rambled on in his usual manner, wearing baggy beige trousers, which appeared wrinkled and worn, a faded blue open-collared shirt and white sneakers. Faith and Gian proceeded to sit, unable to speak. Pablo had a tendency to speak so loudly that the entire neighborhood could hear him, and he could easily monopolize any situation.

"You both are not going to believe the day I had," he declared with his bril-liant green eyes twinkling.

Gian just sat there and momentarily glanced over at the rising moon, which was nearly full. There was not a cloud in the sky, and the stars seemed to hide in the light of the moon.

"Today didn't start out well," Pablo continued, apparently trying to regain his friends' interest. "I was late for work." Pablo was always late for work; in fact this was his third job this summer. "I was only a little late," he stated again aware of Faith's frustration.

"How late is late, Pablo?" Faith interjected.

"Oh, I don't know, maybe an hour," he declared with little thought.

"What?" Gian exclaimed. Faith just laughed. Pablo continued with his tale despite the laughter.

"It wasn't my fault. Look you have to believe me," he stopped and waited for their reaction. Faith was still smiling and Gian tried desperately not to laugh himself, staring at him in earnest.

"Look," he continued, apparently unperturbed, "Yesterday I noticed that my rear bike tire wouldn't turn well. Apparently, the rear brakes had worn and were stuck too close to the wheel, causing some sort of noise. So, I just took the brakes off in the rear and went off to work this morning as usual. You both know I need my bike to go to work, and God knows, I don't have the money to fix it."

"Yeah, we know, Pablo, considering this is your, what, third bike this sum-mer?" Faith retorted.

"Hey, I can't help it if I'm prone to accidents. Well, anyway, once I fixed it, I just took off on my now-adjusted bike so fast that I even amazed myself. I mean, who would have thought that I was a good bike mechanic. I was—I mean, I am…or at least I thought I was this morning."

"Can you please just tell us the story?," Faith pleaded.

"Well, I stopped twice before arriving at work, each time without any problems. Once was at the Eastern Star Café for an espresso. You know I need a cup in the morning to get me going, and this morning was no different. In fact, I needed two. I also ate this great doughnut. Well, then, I had to stop at the arcade to use the john, no problem again. The bike worked great."

"It's funny you always have to use the arcade's bathroom. It wouldn't have anything to do with a certain girl who happens to work there that you happen to like, would it?" Faith teased.

Pablo just ignored her and continued. He was used to her sarcasm.

"I was running a little late at that point, no big deal, right? So I jumped back on my bike and sped off to Vinnie's." He paused. "I was making great time, too. There was hardly any traffic."

"Yeah, well, rush hour was over, like, an hour earlier," Faith interjected.

"You know, I have to tell you both that I never realized this before. I never really noticed until today."

"Can you get on with it already?," Faith pleaded.

"No, really, did you two ever notice how far down hill Vinnie's store was, huh? Did you ever pay attention before? Really, did you ever notice, huh? Well, did you?" Neither one answered. Vinnie's was the store where Pablo worked. His store had been in business for over forty years. Vinnie sold flowers and fruit and vegetables outside in the summer, and inside he ran a good bakery business, selling desserts, cakes, and the like. Vinnie felt sorry for Pablo and gave him a job about a month earlier.

"So I was heading down the street," Pablo continued, "pretty fast at this point, when all of a sudden, out of nowhere comes Vinnie's cat, Bella, right in front of me. I mean right there, right in front of me. I swerved out of the cat's way and had no choice really but to drive right into the fruit and vegetable stand. I had no choice. I quickly applied the brakes and, uh, I forgot they were broken, and the whole bike, with me on it, flipped over, I landed on the floor on top of a lot of apples, and the bike, well the bike sort of crashed through Vinnie's front glass window and into Vinnie's pastry shop. It was a miracle I wasn't hurt."

"Oh no, Pablo! You didn't!" Faith cried.

"Yeah, it was horrible. Vinnie started yelling. I don't think I ever saw him so mad, and he fired me on the spot. He even called the police, do you believe it?"

"Well, what happened then, Pablo?," Gian asked. "You didn't have to go down to the police station, did you?"

"Jail? Did you say jail?The police station? Aren't you listening? It was an accident. I could have been killed trying to save a cat's life. I had witnesses. Hundreds of people saw what happened. They all knew I saved that cat's life. I was a hero!"

"What?!" Gian exclaimed in disbelief.

"A hero?!" Faith smilingly interjected.

"Yep, a hero. Even a nice old lady agreed with me, once she got all of that cake off of her."

"What do you mean, Pablo?," Faith asked, bewildered.

"Well, she had this nice cake in her hands and was walking to the counter when the bike crashed into the..."

"Oh, no," Faith interrupted in laughter.

"Exactly," Pablo responded before continuing. "Look, even the police knew I did nothing wrong. They did take my bike, though. Oh well, after they left, I told Vinnie I was totally innocent, and given that it was an accident, 'cause his own cat ran in front of me, I deserved my job back. Besides, I did save his cat's life. I mean, it shouldn't be roaming around like that. It could have been killed. I mean, I could have been killed. After I thought about it, I thought this would be a good time to ask Vinnie for a raise, I mean, I did save his cat and all. Well, what do you think, Faith? Huh? What about you, Gian? Huh, was I right? Didn't I deserve a raise? Well, huh? Is anyone going to answer me?"

Neither of them answered. Faith and Gian were too dumbfounded to respond.

"Well, anyway," Pablo continued, "Out of nowhere Vinnie goes back into his store at this point and comes out wielding a bat. He chased me at least two blocks, screaming, 'you're fired' the whole time. I've never seen him so mad before—never." Pablo paused and in a more subdued voice asked innocently, "Do you think he meant it?"

His surrogate sister and his good friend laughed so hard for so long that Pablo just left in disgust. He apparently didn't see the humor in his question. Pablo just disappeared across the way, dragging his injured pride and body with him.

Faith and Gian just sat outside that evening talking, Pablo's story had changed everything, at least for a while. For a short time everything seemed to fall back into place. Faith seemed especially radiant this night, her face aglow in the shimmering moonlight. Her smile sparkled. She appeared elegant in a simple sort of way. Gian couldn't keep his eyes off of her. She began to speak of her job at the music store, and how she loved it there.

The music store didn't just sell music. It had listening centers, a snack bar, a coffee bar, and, most of all, an entire second floor devoted to music instruction on practically every instrument imaginable, and even a small recording studio, which was very expensive to rent. Faith would often sneak off during a break and play the piano or the guitar, or work on a song. The music store was her second home.

Gian just listened to Faith and enjoyed every minute of it. He apparently did not want to bring up what had happened earlier that day with Bernadette. He was afraid to, everything seemed so normal, at least for the moment, and he was enthralled by this incredible woman before him. Eventually he couldn't help but interrupt.

"F-F-Faith," he finally stuttered. "Faith," he paused, while she nervously glanced over at him, her smile disappearing as quickly as it had come, for she could sense worry in his voice.

"What is it, Gian?," she questioned. "Please tell me."

"I can't seem to understand what is happening to me. I'm worried—"

"Please, Gian," Faith interrupted, "tonight is so beautiful, please, let's just enjoy every last moment of it together. Together, just the two of us, please, we can always talk about it tomorrow."

She was right, Gian thought. He shouldn't worry her tonight. Instead he reached out and grabbed her in a tight embrace and kissed her as if it was for the very last time, like a soldier kisses his new bride before going off to war. It was indeed a beautiful kiss on a beautiful night. They sat there afterward for some time caught in each others embrace until they had to say goodnight, for it was very late and tomorrow was a workday.

The next morning came quickly, and because Gian hadn't been able to sleep much the night before, he arose early and finished his work by noontime. He had so much to tell Faith, and he couldn't wait, so he decided to visit her at work. He had so much to talk to her about, and he needed to see her. He desperately needed to see her.

He quickly changed out of his work clothes and put on a denim shirt, old jeans, and shoes and ran out. As he walked, he purchased a small bouquet of fresh flowers from a street vendor. Faith loved flowers. He passed Vinnie's and noticed the front window and wondered about Pablo, whom he hadn't heard from since the night before.

He entered the music store, and quickly encountered Budd, one of the store managers, and Faith's good friend. Budd was around thirty years old, a rather tall man with a husky build, dark brown hair, and a tan complexion. He always dressed well and today was no exception, for he had on a fitted shirt, slacks, and dress shoes. He was exceptionally good to Faith. He helped her a lot. He also believed in her talent.

"Hey, Gian!," Budd declared as he entered, "It's always good to see you, buddy." Budd called every guy buddy.

"You know I was just thinking about lunch. Do you want to go and get a bite to eat?," he asked before Gian had a chance to say anything.

"No, I ate a pretty big breakfast, and well, I'm just not hungry. Do you know where Faith is?"

"Oh, of course, I should have known. Look at me, I'm always on a diet or exercising to lose that extra thirty pounds and here I'm thinking about lunch. You on the other hand need a few good lunches. You're full, of course, of course. That's why you've got Faith, and me, I'm lucky just to be her friend!" With that he pulled a chocolate snack bar out of his pocket, unwrapped it, and ate it in two bites.

"Well, are you sure you won't reconsider?" Budd barely uttered as he swallowed.

"No thanks. I think I'll go find Faith. Maybe we'll meet up later," Gian answered as he left in pursuit of his girlfriend. The store was crowded for a weekday afternoon, both bars were full and music played softly in the background.

Gian encountered Faith seated at one of the small tables at the snack bar with another female employee that he did not recognize. Faith was dressed in one of his favorite green dresses that she wore. When she saw him, she ran up and hugged him.

"Gian, you look tired. Your eyes are puffy. You look pale. Is something wrong?," she blurted out, unable to contain herself.

Her friend immediately stood up and left, saying that it was time for her to get back to work.

"No, no, I'm fine, Faith," he reassured her as they made their way back to the table.

"Gian, something must be wrong for you to be here so early", she concluded with a perplexed look on her face.

"Here, Faith, I almost forgot. Here are some of your favorite flowers." He handed her the bouquet he bought for her that was now in disarray, "a little the worse for wear, I guess." Faith momentarily seemed to forget everything, for she smiled and accepted the bouquet from him without hesitation, bringing them close to her face to enjoy their fragrance.

"They are beautiful, Gian," Faith gushed as her emerald eyes reached his. "Thank you, thank you. You are always so kind, Gian." Tears welled in her eyes, her voice trembled a bit before she continued.

"I don't know what I would do without you, my Gian. My life began on the very day that I met you and it will end on the day I have to say good-bye." As those words ended, as usual, Gian could not speak, and all he could see before him was his love bird waiting for his answer. Faith had an incredible way with words, and Gian was just the opposite, so he just reached out and gathered her up in his strong embrace trying to protect her from her fears, trying to shield her from pain. He knew that he couldn't really protect her, like he would want to, but in that moment anything and everything seemed possible.

Faith withdrew after a couple of minutes and immediately sat down again at the table and began to eat her sandwich. Gian sat down across from her and began to chow down on her french fries.

"I finished work early today. I don't know, I woke up early and, well, I wanted to spend the rest of the afternoon with you," he began.

"I finished it today, Gian," Faith replied. "I finally finished it." Faith just looked at him, and at first he couldn't respond, his mouth full of french fries. She just smiled and continued. "I finished the song I was writing, you know, the one I've been working on entitled, 'Without You.'" She paused for only a moment as he took a gulp of her bottled water. "Budd was there, too. He knew how long I had been struggling with it." She paused again, as if waiting for a response at last.

"I'd love to hear it, Faith," he replied. "Maybe that's why I came. It was destiny." Faith just laughed and Gian felt this wouldn't be a good time to talk about Bernadette, at least not now, not here.

"I have to go back to work, Gian, but I'm going to try to leave as soon as I possibly can, so that we can both go upstairs and you could listen to my song."

"Fine, Faith, I'll wait right here for you. Don't be long," And with that she jumped up and turned to leave.

"Faith," he almost shouted, and she turned back around to face him. "I miss you already."

"Oh, Gian, I didn't even leave yet, but I miss you, too." She moved closer and bent down to kiss his head like a mother comforts her child, then Faith disappeared. Gian just sat there for a while, deep in thought, before Budd called out his name.

"Hey, Gian," the store manager blurted out as he approached. "Buddy, hey, can you hear me?" Gian sat there apparently unaware that anyone was calling his name. "Hey, Gian, my man, are you all right? I mean, 'Earth to Gian,'" he remarked as he proceeded to tap Gian's shoulder. Stunned, he turned around and found Budd beside him with a concerned look on his face.

"Is something wrong?" he began. "I mean, if something was wrong with me, I'd have eaten at least three lunches and a supper by now, and you, well…"

"No, nothing's wrong. You just startled me, that's all."

"Startled you, startled you. I walk in here calling your name and you're acting like your own wax figure, and I startled you."

"All right, I'm sorry, I was just thinking…"

"Hey, there's no need to be sorry," Budd interrupted, "I, well, can I help you with something?"

"No, I mean, yes, you can. You can let Faith off early, and join us in the music room later. That will be a great help."

"Sure. I'll see what I can do, buddy, I'll see what I can do." With that he departed as quickly as he had arrived. Gian searched the lunchroom for the time. He'd forgotten to wear a watch, and had no idea how much time had passed. Everything in the lunchroom appeared the same as he gazed around it, and yet everything was different. He had been in this lunchroom at least a hundred times before, and yet today it all seemed so new. Finally he realized that he was different somehow. Somehow—and he couldn't explain it—everything around him appeared different and yet he was the only one who had changed. At this point he had no idea by how much. He must have appeared confused to Faith as she quietly reentered the lunch room and walked right up to him, and yet he did not acknowledge her.

"Gian, let's go," Faith began as he finally recognized her standing before him. "Budd was able to let me leave early and the music room is empty. Come on, Gian, I think you need to get out of this room." He rose from his chair, Faith grabbed him up by his arm, and they made their way together to the studio upstairs. It seemed that everyone they passed knew Faith and was happy to see her. She did appear happier than she had been before, and when she smiled it was contagious.

They entered the studio, and Faith instructed Gian to sit down on a chair near the piano. This studio, although small, was large enough to hold at least twenty people. Faith loved to write songs and perform them; she was always happiest then.

As she took her place at the piano, she looked over at Gian with her enchanting eyes, and he could not help but smile back.

"I've been struggling with this song for some time now, Gian. It was one of my most difficult to write." She paused for a few seconds and her face filled with emotion. In a quavering voice she continued. "It is a song from my heart to yours, Gian, from my soul to yours." With the passage of those words from her beautiful lips, she began to play, and when her eyes met his, she winked, as she began to sing.

Time will begin tomorrow
But our future begins today
Here is where you need to be
And in your eyes I see
My life
My future
My destiny
Whenever I think of life without you
Whenever that might be
I need for you to see
That without you I am lost
Without your touch I cannot feel
Without your kiss I cannot heal
All the wounds of my life
Without you
For my future is with you, my love
Come here
Come now
Come closer still
Together we have a lifetime
Of dreams to fill
Can you see the dawn of our
New beginning
Can you feel the end of my
Long journey
Now that I have found you
Here with me in every way

Now that I have placed you
In my heart
To stay
Time will begin tomorrow
But our future begins today
Here is where you need to be
And in your eyes I see
My life, my future, my destiny
Love is what we have
Love is you and me
Love is what we possess inside
Love is all we see
Together we can create a future
Much better than our past
Where painful memories fade away
And only love will last
Time will begin tomorrow
But our future begins today
Here is where you need to be
And in your eyes I see
My life, my future, my destiny
Please believe me when I say
Place your trust in me
Everyday
For without you
We cannot be
For without your touch I cannot feel
Without your kiss I cannot heal
All the wounds of my life without you
For
I can't imagine life
Without you

Neither one of them spoke at first, not a word. Gian could not say anything despite desperately wanting to. He didn't know where to begin. He just stood there, like the others, staring at a beauty that he was so fortunate to behold. Just as there is silence as the glorious Sun rises across a majestic shoreline, in awe of the miracle of that moment, all were speechless now, waiting for Gian to respond.

He slowly walked over to her and their eyes met as he approached. He stood there, inches away, his heart pounding in his soul as he reached out to touch her face and, finally, to kiss her on her lips, and he held her close within his arms as they embraced.

No one seemed to be able to move. No one was able to speak. For one moment they transcended time and place. For one moment they became one, one last glorious burst of Sun before it sets in the all-encompassing dark sky.

"Hey, you two, do you want to break it up?" Budd blurted out. "We've got an audience now."

With those words reality returned and they both noticed that some people were entering the room, a bit confused by the presence of the three of them there.

"We rented the room for the next half hour," began one of the kids who entered. "We don't mean to interrupt."

"No problem for me at all," Budd chimed in. "What about you two, Romeo and Juliet, care to call it a day?," he laughingly asked Faith and Gian as he left.

They, too, quickly departed. Faith had to return to work because someone had called in sick, so Gian had to say good-bye again, without talking to Faith. He spent much of the afternoon on a park bench nearby. Again, so much appeared the same but so much had changed in the past two days. He was so worried, not so much for himself but for her. He couldn't think of anyone else.

He fed the birds that afternoon, ate a light supper that he bought from a vendor, and proceeded to lie back on the bench in awe of the beauty of this ordinary day. He watched the children play nearby, and recalled those rare times when his own mother had brought him to a local park to play. He had so enjoyed those days. He almost felt like an ordinary kid. He could have sat on that bench forever if it wasn't for the Sun's dramatic departure when he realized that night had fallen, and poor Faith must have gone home without him. He was supposed to meet her after work, so all he could do now was race home to find her. If either of them had had enough money for a cell phone, he would have called her, damn, he knew he should have bought one of those phones.

As he approached her house he could see her beautiful silhouette in the glow of the street's lights as she sat on her porch. The moon's glow was obscured by a band of clouds; its absence was palpable. As he approached, he noticed that she appeared sad. She glanced up as he raced up the stairs and once there, she stood up to meet him. Her eyes met his in the whisper of that moment. She reached out and they embraced, her glistening eyes lay bare before him. She held onto him as a mother might have held her child if it had just escaped danger. She whispered softly into his ear, words that he might never forget. "Hold me so close that even when you're gone, I'll feel your embrace forever." Gian knew then how much he had worried her, and he was so sorry.

He held onto her in that moment and for that short time he felt really, truly loved. He felt we as if they had transcended their meager surroundings to a paradise where only love was felt. They became one in the obscure moonlight joined in spirit, until the door to Faith's house burst open and her father ran toward them.

"Faith—oh, it's you, Gian," her father blurted out, acknowledging his daughter's boyfriend's presence. "Faith, you have to come in to help me. I'm having a problem with some of these damned bills. Please come in now," and with that, he just as quickly disappeared.

"Faith, why are you so sad?" Gian asked as he gazed into her now lifeless eyes.

Faith paused for a moment and then whispered, "I was worried about you, Gian." She paused again before continuing. "I was worried something happened to you, and, and…for the first time in a long time, I felt alone, so totally alone."

"Oh, Faith, I am so sorry. I didn't mean to worry you. I lost track of time. I can't explain it, I'm sorry." I bent down just enough to kiss her head then her forehead, her cheeks, and her neck before he found her lips.

"Without you, Faith, my life would be completely empty, you know that."

"Faith!" her dad screamed from inside the house.

"I have to go, Gian. I'll see you tomorrow," Faith whispered in his ear as she left.

"Tomorrow," he replied.

It was too early to go home. Gian needed to find someone to talk to. He needed to talk to Pablo, and strangely he hadn't seen him all day. At that moment, he knew that he had to find him. Gian went to Pablo's apartment next door and as he approached, he realized that it was slightly ajar. Gian called out a few times as he entered, with no response, but he knew someone was home. He sensed it. The living room was rather dark as he entered; a pale light emanated from a small lamp on a table nearby. He glanced around the room and realized for the first time how colorless it was. He could sense the lack of a woman's touch in the dull, almost desperate surroundings. He had become so aware of the world around him in the past few days. It amazed him how much he had taken for granted. As he inspected the living room, he noticed an open notebook on a small desk in the corner with a lit candle near it. The flame seemed to beckon him toward it. He felt compelled to read this open book; the title of the page caught his eye.

"Pain"

Life is pain
Follow me into a world of shame
A planet screaming
But no one hears
Everyone blames
Everyone else
Everyday
No one sees me
Everyday
No one hears me
Everyday
No one needs me
Everyday
No one loves me
Everyday
I'm crying out
Screaming out loud, I shout
Can't you see me?
Don't you care?
Won't you hold me?
Please, somewhere
Every minute of every day

I cry unseen tears
My heart turns gray
No one sees me
Everyday
No one hears me
Everyday
No one needs me
Everyday
No one loves me
Everyday
Would anyone notice?
If I disappeared
Lost in a nightmare I used to fear?
The Sun would still set
The moon would still rise
No one sees my despair, my disguise
No one sees me
Everyday
No one hears me
Everyday
No one needs me
Everyday
No one loves me
Everyday
No one ever loves me
Everyday
No one ever holds me
Everyday
No one ever cares
Everyday
Can anyone hear me?
Please.

Stunned, he did not recognize the author of this song. He knew that Pablo had collaborated with Faith on some of her songs, but he never knew that he had written some of his own. Could Pablo have written such a desperate plea? Gian could not believe it. Sadly, he continued to read on; he felt he had to.

"Just a Kid"

You trust the universe
To keep you safe
You trust the world
To know its place
I was too small to know
Given not enough time to grow
I was
Just a kid
Looking for safety
I was just a kid
Crying for you
To see me
Just me
Only me
Always me
Just a kid, God
I was just a kid
I looked through
A dirty pane of glass
At a sky smeared with lipstick
Upon the window's bars
A thick layer of dirt
Kept in all the hurt
You could only hear screams
Of a world so sick
A world so sick, a world so sick
Can't anyone see me?

Can't anyone hear me?
Can't anyone help me?
I'm right here
Is there anyone, anyone out there?
Can't you just hold me
Before I go insane?
Can't you just need me
Like I need you?
Can't you just love me
Please, cause I love you?
Can't you see
That I'm just a kid
Looking for safety
Just a kid
Crying for you to see me?
Just a kid
Just me, always me
Just a kid, God
I was just a kid
Just a kid, damn
I was only, just a kid

Gian found himself immersed in a world he barely knew existed, reading the writings of a friend he did not recognize, reading about a pain he did not understand. He felt that he had to read on; an author writes for others as well as for himself, he thought. Sometimes the truth lies hidden within a person's words and nowhere else. He couldn't help but read on.

"Life's Lonely Highway"

I'm in a dark place
I can't find my way
Lost in my nightmares
Almost everyday
I awaken to a different world

Trapped by the shame
I can't find my way out
I can't seem to shout
I'm losing ground
I've lost my way
On life's long lonely highway
I'm losing ground
I've lost my way
On life's long lonely highway
I'm lost now
And in such a different place
Too lost to forget my hidden face
Too lost in the shadows of my soul
Too lost to find
The warmth in the cold
I'm losing ground beneath my feet
I've lost my way
On life's long lonely highway
I'm losing ground
I've lost my way
On life's long lonely highway
I can't hear you anymore
Knocking on my hidden door
To a place only I can go
To a place only I can find
A place away from life
Where pain is left behind
Can't you see I'm losing ground?
I've lost my way
On life's long lonely highway
I'm losing ground beneath my feet
On life's long lonely highway
Please help me to

Find my way
On life's long lonely highway
Please don't leave me here
All by myself
On life's long lonely highway
It's so dark out here
So dark I can't
On life's long lonely highway

Stunned, Gian closed the book, unable to read on. His mind was deeply troubled, his thoughts raced about in his head. Could Pablo have written these painful words? "He must have," Gian thought, "My God, he must have." Gian felt like he didn't really know his friend at all anymore. So much had changed in just a few moments. So much had changed by reading a few pages; so much had changed, indeed.

Suddenly he recalled why he had come, and then he thought that perhaps he was meant to come here on this night at this time, perhaps he was meant to be here.

His surroundings appeared even stranger now as he surveyed them, darker, more desolate, lonelier, almost sad. He felt as if the room itself was trying to communicate with him. "Finally, someone is paying attention" it seemed to say, "Just look around and you will see what is so obvious to me; just look around and you will know."

A sense of urgency engulfed Gian as he struggled to move again, to find his way, as he struggled to find his friend. His heart pounded almost audibly inside his chest. Beads of perspiration broke out on his lips, his breathing quickened, for he could smell the despair about him. He could finally sense it all around him, choking him, almost winning. He could sense imminent danger, and when he finally arrived at the door to his friend's room, he felt as if his heart had stopped for a moment, deep within his chest. For a moment he could not catch his breath, he could not breathe. For a moment he could only see a sad boy before him, one he had never seen before, one he had never known existed.

Once he opened that door, an eerie quiet ensued, and in the absolute darkness ahead of him, he could see a figure, at first unrecognizable, as his worried eyes adjusted to the dim light. He froze. Whoever it was before him stood still, apparently unaware of his presence. Within the stillness he began to recognize

Pablo standing motionless before him in the center of the room with one hand up toward his head. He struggled to see what object Pablo held, and in horror Gian watched, speechless at first, as he realized the object in his friend's hand was a gun pointed right at his temple. Pablo's eyes were closed as he stood there in the agony of the moment. Perspiration dripped down his glistening, boyish face, joining with the tears that flowed down his pale cheeks. Gian froze, unable to speak, unable to move, unable to utter a sound. There before him now stood someone he did not recognize. A long-time friend was now a complete stranger, a figure of absolute pain. In the past few days the world had changed in ways he could never have imagined. He was finally able to see, finally able to listen; finally, he was able to help.

"Pablo!" Gian screamed. "No! Please, no!"

Startled, Pablo quickly opened his eyes and gazed towards his friend in apparent shock. When he attempted to move, he fell backward into a large aquarium he kept on a stand nearby. He quickly regained his stance, but the aquarium shook back and forth spewing forth both water and fish onto the floor around him. They could hear the frantic patter of fins on the hardwood floors. They could almost hear the panting of these small creatures fighting for air, fighting to breathe. They could sense their desperate battle to live, their frantic search for life. Pablo frantically picked each of them up and placed them back into the water. Once finished, he looked at Gian with his baby blue eyes shining in the near darkness about him, like a child frozen with fear and rage. He trembled with the gun still in his hand, now held down at his side. Gian froze at the sight of this boy he thought he had known, unable to recognize the pain contained within these moments—the pain within his friend's eyes. He was indeed seeing Pablo for the very first time, and he couldn't bring himself to cry, though he desperately wanted to. He wanted to cry.

"You could have killed me!" Pablo screamed out finally. "What are you doing here in my house, in my room?" he stammered like a small child. "How did you get in? I mean, what are you doing here? I mean, how could you...come in." He finally ended his search for words in apparent shock and anger. Gian was finally able to run toward his friend and gently remove the gun as it lay within his fingers. He placed it on a table nearby and proceeded to turn on the light. He then quietly approached this frightened, angry young friend as he now stood there before him trembling like a lost child in the darkness, and hugged him like a father embraces his son when he awakens from a nightmare in the isolation of his room on a cold night. After a few moments, Pablo withdrew and sat down on his bed. He didn't speak at first, nor did Gian. Gian searched his friend's face to find the carefree young man he knew, but he couldn't find him. The figure before him was almost unrecognizable. His pain was visible, it was palpable, and as a result Gian could not bring himself to ask any questions, for he feared the responses. Finally, he was able to muster enough courage to speak.

"Pablo," he began, his lips trembling and his voice quavering, "are you all right?" There was no response. Only the ticking of a clock nearby pierced the silence.

"Pablo, did something happen tonight? Is something wrong?" Confused and afraid, Gian could not find the right words. He searched his brain, praying for them, but none came. There must be a reason I'm here tonight, a reason for my finding Pablo like this, he thought, I must find the right words, I must. "Please Pablo, please answer me, I'm scared, please," Gian beckoned for him to respond in some manner as Pablo sat there before Gian, merely a ghost of the boy he knew. "What were you doing with that gun, Pablo?" Gian finally was able to ask. "Whose gun is it?"

Pablo appeared stunned by the question, but he looked up at his friend now with childlike eyes, and was finally able to whisper a response, "It was my mom's."

His mom's? "How was that possible?," Gian asked himself, "if Pablo's mother had disappeared many years ago and never been seen since? How is it possible that this gun would belong to her, and why would Pablo attempt to use it so many years later?" Gian was even more confused and frightened now.

"Pablo," he began again, the words barely uttered across his lips, his voice trembling a bit, "What were you doing with the gun?, Pablo please tell me?"

"No!" came the abrupt response, so detached did Pablo seem from his good friend, and all of the questions at that point. Gian questioned for a second whether or not he could be under the influence of some drug, but he knew better. Pablo just continued to stare off into space as Gian began his frantic search around the room looking for clues of any kind to explain this near-tragedy before him. What could have drawn his good friend to this? He soon realized that everything was as it always had been, except for Pablo.

"I think I need to call your dad; maybe he can help," Gian began.

"No, please, no, Gian, no. It would just break his heart," Pablo sobbed, and again Gian felt so helpless. He knew that Faith would know what to say, and he felt so utterly alone.

"Okay, Pablo, I won't call him," he paused, "But you have to tell me, my friend, please, Pablo, please tell me. Maybe I can help."

"It was my mom," came forth the only words his friend could utter, with a trembling, childlike voice, before he seemed to disappear again into the darkness of his thoughts. Sitting as he was on the bed, Pablo lowered his head as if to gaze downward, and he appeared as if he was about to lose consciousness and fall onto the floor, for his eyes closed and his body slumped forward. Gian lunged toward him, and grabbing hold of him, pushed his body back onto the bed. Gian lay there atop his friend as he lost control and fell unto the bed himself, and he couldn't see Pablo at first, but he could hear him breathing beneath him. Gian rolled over toward the other side of the bed but the scene before him was so totally different that he found himself opening and closing his eyes in disbelief. It was as if he had been transported to another place. He found himself in a small room with very little light emanating from a window behind him, a window whose glass was so dirty one could barely see out beyond it; bars crisscrossed the opening. He could hear the sounds of a busy street outside, though—the chaotic sounds of city life.

The sobs of a child now filled the space, and Gian sat up upon the bed and could plainly see a small boy on an unmade bed before him with tears flowing from his sad blue eyes. The room about him was unkempt and in total disarray. He now visualized another figure standing over the crying child. He fixed his gaze upon the figure of a woman dressed only in a long, worn robe and slippers. He could not see her face clearly; her dirty blonde hair fell at her shoulders and partially obscured his view. In her hand she held a gun with its nozzle right up against the little boy's head. He could see this small, helpless boy clearly as he gazed toward him now with his large, wet blue-green eyes, the gun embedded in his shocking blonde hair. The helpless, innocent little boy gazed at Gian as if he were seeing an angel and his sobs suddenly ceased. Gian attempted to move and then speak, but he was unable to. It was as if he could only bear witness to this tragedy, unable to do anything to help. Gian focused all of his attention on the gun, for it seemed familiar, finally recognizing it as the same one that he had just removed from his friend Pablo's hand moments earlier. With that realization came another: The little boy before him was none other than Pablo. The deafening silence of this horrifying realization was suddenly shattered by an enraged voice.

"I am going to kill you!" the woman screamed as she turned slightly to reveal her pale face and her empty blue eyes that were so filled with rage. "I am going to kill you like you killed me years ago!" she screamed again as she pulled the hammer back with her thumb, the gun now painfully jabbed up against the little boy's head.

"You took my life away; you took my beauty away. You stole my life on the day you were born, and I hate you for it. And now I'm going to take my life back by ending yours. I want you dead, do you hear me; I want you dead!" The woman's voice was so filled with anger that the little boy could only close his eyes to protect himself. Gian became a witness to a horror so palpable the room itself seemed engulfed by it.

Out of nowhere a man ran into the room panting, his face in indescribable pain. He grabbed the gun out of the woman's hand just as she was about to pull the trigger, with such force that he knocked her down onto the floor below. The little boy collapsed on the bed, and the panicked figure of the man gently picked the frightened little angel up into his arms, and kissed his head before he turned to carry him out of the room. Gian at last recognized this man as Pablo's father, but he apparently could not see him as Pablo had, for he rushed by him to leave without hesitation. Gian apparently was only visible to Pablo.

In another instant Gian found himself again on Pablo's bed. At first he appeared a bit confused. Then, as reality resurfaced, he quickly stood up and anxiously searched the room for his dear friend. At last he found him still lying atop his bed, and when their faces met, in the faint light of the present time, tears filled each one's eyes, and they both knew that they had visited such a painful place together. Gian knew that he had seen in that moment what no words could ever communicate. Pablo sat up, and Gian sat back down next to him, both of them traumatized by a past horror. Gian wanted so much to tell his friend that everything would be all right. He wanted so much to hold the little boy in his vision in his arms and protect him from his past, but he could not. Years had passed since that day, and the tragedy of that moment lived on.

"I'm sorry," he was finally able to utter to his sad companion, "I am so sorry for what happened to you, Pablo, so sorry that I couldn't…."

Breaking his silence, Pablo replied at last in a subdued voice. "If it wasn't for my dad, I'd be dead," he began. "If it wasn't for my dad, I'd be dead," he reiterated.

What could Gian say? There seemed no words fit to speak, no words at all.

"My own mother pointed that gun to my head, my own mother," he continued. "My own mother wanted to kill me!" He paused for a moment, as his gaze seemed to fall onto the gun where it now rested upon the table. He reached over and quietly picked it up and held it nervously within his hand.

"My dad doesn't know that I have this. He doesn't know I have it. As crazy as it seems, this gun holds one of the few memories that I have left of her. When I hold it, I can hear her voice, see her face, feel her touch." He paused for a moment as he grabbed hold of the gun tightly within his fist. "That day was the very last day. I've never seen or heard from my mother since. She left before I woke up, and we've never spoken of her—never. Except once, my father told me once that my mother was sick, that she wasn't herself that day. He told me that she was sick, and that none of it was my fault. Can you believe that, Gian? Just once in all of these years, and I can't bring myself to bring it up again; and, dear God, I really want to." He paused and stared at Gian with the eyes of the little frightened boy.

"As crazy as it is, Gian, this gun holds one of the few memories I have of my mother," he repeated again as if trying somehow to explain the unexplainable. "I've never been able to—never been strong enough—to get rid of it."

There are moments in life when Gian wished the words he needed to say would come easily to him, and with them he could make some things better. At that moment, only silence ensued. In that moment only silence could answer such desperate pleas—only silence.

"Gian," his brave young friend continued. "I've never spoken of that day with anyone before, not even Faith. I guess I never could, but somehow, today, you were there…with me. Somehow, when I saw you there, I felt for the first time like I am not alone in this world. Somehow your being there—with me—helped. I am no longer alone with my mother on that day, when her words shattered my soul, even if this gun didn't. Somehow you were able to show that little kid inside of me that God was there on that horrible day; I was not alone; I was never alone. Somehow my pain is less; my fear is gone." He paused and gazed at Gian before continuing in a calm tone. "Thank you, Gian. Thank you for allowing me to see, for the very first time, that it wasn't my fault. My mother hated me because she was sick. I was just a little boy. My father, he…he…he saved my life that day," he paused to stare deep into Gian's eyes, "And you saved my soul today."

Gian struggled to find right the words to say to his friend. He prayed that he would find them. He needed to be strong for him. He needed to be so strong.

"Pablo," he began, quietly at first, avoiding Pablo's eyes, "you know that as children, we fall and quickly get back up. We break a bone, and once its healed, we forget all about it," he looked down to find Pablo with his eyes before continuing, "But the hardest scars to heal are those we can never see. They are the ones that scar our soul."

"The hardest scars to heal," he began again after a brief period of reflection, "are those we cannot see. They are the ones that scar our soul—the ones that form us, the ones that can change a person forever. The very reason criminals are created, or heroes are born. And you, Pablo, are my hero, and everyone who is fortunate to know you loves you for the incredible person you are. You are a very giving and loving and caring young man." He paused to look deeply into the innocence of this youth before him. "I am so sorry for what happened, Pablo. God is sorry, too. He couldn't change what happened to you yesterday, so he must have sent me there today, to be with you yesterday, so that somehow, together, we can be strong enough, strong enough, Pablo, you and I, to finally let go of yesterday, to finally be free."

Gian reached for the gun and once it was in his possession, he hugged his friend like his mother should have. It is finally time to let go of this," he began, "To let go of that night, to let go of all of the painful memories. Together we can find the courage to rise up from the past and defeat it. Together you will never be alone again. Together you will never be alone again."

With those words, Gian let go of his friend, and they proceeded out of that dark room, out of that dark house, not one but two souls united on a path toward forgiveness, on a path toward the light. Gian carried that heavy burden for his friend, at first down the abandoned, cold streets of an exceptionally still city, and then through the woods of a park a couple miles away. Gian carried the gun that had so devastated a life. They carried it together as they walked alone in silence, Gian leading Pablo toward their destiny.

Pablo stopped, and just as suddenly broke the deafening silence, causing his friend to stop too, and look upon him with concern etched across his face. "Thank you, Gian," he began, "For helping that little boy—that little lost boy whose mother couldn't love him—finally find his way."

Gian stopped to embrace his friend again briefly, and then they continued on their journey, only now they spoke of everything. They spoke of everyone. They bonded as brothers as they walked along that never-ending road on that never-ending night. Two brothers, embarking on a journey together, that one could not do alone.

When they finally arrived at the river's edge in the stillness of that dark night, Gian reached for the gun and held it out over the turbulent waters before them, as Pablo grabbed onto it, too, and together they tossed it out into the water. Together they hurled it and all of the tragedy it contained so far out into the depths of the river that they could barely hear it disappear––forever.

The walk home was filled with a renewed spirit, and Pablo finally seemed to revert to the one whom everyone would now recognize, only now his eyes were as innocent as he.

"So why did you come over to see me tonight, anyway, huh?" he began impatiently, as always.

"What?" Gian responded, apparently taken by surprise, "Oh it's not important."

"Look Gian, I know you, and something's on your mind lately, something more than just all of this craziness."

Gian had not realized how much his friend knew him, for there was something he needed to talk about but couldn't. Tonight all of that seemed to change.

"You see, Pablo," he began as he searched inside his shirt and pulled out a gold chain that he wore about his neck, "You see these gold rings, here," he paused as the two of them now stopped upon the pavements not too far from their homes, "One of them is for Faith," he sighed deeply before continuing, "For Faith."

Perplexed Pablo just stared upon the gold articles in the dim light of a street lamp overhead without uttering a sound.

"I want," Gian struggled to speak. "I want to ask Faith to marry me, Pablo, but how can I ask her now?"

"Faith loves you Gian, "Pablo responded without hesitation.

"I work in a homeless shelter," Gian painstakingly responded, "you and Faith and Monsignor Lilli are the only family I have. I have no money. I don't even have a nice place to live, Pablo, and Faith, well, you know, she is everything. She is everything. She loves me even though I have nothing to give her, even these rings are old, and my life, well, it's so chaotic. I don't understand it myself. Most days I don't even understand how she could love me at all—"

"Faith loves you, my man," Pablo interrupted, unable to contain himself, "She loves you. Nothing else matters, and…and, besides, Gian, you're special. Look at tonight, huh? You're just special, and I know that we were all meant to be together, you know, as, a family."

"When did you grow up?" Gian responded, his words filled with emotion as he grabbed his friend by the arm and they continued their short walk home. Each of their faces bore smiles that night in the darkness, broken only by the artificial lights of a sleeping city. They smiled like children do when they finally arrive home, safe at last, safe at home, at last.

CHAPTER 5

It was still so dark that early morning: too dark for the birds to awaken, too dark for most creatures on the Earth. A solitary figure quietly entered a home unannounced through a back window and, once inside, approached a sleeping, peaceful soul on a bed nearby. Sensing something amiss, the sleeping figure stirred, and, through the corner of a half-open eye, a recognizably familiar face stood there in the shadows.

"Pablo," a weak voice uttered quietly, apparently not surprised by neither the visit nor the visitor, "is something wrong?"

"What would I do without you, Faith?" was the equally faint reply. Faith sat up to rub her sleepy eyes and wipe away wisps of hair from her beautiful face. She glanced over at her alarm clock to find that it was only four-thirty. A new day of this late summer season had barely begun. She did not normally have to go to work until nine, and Pablo was still out of school. Pablo had disturbed her sleep many times in the past. His dad worked long hours, and he hated to awaken him. Faith was always just a few feet and a window away, and in the past he would visit often, for comfort from a nightmare or to talk about anyone or anything that was disrupting his sleep. Faith was Pablo's sister, and mother, and friend. Many times he would fall asleep next to her when he was just a child; more recently he would sleep on the floor near her bed. Faith was concerned this time about her little brother, for he hadn't done anything like this in the past couple of years, and she could see that something was different about her friend as he stood there in the dim light of a very early morning. He still had that angelic face and light blond hair, and those innocent green eyes still pleaded with her, but he appeared grown, almost a man. For a moment she could picture him as that frightened little boy who would often just crawl into bed with her without even a word, but then she noticed that he was dressed in yesterday's clothes. Light-blue faded jeans, old sneakers, and a cream-colored T-shirt, mostly wrinkled and worn, adorned his body, and she wondered why. Although he would often come to her for comfort and advice, for she was the center of his emotional world, never had he disrupted her sleep in the past couple of years. Something was wrong. Sensing her obvious concern, Pablo finally broke the silence. He spoke softly so as not to awaken her parents.

"Don't worry, Faith. I'm fine. I'm better than I've been in years," his mouth smiled a boyish grin.

"You wouldn't have come if everything was all right, Pablo," she replied with a noticeable crack in her shaken voice, "and you haven't slept at all."

"But I am. You see, I couldn't wait to tell you; I couldn't sleep until I told you about last night."

"Told me about what, Pablo?" Faith interrupted her friend at this point nervously, "what happened last night?"

"No, no, not here, Faith. You have to get up and get dressed and come with me. I'll tell you on the way." He then grabbed his friend's arm and encouraged her up and out of bed. Faith obliged, and within seconds she emerged from her bathroom in a pair of jeans with her pajama T-shirt top tucked into them. She then slid into a nearby pair of sandals, placing her hair in a bun, and out the window they went, unnoticed. At first, as they both walked along the urban sidewalks toward the park during the pre-dawn hour, there was silence. They held hands as they continued on, each secure in each other's touch, until Pablo began to recount to his sister all of the events of the preceding night. Faith at times would stop to hug her little brother, and twice she cried into his arms, for even she was unaware of the full tragedy surrounding his mother's departure all those many years ago before her friend's arrival at her doorstep. She was also very unaware of the toll his mother's leaving had taken on her little brother.

Pablo was taking her toward the river, where earlier he and Gian had cast aside the gun—a moment that had changed his life forever. As they approached the river's edge, the Sun began to rise. They joined hands and faced the rising Sun together. It was an exceptionally clear, crisp morning, and the dazzling rays of yellow cast their miraculous glow on everything they touched. The water glistened and the grass sparkled, as if by command. The flowers quietly opened and the birds began their morning song. Hues of amber and orange illuminated everything in its path, including these two souls now transformed by this spectacular sight.

"I can't explain it, Faith, but this is how I feel," Pablo said after a short period of silence, "You see how dark it was just a few minutes ago, and now, well, now, you can see the miracle of a new day. One minute there was nothing, and the next, everything. That is what Gian gave me last night, Faith: all of this," he paused as he pointed toward the Sun and all of its glorious gifts. They embraced in the newborn rays of an old friend.

"Today I can feel it warm my very soul," he continued, "and I needed to share that with you. I needed to share it with you, Faith. I needed for you to know that I'm finally all right."

Faith hugged her friend closer, her eyes filled with joyful tears. She could sense her brother's rebirth. She could feel the difference. She could see it in his eyes, and hear it in his voice, and sense it in his embrace. A lifetime of hurt, and finally the wound was healing.

"I am so happy for you, Pablo," she whispered into his ear as she continued to hold him so tight, "I am so very happy for you."

The Sun had risen all around them, as they stood there holding hands by the river's edge. With each sunrise, God renews his faith in this world, his commitment to us. This morning these two souls experienced a different sunrise. The light of this new day not only lit up the sky, but the soul of one of its children, where there had been pain, there was now peace. Where there was darkness there was now light. It is never too late for a sunrise.

"You know that I love you Pablo," Faith began again, "And Gian, he couldn't love you more, we both love you, Pablo. We are a family, and we will always be a family."

"I know," Pablo responded.

"This is only the beginning of a new journey for us, Pablo."

"I know."

"Are you afraid?"

"I'll never be afraid again, Faith, never, not as long as I have you and Gian in my life," Pablo innocently replied.

"I need you too, Pablo; I always have. We need you," she responded before embracing him one last time.

Once the Sun had risen, and the sky's magnificent panorama was complete, the two solitary figures, joined hands in a union of friendship and siblinghood and love, as they gradually began their trek back home. Inseparable since their first encounter many years earlier, their bond was greater, their need for each other grander, their love stronger. As they walked along, they spoke of their future, and then as they neared home, they made plans to meet at lunchtime in the music room to complete a song they had been struggling to write together.

Each of them turned to depart as they arrived home, but not before Faith reached up to kiss her brother on the cheek, as she pushed his tousled hair back upon his head, like she had done so many times before, on so many prior encounters. She could sense that this time was different, as they each walked home apart. She stopped and turned to watch him leave and she could see that her little brother, a once frightened small boy, had grown into a young man. She quickly made her way to her bedroom window and crawled inside to begin her morning ritual to ready herself for work. Once complete, she sat in her comfortable chair with her familiar teddy bear in hand, afraid. Afraid of what today might bring, afraid of losing Gian. Somehow she knew that Gian had always been a very special soul. As she thought back through their years together, and her recollections unfolded in her mind, she realized that there were hints of mystery all along. She refused to see it then, too afraid to face reality, a reality she did not want to comprehend. A reality she knew was inescapable. Tears began to fill her eyes, in an effort to wash away her fear, in an effort to wash away her pain, but they could not. As strong as she was, and she had an incredible strength, she wasn't sure that she could be strong enough for Gian this time.

"Faith are you ready yet?'" a familiar voice pierced the silence, and startled reality into those within listening distance, "Your father and I are going to work, you're late."

"All right mom," was her hurried response.

"I'm leaving in a bit, have a good day," her mom's voice weakened as she left home.

Rushed, Faith gathered up her last-minute items and departed for work, all the while thinking of Gian, almost obsessing about him.

At work the day seemed to drag on forever. It was unusually quiet, so the minutes never seemed to pass. Pablo arrived early for their lunch session, and as usual was disruptive to everyone at the store. He had an uncanny ability to make fast friends, and his smile was contagious. This morning he appeared even friendlier, and of course even more disruptive, if that was even possible, and Budd couldn't take it any longer. No one was getting any work done. He told Faith to take an early lunch, please, and to take Pablo with her. They both quickly left to go upstairs, and Budd breathed a deep sigh of relief.

Once upstairs, Pablo rambled on that had spent a good part of the morning working on their song, and had finished it, or so he thought. Faith had taught Pablo to play the piano, and he had exceeded even her greatest expectations. He had become an incredible musician, a natural player.

"Now Faith, if you don't like it, let me know," he began nervously. "I'll play it for you now, but stop me at any time if you don't like it, do you understand, huh? Huh, do you? Well do you?"

"All right Pablo, of course I understand," Faith replied "go ahead and play the song already."

Pablo sat down at the piano, placed his song in front of him, and began his haunting melody.

"I Reach for You"

When pain came knocking at my door
And I was too weak to resist
When pain came and took away my dreams
When the dark and the moon kissed
I reach for you
To wipe away all of my fears
I reach for you
To wipe away all of my tears
I reach for you
To fill me with everlasting hope
When I can't cope any more
I reach for you
When life weighs more than I can bear
And my past is too heavy to carry
When all around me is despair
And the world is so empty
I can close my eyes and dream of a place so beautiful it seems
As beautiful as life should be
When
I reach for you
When night is all around me and day is driven from the sky

When darkness is all you can see, and life begins to die
When hope is just another word whose meaning is a lie
When all seems lost and happiness is saying good-bye
I reach for you to wipe away all of my fears
I reach for you to wipe away all of my tears
I reach for you to fill me with everlasting hope
When I can't cope any more
I reach for you
For when the stars in the sky beckon me to stay
When the sunrise returns to bless another day
When I see you there in the shadows of my mind
I touch your smile
I kiss your face
I feel your incredible embrace
And my soul searches for a better place
When I reach for you to wipe away all of my fears
I reach for you to wipe away all of my tears
I reach for you to fill me with everlasting hope
When I can't cope any more
I reach for you
I will always reach for you

When Pablo finished playing Faith immediately ran over to him and embraced him, her eyes moist with tears at the sight of her little brother before her. Overcome with emotion, she was at a loss for words. Pablo, sensing her love, spoke quietly into his sister's ear. "Faith, I don't think, I've, um, told you, I mean, um, well, thank you for opening up your home and your heart to me."

At that moment Budd and Gian burst into the music room, and found Pablo and Faith still in each other's arms.

Budd immediately teased, "Hey what's going on here, incest?' he laughed before he bit into a large doughnut he carried in one hand, and then he proceeded to take a quick swig from a coffee cup he held in his other, before continuing, "Do you see this, Gian?" he began again, almost choking on the coffee. "Do you?" He sarcastically demanded. Wearing an oversized shirt with casual pants and doughnut crumbs on his collar, Budd was over the top even for him.

"What? No answer?," he continued in between bites of his doughnut, "See what happens when we're not around?" he swigged back some more coffee before adding, "See?"

Faith turned toward them and Pablo just smiled. Gian seemed so happy to see Pablo smiling again, even though he and Faith had already spoken on the phone about her walk to the river that morning. Gian could clearly see how happy Pablo was, his eyes aglow again with the innocence of youth, his spirit renewed. Faith finally responded to her friend Budd's taunts, "We were just celebrating the completion of that new song we were both working on. Pablo finished it today and it is beautiful." She rushed up to Gian, at the completion of that sentence, and embraced him lightly while whispering into his ear, "I missed you Gian; I missed you so much."

"Hey! Why don't we play it for you both now?" Pablo exclaimed.

"Great idea!" Budd replied, and within minutes the song was sung even more emotionally than the first time, and Budd and Gian applauded them both so loudly that the room seemed aglow with the beauty of renewed life and renewed hope. Gian was so glad to feel all of these great emotions again. It felt like the good old times, even if for but a few moments. Faith shone as beautifully as any angel would. Gian could not take his eyes off of her. Anyone who met her fell immediately under her spell, especially when she sang, for she sang from her heart and from her soul, and for a short while anyone who listened to her was swept up in the moment, away from their ordinary lives into Faith's beautiful world.

"That was fantastic, Faith and Pablo, just awesome! You both deserve congratulations!" Budd yelled out, overwhelmed in the moment, "But remember: We only have this room for an hour so let's get working, we need to practice, so let's go everybody." Everyone immediately got into position to play. They all seemed so accustomed to the need to rehearse in short pockets of stolen time that their preparations took only seconds, it seemed. When they were all ready the music began for a song entitled, "Heaven Sent."

> I close my eyes to loneliness and pain
> With nothing to lose and all to gain
> I close my eyes yet I can't help but see
> Your face in the rain smiling down at me
> For you showed me what love meant
> Heaven sent

For you showed me what love meant
Now that I have you
Heaven sent
Life can overcome your dreams
All too often it overwhelms it seems
Like living on someone else's borrowed hope
For I can no longer see
For I can no longer fear
For I can only see your smiling face
Now that you are finally here
To you and only you I lent
My soul, my life, my love, heaven sent
For you showed me what love meant
Now that I have found you
Heaven sent
For you showed me what hope meant
Now that I have found you
Heaven sent
For I can no longer see
For I can no longer fear
For I can only see your smiling face
Now that you are here
I can no longer see the clouds
I will no longer fear the rain
Now that you are finally here with me
To you and only you my love
My soul I lent
Our love is truly
Heaven sent

"That was great everyone, really. I know how much you all are tired of playing our first song. Even you Faith, you were, as always, wonderful," Budd added.

Faith possessed an amazing vocal range, and performed almost effortlessly. Budd had arraigned for her to have vocal lessons here at the store free of charge, and each time the coach seemed more impressed by her natural talent. Faith always shrugged it all off, and performed each song like it was her first time. She had amazing ability, and yet she never took it for granted, and she never behaved as if she was as talented as she was.

The next song was one that Pablo had written with his music class at school. Pablo was always a little embarrassed by the song, even though it was well written and nicely scored. So much had changed since the last time he performed it with the group, so much. Gian now glanced over at his friend, just as the song was about to begin, and he smiled at him. Pablo winked back in response, and life appeared for the moment normal again. The music began but Pablo did not play at first. Everyone stopped until they seemed to engage their friend again; Pablo just smiled, and started to play.

> I see you almost every day
> I watch you from afar
> I smile when I see your face
> For every moment has its special place
> In my heart forever
> I gaze into your beautiful eyes
> When you cannot see
> I imagine that you see me standing there
> Before you look away
> Why can't you notice me just once?
> Just look as if you care
> Why can't you notice me just once
> As if I was really here?
> I need for you to see
> That I'm waiting,
> Just waiting for you to notice me
> I wait and wait and wait for weeks I search
> And search for what my heart seeks
> A sign from you
> Just one small clue

That you will finally notice me too
Just one small clue that finally you noticed me too
It's been so hard waitin' for what may never come
So hard hoping for a clue
That you'll finally see me standin' right here
In front of you
Why can't you notice me just once?
Just look as if you care
Why can't you notice me just once
As if I were finally here?
I need for you to see
I need for you to notice me
At last
And finally

It was very quiet at first when the song ended, until a group of musicians entered the room, and Budd quickly got his group's attention, declaring that their time was up. They barely said good-bye to him as they exited. The three of them left the building quickly. It was a quiet evening, dark, but not especially hot. Faith, Gian, and Pablo appeared pretty happy with their performances earlier, as they smiled and talked about the songs and they walked along like they had done so many times before. Only, this time, things were different, for they had become even closer over the past twenty-four hours, closer than they had ever been. They were on their way to the arcade, a familiar destination for them some nights. Faith abruptly changed the subject, startling Pablo and Gian into silence.

"Last night I realized how much you both mean to me," she began, "How much we mean to each other. How much we need each other. How much we care for each other." She paused as she quickly looked at each of her companions and smiled, "I love you both more than you could ever know."

Suddenly a beat-up old car arrived nearby, honked its horn, and stopped right there beside them on the street.

It was Nancee. Nancee was a former school friend of Faith's, one of her very best friends. She was far-eastern in appearance, "A mix of the very best of the Orient and Spain," she always laughed. Her hair was a beautiful rich black color, her skin appeared as white as porcelain, her eyes as deep brown as a cup of espresso. Tattoos were quietly scattered about her body reminding everyone who knew her what a free spirit she was.

"Get in," she exclaimed from the car once she had stopped by the curb. Each of them quickly entered, and she sped off in a noisy puff of exhaust fumes. Nancee was dressed in one of her many uniforms, for she worked at least two jobs to put herself through college. She mainly worked at a local cafe and always became the talk of her patrons' tables, for she possessed an incredible wit, with a dash of sauciness sprinkled in.

"So where are we all going?" she exclaimed, after they took off down the city's streets.

"Someplace close, I hope," Pablo began, "in this tin can you call a car."

"Hey! At least I have a car," she shot back, "no one in this city will ever give you a license to drive, considering your biking record."

"Hey, wait just a fortune cookie moment, will you, 'cause nobody here knows what you're talking about."

"Let's see," she began, "what's the tally now? Um, five bikes, four pets, and three pedestrians injured, two car accidents, and, oh, that's right: one store-front."

"Very funny," Pablo could barely reply before the roar of laughter became too intense for it to be heard.

"By the way, where are we going?" Pablo said when he was finally able to speak again, "Oh perfect one," he added.

"To the fair in the town just down the road," Nancee replied, as she sped down the street and out of the city.

"Hey, wait just a junk-yard minute!" Pablo exclaimed. "We were going to the arcade."

"The arcade, what a surprise, I wonder whose idea that was?" Nancee sarcastically replied.

"But, but, but…."

"All right, don't get yourself stressed, my man, we'll go to the arcade after, I promise."

All one could hear for a few moments were the sounds of a graveyard car straining to arrive at its destination intact. Nancee was a true survivor. She had a straightforward, no-nonsense approach to life. She was a joy to be around. She was the youngest of three children who had been raised by her Korean mother. Her dad was "a mixed breed," she used to say, who died in the Persian Gulf War. Her mom was an extraordinary woman who did her very best to raise her children on her own. Everyone who met Nancee's mom couldn't help but be impressed, not just because of her delicate nature, but also by her intelligence, compassion, and sincerity. Nancee had learned a lot from her mom, for she was one determined young woman. Failure was just not a word in her vocabulary. This group, all huddled this night inside this small, quite worn vehicle, were a band of misfits who somehow found each other, fitting together perfectly in the puzzle called life.

Nancee pulled alongside a fire hydrant to let her friend's out, for parking near the fair appeared impossible. They each exited the vehicle and ran for their lives, before Nancee took off to find a parking space leaving all in her wake in a huge puff of smoke.

As the three of them entered the fair grounds, all seemed amazed at how big it was, and how musical, and how magical it seemed.

"I love carousels!" Faith shouted out as they approached a ticket booth next to the merry-go-round. "We'll go on it first, then," Gian replied, for he wanted so much at this moment to grant Faith her wish. They had to wait a long time in line to finally get aboard the carousel. They quickly found two horses together and before they knew it the music started and they were off on a magical adventure. At first Faith noticed that no one was near them. Then they each realized that no one was on the ride but them. They gazed out toward the control booth, and there stood Pablo and Nancee, with a young man, the ride operator, and of course, Faith quickly recognized him as one of Pablo's high school buddies. Pablo proceeded to hold up a cardboard sign with the word *enjoy* on it. Faith and Gian at first seemed a little embarrassed, but soon they seemed to be enjoying themselves immensely.

It seemed like they were all alone in their own magical world. Their horses were majestic, swaying up and down in unison with the grandness of an orchestra's music, surrounding them. It was as if they had entered a world where fairy tales lived, where animals could talk, and dreams came true; to a place where wishes were granted and everyone had a happy ending. Faith wished that they could stay on this ride forever. Gian was holding Faith's hand, and she appeared so peaceful at his side, as if all of the burdens of their lives had been somehow lifted. Faith's face was angelic in this heavenly place, and she smiled a child's smile. Gian leaned toward her, and at first kissed her on her cheek, and then he kissed on her lips. It seemed like a fairy-tale kiss from a book of fairy tales.

"I love you, Gian," Faith proclaimed afterwards.

"I love you, Faith," Gian responded.

Neither one of them could believe how effortlessly their words came out, especially for Gian, but here everything was different. Everything was, in a word, magical. They kissed again as the ride slowed and the music faded. They each knew that this would be a memory that would last a lifetime, a once-in-forever miracle. Gian helped Faith off her horse, and they embraced before they exited the ride. Faith immediately raced over to Pablo and kissed him on both cheeks, embraced him, and yelled, "Thank-you, my little brother," so loud that everyone all around them could easily hear. Pablo responded with a faint chorus of praise for them both, as onlookers watched in appreciation. For the next couple of hours they all had the most wonderful, the most innocent of times. The four of them behaved as if they had not a worry in the world. It was indeed magical. Later, as they made their way to the car on their journey back to reality, even the sky above them was magical, for the brilliance of the stars above revealed a shooting one, as it graced the horizon in its final glorious moment in this universe in that form. They all seemed to acknowledge the meteor in the moment, as they each gazed upward in unison, perhaps to place a wish on this fairy-tale night.

"Don't you think it is kind of odd what just happened tonight, I mean, everything?" Nancee asked.

"No," Faith responded.

"Nope," Pablo proclaimed as he entered the car, "Now, on to the arcade."

In the car they each spoke of the future, as if the past couple of days never happened. For those few minutes Gian, Faith, and Pablo appeared at peace with themselves, their past, and their present. One could just hear it in their voices as each one of them spoke. The ride to the arcade was full of conversation about nothing. A funny reflection of the joys of life around them, as Nancee's car barely seemed to survive the journey. Once the car was finally parked amidst the smoke and noise, Pablo darted out of it and into the arcade. The rest of them just took their time exiting, in no apparent rush to follow their friend.

Once inside, the search for Pablo began. At first none of them could find him. Aimie, Pablo's secret crush, was there as expected, dressed in designer clothes. Her blonde hair flowed about her shoulders. She was not only beautiful enough to be a model but also the owner's daughter. Her father probably owned most of the real estate in this section of town. Aimie attended private schools, and no one was quite sure why she worked here to begin with. The eyes of every young man in the place were focused on her. She barely acknowledged most of them. Pablo definitely had his work cut out for him.

Pablo appeared out of nowhere with a ten-dollar bill in his hand, definitely not his own, as he and a friend approached Aimie for change. Once the way was clear of patrons, Pablo went in for the kill, almost knocking Aimie over in the process. Aimie didn't even acknowledge him with a response or even a glance, she just handed him his change in her usual manner. What happened next no one could explain, for somehow Pablo lost his balance and fell onto the object of his secret affection, and they each fell to the floor with a thump.

"I'm so sorry," Pablo exclaimed as he quickly arose and tried desperately to help Aimie up, but he tripped on his own shoelaces, and down again they both went for knockdown number two. Aimie quickly got out from under him while the entire arcade looked on. She stood up and yelled out, "Don't touch me!," as she ran into a back room. Pablo quietly stood there at first, his face reddened from embarrassment. Then he slowly followed her to a dark corner of the arcade where she proceeded to light up a cigarette. She fumbled with it like a novice would and did not anticipate Pablo following her. Pablo called out nervously, "Are you all right?," as he approached, startling the poor girl so much that the lit cigarette flew out of her hands, and onto a sprinkler head on the ceiling above. A deafening alarm and streams of water followed and total chaos broke out. All present quickly headed towards the exits. The arcade manager sprang into action immediately and shut the sprinklers down with minimal damage to the place, and even notified the proper authorities of the false alarm. Outside, Gian, Faith, and Nancee quickly found and huddled near their humiliated, wet friend.

"Hey Pablo, my friend, don't fret. At least you got Aimie to notice you," Nancee began mercilessly. "Actually, I don't think she'll ever forget you," she laughed.

"Drop dead," was his frustrated response.

"Oh, come on now, Pablo, you know I was only kidding. Just think about this for a moment: Every guy in there envies you."

"Sure, Nancee, sure, whatever you say," came Pablo's sad response.

"Look, I've got to go now. Tomorrow is an early day for me. Does anyone need a lift?" Nancee politely asked.

"No, we're fine. We can walk from here, don't worry yourself about us," Faith began in reply, actually a little relieved that her friend was leaving, for she could clearly see how upset Pablo was. "And thanks for the great time at the fair," she stated as she kissed her friend on the cheek. Just as Nancee was about to leave, she grabbed Pablo by the hand and asked innocently, "Friends?"

Pablo responded with a polite, "friends," before turning to face Gian and commenting, "I'll probably get arrested if I ever go back in there."

"It was an accident, Pablo. And besides, she shouldn't have been smoking in there," Gian replied.

"Nothing ever seems to go the way I want it to," came his childlike response.

"You know," Faith uttered as we began our walk toward home, "Somehow this will all work out for you, Pablo. Trust me: It may be just what the doctor ordered."

"Yeah, that and a cold shower."

"Well, you just had one," Gian chimed in, and they all laughed. They all needed to laugh. After a while Faith and Pablo continued their conversation, but Gian seemed distracted, distant, and aloof. The usual noises of the surroundings seemed artificially subdued. Something seemed amiss. Tonight it was exceptionally quiet, eerily so. As the three of them crossed an alleyway near Gerard's Place, Gian froze, finally alerting Pablo and Faith to his hidden concerns, but it was too late. Out of nowhere there appeared a gang of thugs, and they surrounded the three of them like a pack of wolves encircling their prey. Two of them were wielding knives, as the others grabbed hold of each of them, before they even had a chance to fight back They were easily outnumbered. Faith let out a scream, as one of the gang, knife in hand, approached her, removing his headgear and quickly stuffing it into her mouth. She responded with a swift kick to his outstretched hand sending the knife hurling out of her attacker's hand. Gian and Pablo each fought to get free, but several of them held them at this point, and their efforts were futile.

"Hey, now, pretty thing, how's about a dance?" the apparent leader taunted Faith.

"Leave her alone!" Gian yelled out, resulting in a sudden punch to his gut.

"If you want money," Pablo uttered nervously, "we don't have any, so please just leave us alone."

"You see," the leader responded in a cold, almost dead voice, "I mean, she's beautiful and all, but all I really want is you," he proclaimed in Gian's face, with his knife one inch away from his intended victim's neck. Gian broke free, startling his captors, and jumped upon his attacker with a force that could only have come from sheer terror. Pablo struggled free in response, but was quickly subdued again. Gian fought with this now unmasked attacker, his face exposed for all to see. He was only a teenager himself, a tattooed, tan-complected youth with curly black hair, sweat beading on his brow, and anger in his eyes. Gian was finally able to grab hold of one of his assailant's wrist, as each of them fell to the ground. In an instant, everything seemed to change, as Gian found himself in a small, very dark room, overcome by the cries of a child nearby in the shadows. He glanced down at his feet, only to find a scared little boy with big brown eyes staring up at him in shock. The child quickly turned away, as if more frightened than before, and began to plead, "Please open the door, please? I'll be good!" he cried out over and over again, "Please, please, let me out!"

The door to this room suddenly opened, and a flood of light blinded them both at first. They were in a closet. Gian peered out at the jailer, and there he stood, a grown man with the devil in his eyes, and a stench emanating from his body, wielding a belt in his hand. Gian looked down upon the small boy there with him and he could only see his frightened eyes staring back at him. He reached out to his little fellow prisoner, and touched his hand. At first, he felt only emptiness. He had never felt anything like this before. He felt lost, forgotten by a world too busy to remember this little boy. He felt hopeless, lifeless, futureless. He felt a cold—the cold of the forgotten youth, the ice left behind when the warmth of life is gone, when the hope of life is buried so deep that it seems lost forever.

"You're quiet," came the abuser's voice, piercing the silence, "Good!." He closed them in again as he slammed the door shut and locked it up. "Why doesn't anyone hear the cries of this innocent child?" Gian asked himself. "Where is everyone? Where is anyone?" The silence of the neighbors and friends and family was overwhelming. The silence of the forgotten was deafening.

In an instant Gian was back on the ground fighting off his attacker, but something was different. This time his attacker wasn't fighting back, and when he gazed into his eyes, Gian recognized them immediately as those of the little trapped boy whose hand he touched in the boy's hellishly hopeless prison. The startled teen immediately stood up and yelled for everyone to leave, and before he disappeared again into the shadows where he had lived his entire life—the shadows from which he had come—his eyes met Gian's one last time, and all Gian could see was that little boy. The face of a scared child who was so afraid of the dark, and now he lived there. Before he disappeared into the shadows again, a single tear could be seen growing from his tear duct, a sign that he remembered—a glimmer of hope, a ray of light in an otherwise black world.

Faith and Pablo each ran up to embrace Gian, as he stood there frozen by what he had just experienced, and Faith was crying. Gian did not move at first. He did not speak.

"What just happened, huh? Can someone please tell me, and why did they leave?" Pablo was barely able to ask as they each stood there in the shadows.

"A change of heart," Gian was finally able to reply as he hugged Faith tighter still and held her close.

"But he wanted to kill you, Gian!" Pablo insisted.

"Not anymore, Pablo," he responded as he reached out to him and repeated, "Not anymore."

Relieved, the three of them just stood there together in an embrace for a few more moments. When it finally came time to leave, they each walked quietly toward Faith's house. On her front porch Faith was finally able to speak, "Something dark is all around us, Gian, and I'm frightened." Gian could sense the danger, too, but he did not want to alarm his friends.

"Something happened back there, Faith," Pablo quickly added, "something stronger than the darkness."

"Let's go home," Faith quietly added as she entered her home and Gian and Pablo followed, "tomorrow is another day, and tonight we will be stronger together."

They each quietly entered Faith's home, and once in her bedroom, she placed blankets and pillows on the floor, and each of them lay upon them, Faith in the middle of her family, each in each other's embrace. Together they fell asleep, together they were safe in each other's arms, safe, at least for now.

CHAPTER 6

Around dawn, Gian was the first to awaken. Faith and Pablo were still peacefully sleeping. There was a slight chill in the air that morning, a chill that had only awakened Gian, and once awake, he could not fall back to sleep. His mind was filled with questions and very few answers. A part of him knew that he was partially responsible for the chaos of the past couple of days. He felt he alone had put the lives of those he loved in jeopardy. His only real family, the only family he had left. He knew that he had to leave the room to think, so he quietly did so. Faith's mom was asleep on the sofa, and as he walked past her to the front door, he could not help but wonder how this poor woman would feel if she became aware of the events of the prior night. He exited the house, onto the porch, as the Sun was just beginning to appear in the sky. Faith's dad was snoring on a porch chair nearby, one of his favorite places to wander. Gian gently awakened him and walked him inside. His breath smelled of too much beer, and Gian helped him to his feet, and walked him inside like he had done several times before. Once he settled him onto the sofa near his wife, he quickly fell asleep again. Gian quietly retreated back outside to witness the birth of a new day. He sat upon a comfortable old chair, and watched the Sun rise over his body. Its warm rays seemed to soothe him, and warm his soul, and he fell peacefully asleep within their glow, like an infant would in his mother's gentle arms. The Sun seemed to embrace him fully there on that lonely porch, this early morning, and within its rays he slept as a young child does. He slept as he had not done in years, in peace, finally in peace.

"Gian, there you are!" he heard a familiar voice say just before the outside screen door slammed closed. He startled up from his deep sleep and sprang out of his chair. The bright sunshine momentarily blinded him as he rubbed his eyes, all the while knowing that it was Faith's beautiful voice that beckoned. At first he was a bit bewildered not remembering where he was, and what had happened. He felt so warm, so rested, and so at peace, and then he suddenly remembered it all.

"I was worried about you, Gian," Faith stated quietly as she approached to gently embrace him and kiss him on the cheek. "I am so happy to see you."

"Where is everyone?" Gian asked half awake.

"Pablo left already, you know, window to window. His father would be checking in on him before he left for work. My mom and dad left for work, too. It's funny that they left you here asleep on the porch."

Gian just stood there, semiconscious, semiaware, and sat back down into the chair in the warmth of this new day and closed his eyes to sleep again. He so desperately needed to sleep; something powerful drew him back, something overwhelming. Once asleep a single calming voice was heard repeating, "You are not alone, Gian," a simple voice repeating simple words in his dreams, a soothing voice, "You are not alone, Gian. You are not alone."

"Gian, Gian," he heard over and over again, the frantic voice of one who was so worried for him; the one person who began to forcibly shake him awake. "Please wake up. Are you all right?" she screamed.

He finally opened his eyes to the panicked ones of his dear Faith before him.

"Gian, is something wrong? Are you all right?" she repeated in desperation.

"I'm fine, Faith," he quickly responded, sensing her concern and wanting so desperately to reassure her. "I'm fine, Faith, really," he repeated. "I don't know what happened exactly. I was just so tired that I couldn't help myself, but now I'm all right, really I am."

"Nothing's all right, Gian," she blurted out, "You were almost killed last night. You've been having these strange visions. You blacked out a day ago, and, and, well, I'm scared, Gian. I'm scared."

"I'm sorry," came his quick response, as if he were five years old and he was apologizing to his mother for writing on the walls.

"Oh, Gian, what am I going to do with you?" Faith whispered in response. How could she get mad at him when he almost never fought back?

He could see the concern etched all over his beloved's face, so he quickly stood up from that old porch chair and smiled, before kissing her on both cheeks and exclaiming, "Buon giorno." Faith smiled in response, that incredible smile, and her eyes began to twinkle with light again.

"Well, buon giorno to you too," she rejoiced, sensing a hint of normalcy at last. "Come on inside, Gian, and I'll make us a quick breakfast."

She grabbed his hand and pulled him in, "Come on." Gian followed her into the house, as a dog would its beloved friend. He marveled at her now, clad in pajamas, busily making coffee and placing bagels in a worn toaster nearby as he sat quietly at the kitchen table. He had always admired Faith for overcoming so many obstacles in her life. She rarely complained. She tried desperately to support her parents, to help them to cope with their life. She was determined to make a success of herself someday, so that her parents wouldn't have to work anymore, and then they would finally remain sober. Even though she struggled to support herself through college, she never once asked them for money. She always defended her parents to anyone who ridiculed them. She had an unconditional love for those in her life that almost never wavered. She felt they did the best they could to raise her. She always seemed to sense the good in people; she only seemed to recognize everyone's better self. She helped maintain the house and took care of the household finances. Her parents struggled to pay the bills, and balance the checkbook, and she was always there to pick up the pieces when all around her, life appeared to be falling apart. She knew that her parents loved her in their own special way, and she was grateful for their love. Everyone who came to know her recognized in her a giving and warm and exceptionally kind and wonderful soul. She was a gift to all that knew her and were fortunate enough to have her in their life. She was his gift, and he knew how lucky he was to have found her, and he thanked God for her. There she was taking care of Gian that morning, rarely thinking of herself, and yet this morning Gian couldn't stop thinking about her.

Faith raised the volume of a radio near where she worked as a special bulletin was announced. "The Pope has arrived unexpectedly this morning," a news reporter began. "This visit is unannounced, unprecedented, and veiled in mystery," the male correspondent paused before continuing. "He apparently arrived a short while ago aboard his private jet, and was greeted by our city's Cardinal McGarrick. He was whisked away by a private limousine to the cardinal's historic residence here in the city, but questions remain regarding his mysterious visit. Is he here to help a church in crisis? Is he here to meet with local public officials? Is he here to meet with Cardinal McGarrick? The official comment has been 'no comment,' and the president himself, when asked, also had 'no comment' on the matter. The eyes of the world are watching as these events unfold, and we will bring them to you, live, as they happen." With that, Faith turned the radio off, served breakfast, and finally sat down herself next to Gian, before commenting on the report.

"Isn't that odd, Gian," she began after sipping her coffee. "I wonder why he's come." Gian wondered, too. Why had the Pope chosen to come now? Why was he here? What did this mean?

"I really don't know, Faith, but I'll tell you this, if I ever have the honor of meeting our Father, I know exactly what I'd say to him," Gian meekly replied, before changing the subject. "Did I ever tell you that I don't know what I'd be doing, or even where I'd be today if it wasn't for you, Faith?"

"Gian, you have it all wrong," was the quick response, "it's definitely the other way around."

"Last night," he began, but then he seemed unable to find the words to continue.

"Last night," Faith took up where he left off, "my only thoughts were of losing you, Gian," she paused, "I'm so afraid of losing you." Gian arose from his chair in response, and walked toward her to stand behind her as she sat in her chair, caressing her beautiful hair, and then he bent down to kiss her head.

"You were so brave last night," he spoke, and an incredible smile filled his worried face, "And I guess all those years of martial arts training paid off," referring to her swift kick of her much larger assailant the night before. They both smiled, unable to contain it any longer, and Gian kissed her again.

The front door burst open at this point, and Pablo and Nancee stormed in. Surprised, neither Gian nor Faith could speak, as each of them surrounded their friends now, out of breath. It was then that Gian noticed that they both were dripping wet, soaking wet from head to toe. Pablo's blonde hair was almost glued to his head, and Nancee's black hair seemed plastered to hers. Each was wearing a t-shirt and jeans, their sneakers squeaked as they walked, leaving water behind. Pablo reached over to grab half a bagel and proceeded to munch it down before even speaking.

"I heard what happened last night," Nancee began, "And I'm sorry, I should have insisted on driving you all home, then nothing would have happened. I mean, I should have driven you all home."

"It's not your fault, Nancee," Gian began sincerely, "Those men were waiting for us, just outside. Once you pulled away, they would have attacked."

"I don't understand," Nancee replied. "Why would they want to hurt you?"

"I don't know," Faith began, "but they were only after Gian."

"Pablo told me about it on the way to work, and I couldn't believe it. I mean, nothing like this has ever happened to one of us before, and right here."

"Horrible things can happen anywhere," Gian painfully recalled.

"Oh, I'm sorry Gian, I'm such an idiot, I forgot what happened to your own mom."

"Don't worry about it," Gian reassured her. "It's over. They're not going to hurt us anymore, later, we all have to go to report it to the police."

"I pray that you are right," Faith sighed.

"So could one of you tell me why you're both dripping wet?" Gian stated with a smile, "and you're making a mess of the floor, I might add."

"I'm glad to see that nothing's changed around here, except maybe that you can't seem to stop kissing each other," Pablo sarcastically added, referring to his encountering them kissing at the table upon entering the room.

"Look, will someone tell me what happened?" Faith demanded.

"My story is always the same. I try to do good and…," Pablo began before Nancee interrupted.

"Your story," Nancee retorted in a mocking tone, "Your story, I'm standing here like a fish out of water and this is *your* story to tell? Oh no, buddy, no way, go peddle yourself to work on that broken down bike of yours, 'cause I'm telling this one!"

"Oh no, sister, no way," Pablo insisted. "Go tumble in a dryer somewhere and let me tell my, I mean, our story. Anyway, it's all your fault, if you didn't insist that I drive your car this morning…."

"I what? I insisted? You're the one who begged like a baby to drive my car!"

"What?" Faith interjected. "Is this right, Nancee, you allowed Pablo to drive your car?"

"I felt sorry for the poor goldfish, after he told me the story and all. Who knew?"

"Finally, I can begin," Pablo replied.

"Who said anything about you telling this story? I'm nearly drowning here and…"

"Look, will one of you begin? I mean, we do all have to get to work, you know," Faith said in exasperation.

"Okay, well, let's see, first Nancee offered for me to drive her car," Pablo began.

"Here," Nancee interrupted, "hold onto this toaster, Nemo, while I go plug it in."

"Hey, will you two stop already," Faith scolded, "and one of you tell us the truth."

"I'll stop if she'll stop," Pablo childishly replied.

"I feel like a kindergarten teacher!" Faith exclaimed.

"All right, all right, "Pablo began again. "I did beg Nancee to drive her car this morning, after she insisted she was too tired to drive, and that she knew I needed some experience behind the wheel, since I'm going to be taking my driver's test soon, and…"

"Oh brother," Nancee interrupted, "there he goes again."

"All right, all right, I insisted on driving."

"And what about leaving early, because you wanted to make a good first impression?"

"So I really wanted to drive by the arcade when Aimie arrived. I needed to, really, after last night, you know. It was a short cut anyway."

"A short cut, a short cut. I work on the other side of town. Oh boy, that's it, that's really it," Nancee yelled out, too upset to stop. "This is all my fault, why I let this clown convince me to drive my car in the first place, I'll never know. I just wanted him to get some driving experience, is all. I just wanted him to get a job at my restaurant, as a bus boy or something. I felt sorry for him. I mean, how many jobs have you had this summer, anyway? Five? Well, I arranged for him to meet the assistant store manager for a position, I mean," she paused and continued in a mocking tone, "I put my job on the line, here, and look, I'm to blame. Really, my job's on the line here. I'm late for work, and…"

"All right, all right, you're right," Pablo quietly interjected. "I should never have taken that short cut past the arcade this morning."

"For the last time, there's no short cut past the arcade to my work!" Nancee exclaimed.

"Okay, okay, all right already," Pablo finally condescended. "I'll admit it, but only to you three. I wanted to pass by the arcade this morning. I needed to pass by at the exact moment Aimie was arriving for work. I mean, after last night and all."

"Finally, the truth."

"Yeah, yeah, well, I mean, you know how I feel about this girl, and, and everything's been going wrong lately. In fact, I thought it couldn't get any worse. I mean, after last night and all."

"Okay, Pablo, we get the point, now continue."

"So I was driving along and there she was, just ahead of us, getting out of her car in front of the arcade. And she looked great, too. She was wearing this really great skirt…"

"Hey, Ralph Lauren, could you please just get on with it," Nancee joked.

"All right, already," Pablo continued, "Oh yeah, that skirt, yeah, she did look hot, oh brother…"

"That's it, that is *it*," Nancee interrupted again," I'm telling the rest of this story, P. Diddy."

"Over my dead body," Pablo sarcastically replied.

"That is not a stretch…"

"Look you two, I need to get to work," Faith shot back.

"Okay, all right," Pablo began, as Nancee rolled her eyes, "So there I was driving along, coming right up to the arcade, and there she was looking stunning, but she wasn't looking at me, I mean, we were gonna pass her by and she wouldn't even had known it was me, so I innocently honked the horn…"

"Innocently honked the horn, innocently honked the horn. Is that what you just said? Did I just hear that?" Nancee blurted out at this point, staring down Pablo as she spoke. "You mean to say that you played my horn like you do your drum set and then, worse than that, he started to wave his hands around like a madman, screaming her name, and…"

"Look, I forgot I was driving for a second, I mean, this is all new to me."

"The next thing I knew, I had to take control of the wheel, but it was already too late. We hit the fire hydrant right in front of the arcade, no less, and…"

"I did try to stop the car, Nancee, honestly, you know…"

"What!" Faith exclaimed aloud, concerned. "You two were in an accident this morning. I mean, is everything all right? My God, I didn't know. Are you all okay?'

"Look, don't worry, Faith," Pablo hastily responded. "We're fine. Can't you see that we're both fine, really. We are. Everyone is okay. No one was hurt. Somehow I lost control of the car for a moment. And yes, we hit the fire hydrant and all, and yes, the next thing I knew, we were soaking wet. But we're not hurt. See, it was just a little accident, that's all."

"A little accident, a little accident, did I just hear this little wet rat say a little accident?!" Nancee screamed out as she lunged toward Pablo with her arms outstretched, and her hands ready to grab onto his neck before Faith ran over to stop her. "Oh, I'll give you a little accident," she continued as Faith stood in front of her. "I should have known all along. I'm the more mature one. I'm the older one. I'm the sensible one. God knows I'm the smart one. So this is all my fault; I realize that now. I mean, just look at him. He's a kid. I don't know what I was thinking about, really I don't."

"Please, Nancee, please," Faith began in a calm tone. "Please just tell us what happened. We all have to get to work."

"All right, all right, already," she began. "Last night I asked Pablo to meet me outside my house this morning. You see, when he arrived, he told me the story about what happened to you three, and I couldn't believe it, I just couldn't."

She paused suddenly and returned to sit at the table. Faith poured her a cup of coffee, and she sipped at it before continuing. Everyone sat down at this point, hoping to hear the end of this story at last.

"I mean, I still can't believe what happened to you three. You three are my best friends and all. I don't know what I'd do without you."

"Really," Pablo interrupted, "you mean it? I'm one of your best friends even after all this, huh, really?"

"Yeah, I guess so, Pablo," Nancee continued, "even after this morning."

"Thanks, Nancee. That means a lot."

"Look, can one of you finish this story please?" Faith pleaded again.

"Yes, here it is," Nancee began. "I allowed Pablo to drive past the arcade. Yes, he did blow the horn a lot. Yep, he even waved his hands around like a madman for a few seconds, and yes, we did hit the fire hydrant near the front of the arcade. There, I can't believe it. I said it. It's done."

"Done, done, well, tell us what happened after that, I mean, how can that be all?" Faith interjected at this point.

"Look, I'll tell you about everything," Pablo began.

"Oh, no, I'll continue," Nancee insisted. "So I reached over, grabbed the steering wheel, and screamed for him to brake, which he did, a little too late, I might add, but he did, thank God. After we hit the fire hydrant, a steady stream of water nearly drowned us both. My car was flooded in seconds. I mean, I almost drowned on a city street, and worse yet, in my own car."

Nancee couldn't help but laugh now, and they all began to laugh. It felt great to laugh again.

"I don't know why I'm laughing. My car is totaled," Nancee was finally able to say, once the laughter died down. "I'm late for work and I don't know how I'm going to get there, and, worse yet, I don't know where I'm going to get the money to buy another car."

"Nancee," Pablo replied concerned about his friend, "You know I said I would help you buy another car. I'll ask my dad for some money. We could ask him today."

"I'll help out, too," Faith added, "I have some money saved up."

"Me too," Gian happily informed his friend.

"Wow, between us, I should be able to afford a tricycle," Nancee joked quietly.

"Well, for now you could borrow my old car, the one that Monsignor Lilli gave me," Gian remembered.

"Great," Nancee replied, as she walked over to him and gave him a great big hug.

"Wait a minute," Faith interjected. "Weren't you both issued tickets and summonses or something? Aren't there going to be fines? And who is going to fix the hydrant?"

"No, nothing," Nancee chimed in. "The first officer on the scene comes into my diner all the time. He was so nice. He just wanted to make sure we were all right. He never asked us any questions about the accident, and we never volunteered. He just wrote that it was probably a mechanical failure, and that was that." She paused for a moment before continuing. "He told us how lucky we were that we weren't hurt, and that we didn't hurt anyone else, and with an old car like mine, he was surprised something worse hadn't happened."

"Hey, wait a minute. I forgot to tell you the best part!" Pablo exclaimed excitedly. "When the accident happened, even Aimie was all wet, so while Nancee was explaining everything to the policemen and the firemen and all, well, Aimie and I just laughed, and we talked, and well, I got a date with Aimie tonight at the rally. Do you believe it? She said that she thought I was cute, and she just loved all the attention I gave her, and she asked me about the rally tonight, go figure."

"Yeah, I was trying to explain to everyone what happened, and he got a date with his idol? Go figure," Nancee complained. "And a kiss no less."

"A kiss!" Faith exclaimed.

"Look, no comment. I don't want to talk about it," Pablo responded with a semi-smile on his face.

"Pablo, Pablo," Gian interrupted, "What do you mean, the rally is tonight? The rally is tomorrow night."

"Don't tell me, Gian, that you forgot that the rally is tonight," Faith asked in disbelief.

"Oh, no," Gian replied so worried that he almost couldn't continue. "I have so much work to do and I'm already late. There is so much more to do before the benefit rally for Gerard's Place tonight, and we each have to practice our songs, too."

Each year one of the fundraisers for the church was a benefit concert of sorts, where all of the local bands and groups performed. There were also food vendors, games, and some amusement rides. It was one of just a few community events, and the first time that the band was going to perform live before a large audience. Gian could not believe that he forgot, and worse yet, that he was late for an important meeting.

"I've got to go and shower and change, everyone. I'm already late. Father Thom is going to have my head!" he exclaimed as he made a quick exit.

"I have to go, too," Nancee quickly followed. "Remember, you are going to let me borrow your car."

So all three of them left Faith behind, but not before agreeing to meet later that afternoon to practice once more before the concert. They all had too much to do before the rally, including Pablo, who was committed to setting up the chairs later that day.

When Gian finally arrived home soon after, something was noticeably different about his apartment, but he could not figure out what. Something had changed, but he couldn't pinpoint it. It seemed unusually quiet, uncharacteristically neat, and perhaps a little cleaner too. He startled as the bathroom door opened, and out walked his friend, Monsignor Lilli. As soon as he saw Gian he ran toward him, and he hugged him, exclaiming, "Thank God you're all right! I was so worried when you didn't come home last night, and then when you were late for work this morning…Oh, Gian, I was so worried for you."

"Don't worry, Bishop, I'm fine. I forgot that you were arriving last night. I completely forgot."

"That's okay, Gian, as long as you are all right, that is all that matters, and please don't call me bishop, around here I'll always be Monsignor." Gian couldn't help but notice that his friend seemed a little more frail than on their last encounter, a little more gray, a little more worried, but as always his face was full of joy and hope, his smile contagious. They proceeded to sit down upon the room's sofa bed, and they began to discuss all of the events of the upcoming day and night. Gian gazed into his old friend's wrinkled face as he spoke and could not help but be sad. His good friend was well into his seventies, weaker than he had remembered him. How could he tell him about the events of the past few days? He just could not. Once finished speaking, the good bishop apparently sensed his friend's unspoken concern, and asked again if he was indeed all right.

"Monsignor," Gian began again, trying successfully he thought, to hold back his fear, answering as convincingly as possible. "I'm fine, just busy with the craziness that is my life, I guess, so busy with life's craziness. I didn't mean to worry you."

"You know, Gian, Father Thom and some of the other residents at the house had some interesting stories to share with me last night after I arrived."

"Believe me, it is nothing to worry yourself about, Father. It's really nothing. I'm fine, can't you see for yourself, just fine." Gian tried so hard to convince his old friend that everything was all right. He did not want something to happen to him; he could not risk it.

"Gian, I came here last night to wait for you because I needed to speak to you, my friend; I needed to speak only to you." The concern in his voice was obvious. His entire facial expression had changed.

"What is it?" Gian asked so quietly, afraid of his response. "What is it, monsignor?"

"I know, Gian," he began, "That you are just trying to protect me because that is who you are, but there is no need. You are the one who…," he stopped speaking suddenly, and reached out to grab his friend's arm.

"What is it, Monsignor? Please tell me," Gian repeated again as the monsignor quickly withdrew his hand, and appeared to be gathering his strength for me.

"Gian," he finally continued, "in a dream two nights ago, I saw glimpses of you, and what has been happening to you. I didn't know it then, but after speaking to the others, I know this to be true. I have seen what they told me, and more, what has happened, and part of what may happen still. I tried to get here sooner, but it was not meant to be. What happened to you last night was meant to happen. I foresaw it, but I could not change it, and I am sorry."

"But how did they know?" Gian asked in disbelief.

"Pablo and Nancee stopped in looking for you," came the unexpected response.

A silence ensued as Gian's eyes filled with tears, at once so happy that his trusted friend knew some of his secrets, and perhaps he could help him to understand, and yet again so sad that he could not spare him the pain.

"I saw glimpses, Gian, glimpses of your past and of your future, enough to make me realize what I had known since the very first day that I met you. It seemed my destiny there and then; and now, I know it to be true. You cannot spare me my destiny just as I cannot spare you yours."

He paused to take some deep breaths. He closed his eyes as if to meditate, as if to ask for strength and guidance. "Glimpses, you see, Gian," he continued, staring deep into his friend's eyes, and Gian was transfixed, "Glimpses of your amazing gifts, gifts from God, my son, and these gifts always come with a high price." He paused again and bent his head down, and made the sign of the cross, before continuing.

"You see, Gian, that you are not the only one. There have been others, and there will be others. Ones who, with Divine help, have appeared in the worst of times. Each of them reluctant souls like yourself; each of them inspired to spread His word and to show us that He is indeed very much alive."

The good bishop paused again as if to collect his thoughts. "You, Gian, are one of those chosen, that I know. You have been given Divine gifts that the world of today needs. It needs you, my son. Don't be afraid, Gian, for I will be here to help in any way I can. I will pray for you to be as strong as the world needs you to be. The world is crying out, Gian, they are crying out for a sign, any sign that God exists. You are that sign, Gian. You follow in the footsteps of so few before you, given these special gifts while still here with us on Earth. I cannot explain it to you any more than this, for I do not understand it all myself."

The good bishop now stood up, his body trembled so much that Gian rushed up to help support him. He embraced his frightened friend once again and whispered into his ear, "Go now, Gian, for you must go, for I have already interfered. I will pray for you, and I will always be here for you. Remember that. But now you must get ready for Father Thom, for he awaits you. Go in peace, my son, and may peace follow you," he declared before he left.

In the next few moments, Gian sat there upon his sofa and recalled the words of his dear friend, and even though he was gone, he felt his presence still, and for a moment during these past few days, he felt at peace. He knew now that he was not alone in this, and that his good friend would be there for him no matter what.

He quickly gathered up his clothes, showered, and changed. He knew that he had so much more work to do, and that he needed to get started right away.

Upon entering Gerard's Place, Gian noticed that everyone was so busy with their last minute preparations that no one seemed to be aware of him. He made his way to the conference room in search of Father Thom, and as he entered, all of the commotion inside the room ceased. Seated at the head of the conference table was Father Thom, himself, and surrounding him were members of the church council, some of the Sisters of Poverty, some volunteers and a few inhabitants of Gerard's Place. All seemed to turn their attention towards Gian in silence until Father Thom spoke.

"Gian, where have you been, and why are you late?" he began forcefully and continued before Gian could reply. "We have all been working here so hard this morning since well, very early. And you, well, you know what you were supposed to do, and what is expected of you, and you will finish all of your duties, all of them, do you hear me? Before you can attend the rally tonight. You, of all people, should know how important tonight is for this parish and for this institution. Without these fund raisers we would have to close our doors." He finally seemed to pause long enough for Gian to respond, but what could he say. He was suddenly speechless.

"Yes, father," he was finally able to reply. "I know what I have to do and I will do it to the best of my ability. I'm sorry." He stood there for a moment waiting for a reply that would never come. As he left the room, the previous banter recommenced, and he stood there for a moment just outside the door, overwhelmed. There was no way he could perform all of his tasks and still make the rehearsal for the band, he thought, no way.

As he stood there, he could feel someone behind him tapping him on the shoulder. When he turned around he could see Marc there before him. Marc was a very good friend of Gian's, and of the parish, especially to the residents of Gerard's Place. He was a proud man, just over six feet tall, strong and energetic. He was a black man who never let his past dictate his future. His face alone could tell a thousand stories. For a man in his fifties, he had already lived so many lives. A paramedic who was drafted into the Vietnam War and survived, as he often called it, 'a tragedy of modern-day humanity.' He now worked as a physician's assistant at the local veteran's hospital where he was an admired colleague and trusted friend and confidante. In his spare time, he worked at Gerard's Place. He took care of the sick, both physically and emotionally. He was a friend to everyone there, and a source of constant inspiration and courage.

"I'll help you to finish, Gian," Marc explained to his friend as they both stood in the hallway facing each other. "In fact, I was up very early and encountered the good Monsignor Lilli. I have already completed most of your chores, so don't worry, my friend, we will accomplish the rest in no time at all, no time at all." Gian, at first, just stared into his savior's gentle, bloodshot brown eyes, eyes very weary from lack of sleep. His face was wrinkled beyond his years, but so gentle nonetheless. His hair, although cut very short, was a rich, incredible black hue, and his smile could make everyone smile around him.

"Marc, you didn't have to do that. You have too much to do already." Gian began, "and besides I promised to help *you*, remember?"

"Gian, we have been friends from that very first day you showed up here with the good monsignor. I knew then how special you were, and when I heard what's been happening of late, I wasn't surprised. I just want you to know that

I am here for you, Gian in any way I can. I will always be here for you Gian, my friend."

Gian was overwhelmed, and before he could speak, the doors to the conference room burst open and Father Thom almost ran into the two of them in his haste. "Gian, you are still here? Didn't you hear me? Marc, if you intend to help him you better bring along your entire family to help you. You'll both need them." With that, he rushed past, leaving them and the rest of the conference room's inhabitants aghast. Everyone there knew that Marc had no family. He was a loner who never spoke of any of his family, and who had never married. He told everyone close to him that he had seen enough during the Vietnam War to last him a thousand lifetimes. He often said that Gerard's Place was his family, and if you looked deep into his eyes, you could see that indeed this was the truth.

Marc finally broke the silence. "Oh, Gian, pay him no attention. He is just too worried, too nervous, and too afraid for us to pay attention to what he says. You know as well as I, and everyone else here, how much he cares for this place, and how much he just wants for this night to be a success. As cranky as he can get, we all know, he tries his best to help."

"I know," was all Gian could say in return. It was so much like Marc to ignore cruelty, ignorance, and meaningless words.

"You know Gian," Marc began in a tone he rarely used, "You are one of those few people who judge a man by what's on the inside, not the outside. You've always seemed to be looking deep inside of me, and you see what very few people see, you see the real me. I love you for that Gian, and I will always protect you, no matter what, because that is my calling."

Gian did not know how to respond. He was so overwhelmed by all of this sentiment from this dear friend and he didn't quite know what to say, so he simply said "Thank you."

"Let's go, Gian," Marc reiterated his need to move on, having said what he needed to. "We still have a few important tasks left to finish, so we better go."

"Sure, Marc," Gian was barely able to say, "and thanks, my friend, thanks for everything."

With those words the two of them took off, and within the next few hours, completed everything. As the morning quickly faded into mid-afternoon, all of the preparations were done.

The stage was set in the church's enormous parking lot and adjacent field, with an assortment of food vendors and games and rides, for one of the largest celebrations ever. Gian bade farewell to his good friend Marc, and he may not have known it then, but that night marked the beginning, the real beginning of his incredible journey.

CHAPTER 7

Gian arrived at the Music Store late that afternoon. Practice had already commenced, and since he was late, Nancee was there filling in for him. Nancee could play a few instruments herself, and often subbed for any one of the group if she could. Relieved to see Gian, Faith interrupted the session to greet him, and gave him a quick hug and a kiss. Budd remarked something to the effect of never being on time, as he took a quick sandwich break. Pablo seemed especially nervous. Gian was later informed that Pablo and Budd had been practicing prior to the rest of the group arriving, and everyone was talking about it. Initially everyone appeared calm.

The group practiced together for a couple of hours, and even though it seemed to go well, the anxiety of playing to such a large audience was palpable. As a group, they had only performed at small venues before, and tonight there was a possibility of thousands of spectators. By late afternoon, they disbanded, each to their own homes to dress. Nancee was kind enough to drive "the three stooges" as she sometimes liked to call Faith, Gian, and Pablo, in her new 'old' car that each of them had somehow contributed to. They laughed together on that short ride home. It was hard not to, since the four of them literally squeezed into a car made to comfortably seat three small people, and to save time, each one of them tried to gulp down dinner—a bagged lunch and a soft drink—that each of them had purchased at the cafeteria before leaving. Most of Pablo's dinner and drink didn't quite make it into his mouth, as Nancee tried desperately to ignore him and drive, with little success. Nancee finally pulled over.

"Look, Curly," she began, referring to Pablo, "Just because you're sitting behind me, doesn't make me your human napkin."

"Oh, no, I'm sorry, really, since you're dressed in a tablecloth," referring to her red plaid top, "I thought I could eat off of you."

"A tablecloth? A tablecloth!" she retaliated in a loud voice, "Did you say 'a tablecloth?'" Nancee paused for a second before continuing in a calmer voice, "Do I really look like a tablecloth?" she asked in earnest, glancing down at her top.

"When you dress like a table…" Pablo jokingly began.

The laughter interrupted him mid sentence, and it lasted for a few minutes. They all needed to laugh. Nancee restarted the engine afterwards, and they all were home within a minute.

It was nearly evening by the time Gian showered and changed. He could hear the excitement of the crowd nearby from his apartment. Once he stepped outside, he noticed that the sky above was a brilliant blue, and a rather low and glorious Sun kissed it gently with its dazzling glow. He exited out the back of Gerard's Place, hoping to avoid everyone, since he was, as always, running late. He stumbled and almost fell over what he had initially thought was garbage on the side of the house, but it stirred and he knew then, that under the camouflage lay a person. He froze, unable to move, unable to leave, as he waited for this stranger to clumsily stand up amidst the debris. He was shocked at the condition of the woman in front of him. Her golden brown hair was ragged and filled with debris, her clothes were multilayered, and her shoes were worn and ill-fitted, yet her face was remarkably gentle and her eyes were so incredibly earnest. Upon recognizing him, she at first smiled, and then proceeded to cry.

"I, uh, well, I, um," she began amidst the tears. "I've been waiting for you, kind sir. I've been waiting for you, Gian."

He was struck by the mention of his name, and struggled to recognize this poor woman, and yet he apparently could not.

"I have heard that you can help me, but I don't know how," she continued in a somber voice. "No one can help me anymore."

He reached out to touch her but felt nothing but the coldness of her hands on this warm day. Maybe she was right; maybe he could not help. He did not know what to say. At first he could not say anything, but then he asked her one question, and her face changed.

"Is there someone I could call," Gian finally was able to say, "Someone who could help you?"

"Maybe no one can help me," she replied sadly, "I thought, well, that you could, but now I see that no one can," she suddenly turned away from him to leave.

"There must be someone that I can call," Gian repeated. This frail figure of a woman turned back around and her response was chilling.

"Yes, there is. There is someone you can call, my beautiful daughter, just sixteen, you see. When I found her dead on her bedroom floor, her wrists cut by her own hand, my baby, my little baby, had taken her own life, and I couldn't—" she struggled to finish the sentence.

Gian could sense her agony, and knew that there was nothing he could do now. She then fell onto her knees and cried there as the Sun's rays seemed to intensify around them, still unable to offer her warmth.

Gian fell on his knees beside her and grabbed hold of her cold hand, hoping to help in some way, but again, he could not. He felt the need to approach her ear and whisper in it as she sobbed.

"Gloria didn't mean to hurt you," he began, "She wants you to know that she is all right, and that it wasn't your fault. She wants you to go home to Alic, for he prays for you every night to come home."

Gian awoke a short time later on the path leading to the street alone. He struggled to stand, so weak and so confused. No one was around him, so he wondered if it was all a dream. It had seemed so real, and yet here he was, alone, and he could hear the loud boom of the festival's firecrackers overhead. In his hand he felt a paper of some sort, and when he looked upon it, his eyes filled with tears. It was a worn photo of the woman of his dream, only here she was happy, and surrounded by her husband and two children, her beautiful daughter Gloria and her son Alic, for their names were written across the bottom. Scribbled on the back was written the words Gian needed to read to understand that what just taken place was indeed real. The words read simply, "Thank you, Gian. I'm going home." Gian felt a peace descend upon him in that moment, another reason to be joyful, and continued on his way toward the fireworks, no longer nervous, but tranquil. No longer anxious, but at peace, as the warm summer Sun warmed his soul.

As he approached the church fair grounds, the sheer number of spectators and participants, far greater than he had ever seen before, amazed him. There had to be thousands about. This was one night when everyone felt a part of a real neighborhood, a real community. He could see Bernadette, and some of the other residents of Gerard's Place, and they smiled and waved as he passed nearby. Bernadette raced up to him, which at first, in and of itself, startled him, she hugged him as he stopped to greet her.

"Thank you, Gian," she began with tears in her eyes and a tremble in her voice, "Thank you for everything."

"Don't thank me, please, Bernadette, it was—" Gian began before he was interrupted.

"I have a new job at the shelter, Gian, I'm helping people like me," she began enthusiastically, "and I'm going to get my G.E.D., all thanks to you."

"I'm so happy for you," Gian emotionally replied.

"I know you have to go now," she acknowledged as she finally let go of him, "I love you for what you've done for me, Gian, and I will work the rest of my days helping others, praising God for his great gifts, and praying for you." She quickly reentered the crowd, as Gian searched the crowd for her, for he had so much to say in return.

Father Thom and Monsignor Lilli were in the distance laughing with the children surrounding them as a clown amused them all with his tricks. Tonight was already a success. Everyone here, if only for a short while, could escape their troubles and just enjoy. This fair offered hope to an urban area where hope was scarce, and life was hard.

Fireworks began again to alert everyone to the start of the show, as hundreds gathered about the stage to hear the musicians play. The high school band assembled on stage, and began to play to great applause. They were the first of six local acts to perform; Gian and the group were scheduled to perform next. Gian rushed past many, knowing that his friends were probably worried.

Faith seemed exceptionally nervous as he finally approached. "Don't worry, Gian," she began as he neared, "I know you had a good reason to be late. I could feel it." They hugged each other before Budd interrupted them.

"We're ready, people, we're finally ready and tonight we are going to take this audience by storm!" he exclaimed, as he approached them both, and joined in their hug.

Faith looked exceptionally beautiful this evening in a new dress her parents had bought her for just this occasion. Her parents were here tonight too, seated right up front. They had been sitting there for hours, waiting for their only child to perform. They were so proud of her. They were always so proud. They were disappointed in themselves, but never in their daughter. They knew that they had been handed a gift, and they were here tonight to see her shine.

Gian, Faith, and Budd felt Pablo join them in a group hug, and finally even Nancee. Together they grew stronger. Once they separated, each one of them commented on how great each looked. Budd looked ever the professional with his curly black hair slicked back, and in a new shirt and slacks. Nancee seemed aglow in a fitted dress adorning her cute figure, and Pablo wore an intense blue shirt that made his eyes seem even more revealing, a blue as blue as the clearest of skies. He seemed preoccupied though, as he continually searched the crowd for her, for Aimie.

"Everyone, don't be worried," Budd began. Being the oldest of the group, he was always reassuring. He had believed in this group since the beginning, and most especially, he believed in Faith. He knew that her talent was nothing short of amazing. "Everything will be just fine," he continued, "Just fine."

It was then that Aimie appeared backstage with them, her blonde hair swept upward, revealing her searching light blue eyes. Her mouth formed an incredible smile as she met Pablo nearby. They quickly embraced, and she gave Pablo a quick kiss on his lips, whereby he almost fell over, and they both laughed.

"I just wanted to tell you that I wouldn't have missed this for anything, Pablo. Thanks for inviting me," Aimie declared, as she stood there facing him. It was as if no one else was around.

"I'm glad you came," Pablo responded, "It wouldn't have been the same without you."

"You look great," Aimie interrupted, "just great."

"Thank you," was all Pablo could utter before Budd began to yell, and Aimie immediately turned to leave, and take her assigned place in the front row.

"We'll be up there shortly," Budd began again, "and we'll be great, you all will see."

By now Gian noticed that Faith had wandered off alone not too far from everyone. He ran over to her and startled her by hugging her from behind.

"I don't know why you worry so," he began to whisper in her ear. "You're perfect and tonight is going to be perfect. Everyone here will finally see how talented you are; they will hear how amazing your voice is, and everyone will fall in love with you," he paused as he turned her around to face her, her glistening eyes, now met his before continuing, "like I have."

He leaned forward to kiss her, a kiss that seemed to last forever on this beautiful night, a kiss that he wished could last forever.

"I can't," Faith finally uttered as she faced him after their kiss, "I can't breathe without you, Gian."

Gian hugged her close for he knew that he couldn't live without her either, but he couldn't respond at first.

"I—I couldn't live without you, Faith," Gian whispered.

Pablo screamed out for his friends to join him. He suddenly seemed so concerned. As Gian and Faith approached, Nancee began, "I just realized that our band doesn't have a name. Who will introduce us and what will they say?" Remarkably, she was right. The group had never thought that it would ever get this far, and when they performed previously, they were always introduced as "our favorite local group."

"Don't worry," Budd exclaimed when he became aware of the dilemma. "I took the liberty to name us earlier, and well, you'll all see soon enough." With that, Budd was called to the stage and Pablo shouted out, "Let's go everybody. It's finally our turn. Come on," he continued, "Let's show 'em how it's done!" The group scrambled onstage together to light applause, and assumed their positions. It was a clear night, and above the crowd, the stars shone brightly, dimmed only by all of the lights onstage. Gian looked out at the crowd gathered before them, and scattered throughout, he could see its diversity, from the well-to-do, to the homeless, from the healthy, to the sick. Wheelchair-bound individuals were scattered about, and near the front the children played, all of them familiar, all from the surrounding neighborhood. Some lived at Gerard's Place, hoping for a family and a home that they could call their own. From the most fortunate to the least, tonight everyone was equal. Tonight, in the calm of this mild, clear evening, as the Sun started to bid its farewell, everyone present was equal.

In the front row Gian could see his many friends and family. He could see rows of the religious community, including the local archbishop. Politicians for the local community, including the mayor, were there, and representatives from regional synagogues and mosques and churches came too. Gian's good friend, Monsignor Lilli, smiled as their glances met, and Father Thom sat nearby, his face beaming with delight. Everyone seemed to be enjoying themselves. This neighborhood had never felt so alive before. You could feel its heart beating for the first time in a long time.

Off to the side of the stage, a camera crew caught everyone's eye. Gian recognized a well-known local television news reporter speaking to her audience amidst a glare of camera lights. It was strange to see the media here; it made it all the more magical.

Faith took center stage, guitar in hand, for her first song. She appeared radiant in the intense lighting, angelic appearing in the backdrop of stars. Budd approached the mike and after gaining the audience's attention, introduced the band, each one separately at first, to polite applause. Lastly, he introduced Faith, and finally the band's name was heard above the quiet chaos this evening, as he called out for some applause for, "Yellow Brick Road." He then proceeded to thank everyone for attending and supporting such a worthy cause on this very special night. The crowd was so polite as the group began its first song. It all seemed perfect as the song began. A peaceful silence ensued before Faith broke it with her angelic voice, as the music began flawlessly around her.

> Searching for tomorrow
> Praying for a sign
> Hoping that forgotten dreams
> Will finally be mine
> Searching for tomorrow
> For today is all we know
> For tears can form in any place
> A smile hides on every face
> This pain can't stop tomorrow
> And the hope we need to find
> For together
> We can make a difference
> Together we can make it grow
> For together
> We can make life better
> Together forever
> I know
> Searching for tomorrow
> Praying for a sign
> Hoping that forgotten dreams
> Will finally be mine
> Searching for the answers
> Long hidden within my soul
> For today
> Tomorrow

Is so very hard to know
This pain can't stop tomorrow
And the hope we need to find
For together
We can make a difference
Together we can make it grow
For together
We can make it better
Better than you know
Raise your hands
In search of justice
Raise your hearts
In search of truth
Raise your voices
In search of eternity
For together
We can make a difference
Together we can make it grow
For together
We can make it better
Better than you'll ever know

Quiet at first ensued, a lingering quiet as the song finished before the immense applause erupted, and everyone on stage went numb. An incredible feeling came over everyone on that stage, at that moment, like never before, an intense, indescribable feeling. Once the applause subsided, Faith took her place at the piano, and lowered the mike closer to her lips. She thanked the audience for their kindness, and introduced the next song; asking everyone present to dance if they felt like it, just dance. The music was louder for this number, and the audience was enjoying it already.

Live and make every second count
Live 'cause that's what life is all about
Live as if every moment was your last
Live for today

'Cause you can't change your past
Live for today
'Cause life travels fast
Live
Just live
'Cause life's a blast
Enjoy the music
Get up and dance
Forget who you are
This may be your last chance
To live
And make every second count
Live
'Cause that's what life is all about
Live
As if every moment was your last
Live for today
'Cause life travels fast
Live, just live
'Cause life's a blast
Dance 'cause you are alive
Dance and let it all out
Dance till you almost shout
Dance
Come on get up and dance
Dance that's what it's all about
Who cares who you were yesterday?
All that matters is today
So live
Don't be afraid to change who you are
Live
Don't be afraid to wish upon that star
Live

Don't be afraid to stand up and change
Enjoy the music
Get up and dance
Forget who you are
This is your chance to live
Live
'Cause that's what life is all about
Live
As if every moment was your last
Live for today
'Cause life travels fast
Live
Just live
'Cause life's a blast

The band continued to play the music as the lyrics ended; everyone in the crowd was up and moving to it. Everyone in the band played on, and this was one of the few songs where everyone sang backup for Faith during the chorus. Pablo sang more alternating lyrics in the chorus near the end with Faith. It was a song they had both written, and they really enjoyed performing it. Once the music had ended as abruptly as it began, the applause was deafening. The band received its first standing ovation, and Budd noticed that even the TV crew had recorded some of it. The group played better than they ever had before. Each member looked at each other now, so proud of their accomplishment.

Suddenly, Faith began to speak over the crowd, and finally the commotion died down and allowed her to continue.

"This next song I wrote recently," she started, "to say something from my heart to someone that I care so very much about." With those words, she paused and turned to face Gian and smile; she blew him a kiss and the audience applauded.

"This song was written for everyone who is in love, Gian. This song was written for you. It is called 'Forever.' Gian appeared stunned as the music began and the audience hushed. This was not the song the group had rehearsed. Members of the high school band joined them onstage once Faith began to sing. Gian walked up next to Faith and stood at her side. He couldn't take his eyes off of her.

Once in a thousand lifetimes
Once in a million years
Along comes that special someone
Close your eyes
Forget your fears
Hold on forever
Hold on tight
Hold on as if the future
Were only tonight
In your eyes I see my present
In your eyes I forget my past
With your kiss I can see our future
With your love, at last
I will want you
Forever
I will need you
Forever
I will trust you
Forever
I will love you
Forever
Whatever tomorrow brings
I will always hold on to today
You can change the world
with me forever, I pray
Hold on to me forever
Hold on to me so tight
Let only light enter
Never the night
I can hear your voice in my dreams
I will trust in you, forever
I will need in you, forever
I will love only you

Forever
Hold me close in your embrace
There is nothing that we cannot face
Together
We will become as one
And start anew
Together forever
Just me and you
I will
Want you forever
Trust you forever
Need you forever
Love you forever
And ever
And ever
And ever still

As the song ended, Gian embraced Faith in the twinkling of the stars that evening to the applause of hundreds. He kissed her and in that moment they seemed alone together in a place where no one else could enter, in a place where together, they were safe.

Interrupted by cheers for more, they quickly looked around at their friends who were standing nearby and applauding too. Overjoyed, they smiled at them, and out into the crowd before them. Gian knew then that everyone there recognized what an enormous talent Faith possessed. In that moment, a part of their lives would change forever, for others could plainly hear Faith's tremendous gift, and there was no turning back, their numbers would only grow.

Budd directed Gian and Faith's attention back to the group. He told everyone that he had an important announcement to make. Once the band gathered near Nancee onstage, Budd reengaged the audience's attention. "Our next song will be performed by the youngest member of our group." He paused and pointed to Pablo. Faith and Gian looked on in disbelief. "Pablo wrote this song for his sister, Faith, and he will perform it for you now."

The audience applauded politely as Pablo nervously took his place at the piano, center stage, and Budd accompanied him. He looked over toward Faith, and proclaimed, "This is for you, sis." He began to play the music of the song, a haunting melody that immediately caught everyone's attention. After a couple of minutes, he began to sing.

> I was so young
> When my Sun disappeared
> When my sky turned to gray
> And it rained every day
> I was so small
> Just a shadow of who I am
> Just a fragment of the man
> I was to become
> I was so innocent
> I believed in talking dinosaurs
> In walking mermaids
> In magical places
> In far away lands
> For
> I was so young
> I was so innocent
> I was so small
> After all
> I was so lost
> Until I was found
> Until I was loved
> After all
> You picked up my pieces
> You sewed up my heart
> You put me together
> After life tore me apart
> You are my beginning
> My everything
> My start
> For
> I was so young

I was so innocent
I was so small
After all
For
I was so lost
Until I was found
Until I was loved
After all
A wounded bird
Hurt so long ago
Lost in my world
Out in my cold
A wounded bird left to die
Until I was found
And now I can fly
Thanks to you
You picked up my pieces
You sewed up my heart
You put me together
After life tore me apart
You are my beginning
My everything
My start
For
I was so young
I was so innocent
I was so small
After all
For
I was so lost
Until I was found
Until I was loved
After all

Pablo continued to pound out the ending of his song, so different from the others performed so far. His voice seemed to reach out and touch everyone; his music was haunting and real. When he finished he just sat there with his head down, and the audience at first stood still, numb. Faith walked over to him and touched his head. He stood up and they embraced, and the entire audience then stood and the applause was deafening. After a few moments, all of the members of the group gathered around them at the piano, as the crowd cheered on and screamed for more. Budd quietly agreed to play a few last stanzas of their song, "Live," and soon the five of them began to play amid the chaos.

> Live
> Don't be afraid to stand up and change
> Enjoy the music, get up and dance
> Forget who you are, this is your chance
> To live, live and make every second count
> 'Cause that's what life is all about
> Live, as if every moment was your last
> Live for today, 'cause you can't change your past
> Live for today, 'cause life travels fast
> Live, just live

"Can you hear me!?" Faith exclaimed, changing the song's ending, "Live, just live, just live everyone, just live!"

When the music ended, Budd thanked the audience and left the stage as each member did to resounding applause. Backstage, the group could hear the roar of the crowd, and all were silent at first, overwhelmed by it all, then they all hugged as a family. Aimie joined them, and singling out Pablo, embraced him, and they kissed. Their lives in that moment seemed forever changed, in ways they could never imagine.

Grabbing hold of Faith so close to him that she could hear Gian whisper despite the noise, he spoke words so difficult for him to say, "I love you, Faith, and I could not imagine my life without you." He fell into her arms, and they held onto each other so tight, as if this was their final embrace.

Budd congratulated each of his friends for an incredible performance. Pablo and Aimie still huddled in a corner. Faith and Gian appeared oblivious to all of the commotion around them, as local news reporters surrounded them all. Budd began to address their questions, and Nancee called for Gian's help nearby. He approached her, and before Faith could join him, Pablo interceded. Together for the first time since Pablo had sung his song, Faith kissed her friend, her brother, on the cheek and hugged him close, whispering into his ear, "Thank you, Pablo, for everything. I love you, little brother."

"You know how I feel about you Faith, big sis', you just know, don't ya'?" he was barely able to speak such simple words, when he had he just sang so eloquently, but Faith did know, and he knew that she did. She knew him more than anyone.

"Of course I do, now how could you leave, you know…"

"I luv' ya' sis'," he laughed as he literally ran into Aimie, who was standing nearby.

"I had no idea, Pablo, I didn't know…" Aimie began, once they had stopped smiling after their clumsy encounter, and they stood, face to face, close enough to kiss.

"You didn't know what?" Pablo quietly asked, in awe that he was spending any time at all with a girl like Aimie.

"I didn't know that you were such a poet, such a gifted singer and performer. I didn't know that you," Aimie paused to collect her thoughts, "well, I just didn't know."

"Neither did I," Pablo quipped with a smile, and for the very first time he initiated a kiss with Aimie.

"Gian," Nancee began aloud, "This is all so crazy, but I need you to know what I just overheard, and Gian you really need to know that you are going to be asked to say…"

The commotion surrounding the five of them became so intense, that Nancee couldn't finish her sentence.

Until then the band seemed oblivious to the chaos surrounding them. Oblivious to the goings on at the rally as it continued nearby, until Marc rushed backstage, shouting Gian's name, his face perspiring more than anyone had ever seen before, his voice loud but shaken.

"Gian, didn't you hear?" he yelled at all of us as he neared him. "Didn't you hear?" he repeated in exasperation to his face. Realizing now that all seemed oblivious to his question, he lowered his voice and began to explain.

"Monsignor Lilli spoke," he began nervously, "after the mayor did, you see, and he asked Reverend Martin to say the final prayer," Marc paused to catch his breath before continuing," but the reverend instead asked for you, Gian. He asked for you to give the closing prayer." Silence ensued as Marc panted audibly at this point, awaiting a response.

"Did you hear me, Gian?" he again repeated. "You've been asked to say the final prayer. Please come with me. Everyone is waiting."

No one spoke. Marc then grabbed hold of Gian's arm and began to pull him closer to the stage. "Marc, wait," he was finally able to respond, holding his ground again, hoping he misunderstood.

"Please, Gian, come with me," Marc continued, "everyone is waiting."

"This must be some mistake. Please, what could I say to all of these people?" Gian nervously asked of his good friend.

"It's too late to ask questions, too late to say no," Marc responded as he coaxed his friend along to the entrance to the stage.

"Marc, wait! Please, "Gian pleaded, "I won't know what to say."

"Trust in God, Gian," Marc replied as he gazed into his friend's nervous eyes with his supportive ones, "I believe in you."

Faith quickly joined them. She grasped hold of Gian's free hand, nervously smiling as she offered him her support. "Go out there, Gian. Don't be afraid," she spoke lovingly. All could see the concern etched all over her pretty face, the worry evident in her eyes, despite her reassuring words.

Within seconds the three of them were back on stage and Monsignor Lilli quickly approached them. "Come on, my son. I will walk with you and pray for you," he began as he separated Gian from Marc and Faith, and together the two of them began their journey to the center of the stage. "I will be right here with you, Gian. Do not be afraid." His kind face tried to reassure him. "We will all be here for you."

Once they were center stage, Reverend Martin greeted his newly found savior with tears in his eyes. He quickly embraced him, and then turned to the anxious crowd to introduce him. Monsignor Lilli helped Gian to the microphone, and then both departed as Gian faced the awesome crowd alone. He appeared totally bewildered and afraid. His eyes searched the crowd and found many friends, and many of the members of reverend Martin's congregation, who like their good reverend, had tears in their eyes.

As Gian began to speak into the microphone, though, with words he at first could barely utter, his demeanor suddenly changed. He appeared tranquil and at peace.

"I am here before you, to say a prayer with each of you," he began, as the crowd quieted around him, "for all of us. I ask now that my friends please join me onstage." He paused as they approached, "and please join hands with me."

Faith was the first one to grasp his outstretched right hand, Monsignor Lilli was on his left, and each of his friends took hold of one another's hand on the stage, friends and family uniting as one in support and prayer.

"Please everyone, everyone here, please join hands with each another, young and small, so that finally one by one, we will all be connected in spirit, one in body, as we stand here today, united."

Quietly and quickly all of those in the audience seemed to form a circle with those onstage, physically connecting everyone at the event. All present were joined in body with everyone else.

"I am here tonight to offer a prayer of peace," Gian began again, "an inner peace that will extend outward for all to see." He paused to gaze out to all before him, as they stood in silence, amazingly quiet, together.

"Please turn to face your neighbor, and look deep into their eyes." Everyone did as instructed, even those on stage, although Gian's eyes focused on what lay ahead of him. "Look deep enough and you will see your friend. Look deeper still, and you will see a loved one, even deeper and you will see yourself, for we are all our neighbor, all one, and in each other's eyes we can no longer see our differences, only our selves. And if you look deep enough, you will see a glimpse of God Himself. You will see Him there, in the eyes of your neighbor, in the eyes of a stranger, in the eyes of a child, for we are all His children, made in His image. We are all children of God."

Everyone stood there, united in a pure silence, a peaceful silence.

"I pray that we will always remember this feeling, that we will always embrace each other as brothers and sisters, all of us, children of God. We must accept one another; love one another. We must not let our differences divide us, and remember what all of God's prophets, our religious leaders, have taught us. They have taught us to be patient and kind. They have taught us to love, not hate. They have taught us the way to peace, not war. They all believed in life, and not death. If we believe in what they have taught us, then we will see life, not death, love, not hate, happiness, not sorrow, safety, not fear, peace, not war. Together we can create a world built on trust. Together, and only together, can we see that killing darkens the soul, it captures the heart, it destroys the light. No good ever came of evil." Gian paused as if in reflection, before he continued in an even louder voice, "hate only breeds more hate, ignorance more ignorance, despair more despair, murder more murder, and on and on."

"I ask each of you, all of us here present, to close your eyes and invite God in. Invite God in, to a place inside your soul, a place inside your mind, where no one else has been, where no one else has ever been. Allow Him to see what only you see. Allow Him to feel what only you feel. Allow Him to enter, and He will be there with you, by your side. He will follow you and be one with you, and together one by one, He will offer you peace."

Gian began to see images of crying children, to witness some of humanity's tragedies, one by one. God reached out to each of his sons and daughters, in their time of need, and Gian could feel it. Gian could see it. Gian watched as some committed these acts before him, acts of rage and prejudice, violence, and murder. He watched as God reached out to them, hoping to reach a place inside long neglected, hoping to offer them light where there was once, only darkness, forgiveness where there was once, only despair, love where none before existed. He remembered vividly seeing Monsignor Lilli before him, as he alone survived a car accident that tragically took his grandparents' lives. He felt Father Thom crying at the back of St. Gerard's church for forgiveness for his own weakness. He felt Marc crying out, again and again, in fear and anguish and pain, in war, as he watched those he loved kill and be killed. He saw all of their faces, and one by one, they each knew, he was there with them, sometimes in a place so dark that no light had ever entered before. And one by one they opened their eyes in wonder, for in the sky above, there appeared a star so bright that it lit up the night with its glow. Its luminescence offered hope, its mere appearance they took to be a sign of God's presence and His love. Gian finally opened his eyes at last to behold the beauty of that star above him, as silent tears fell down from his smiling face, and from everyone present to form a river of hope that surrounded them all.

A few minutes later, Gian awoke to the frightened faces of his friends above him, Pablo, Faith, Reverend Martin, Monsignor Lilli, and Marc. He must have fallen into unconsciousness. He still could not remember what happened, nor could he adequately describe what had taken place. In that moment he felt the love that a child feels when his parents arrive in the middle of the night to comfort him from a nightmare, to bring light into his world in the darkness. He felt at peace, truly loved and truly blessed. Faith later told him that when his blue eyes opened and he smiled, everyone present smiled, too.

Gian was quickly helped up and taken off the stage, many feared for his safety as the crowd approached to touch him, to thank him. Police secured the stage, as Gian was escorted off and into a nearby police car. Once inside with Faith and Monsignor Lilli, he quickly fell asleep.

CHAPTER 8

Pablo and Aimie were suddenly surrounded, almost suffocated, by the crush of curiosity. They tried to follow their friends, but could not. The local TV news reporters had apparently filmed the entire concert and sermon, and were swarming around them like killer bees with pointed questions. Confused and concerned, they pushed their way through the crowd with Pablo leading the way. Aimie held on for dear life. They managed to disappear into the chaos as more police and regional news agencies arrived, armed with even more cameras. Pablo led Aimie quickly toward his house. Once inside his apartment, they felt safe, if even for just a short while.

Aimie appeared out of place in Pablo's and his dad's small apartment. Her cosmetics, wardrobe, and fragrance allowances combined probably cost more than all of the furnishings in the place. Pablo quickly turned on all the lights as he gazed over at his visitor in disbelief and worry. He could not believe that she was finally in his home. He was so afraid she would leave.

"You live here with your parents?" she asked innocently, as she gazed around the living room.

"No," Pablo abruptly answered, "just my dad and me live here. My mom," he stammered as he hesitated to answer, "she, she doesn't."

With that, Aimie noticed that of the few pictures scattered about the room, most were of Pablo, some of his dad, and none of his mother.

"It seems like a nice home, Pablo. Your dad must be a good man," she declared.

"You're just saying that, Aimie. This place can't compare to your house. You could probably fit the whole apartment in your garage, I bet."

Aimie, sensing her newfound friend's embarrassment, replied in earnest, "You know, Pablo, what matters most is that it's home."

"You must have a great family, Aimie, to have taught you all of that," Pablo innocently replied.

Aimie lived in Bellmere, a wealthy suburb of the city, with her parents. Her oldest sister was in New England studying pre-law, and her brother was in law school on the West Coast. Her mom had two advanced degrees, and her dad was a successful real estate entrepreneur, like his dad and granddad before him.

"You're right Pablo," Aimie began, "I do have a good family, because they taught me about helping others. They bought that abandoned building downtown and transformed it into an arcade, and the upper floors into great low-income housing. I volunteer there, and my mom, well, she volunteers everywhere. She sits on the boards of many local hospitals and charities, and since we were kids we've always helped out."

Pablo just sat there, amazed that his dream girl was in his house talking about her amazing life. "You're so lucky, Aimie," Pablo responded, "you're one of the lucky ones."

"I guess you're right, Pablo. I'm lucky I'm here. I'm lucky to be with you."

Pablo, feeling a bit embarrassed and awkward, tripped over himself as he left the room, proclaiming, "I think we need some music in here," he stammered before he departed.

Aimie proceeded to walk around the room before settling into a chair. She lifted up from the table nearby a headset attached to a tape player, and she placed the headset on, and pressed play. At first she could only hear a piano playing, and then finally Pablo's voice.

> I tried so hard to make you smile
> So hard for you to notice me
> Just for a while
> So hard to be true
> So hard for you to love me, too
> I could have given you
> All the stars in the sky
> All the planets in the heavens
> I could have given you my heart
> If you could have loved me
> Why couldn't you love me?

Why didn't you care?
Why would you just up and leave
To faraway places
To nowhere?
Why couldn't you love me?
Why couldn't you see
That I loved you more
Than anyone
More than everyone
More than
Me?
Why couldn't you just hold on tight
And never let me go?
Just keep me safe like others do
Why couldn't you believe
Like I believed in you?
I could have given you the world
If you just loved me, too
I can see your tears
I can feel your pain
I wished to help you
See the sunlight
And stop the rain
In your eyes I saw my own
Years before your dreams had flown
The Sun had set upon a day
In a place where your dreams lay
Why couldn't you love me?
Why couldn't you care?
Why would you just up and leave
To places unknown
To nowhere
Why couldn't you love me?

Why couldn't you see
That I loved you more
Than anyone
More than everyone
More than me?
I loved you then
I love you till
I'll always love you
I love you still

Aimie was stunned by such raw emotion. As her tears began to flow from her bright eyes, and the music ended, she shut off the recorder. Pablo reentered the room at this point, carrying at least ten CDs, unaware of what had just taken place.

"I didn't know which one you would like, so I…" Overcome by the sight he beheld, of Aimie crying, with his headphones on, he dropped the CDs all over the floor around him.

Aimie took off the headphones and rushed to help him pick up the CDs. Once finished, they both stood there, initially at a loss for words.

"I'm sorry, Pablo. I didn't realize this player contained your personal songs. I just wanted to listen to music and…" she could not continue.

Pablo, sensing how upset she was, neared her silently and whispered, "Don't worry, Aimie, it isn't your fault," he began quietly, as he reached out to touch her hand.

"This day has been crazy, Pablo."

"I know, Aimie. I'm sorry that I made you cry."

"No, no, there's nothing to be sorry about, Pablo. I mean, that song sort of reminded me of what had happened earlier this evening, at the concert. I mean, I felt things that I hadn't felt in years, saw things that I'd forgotten."

"I know," Pablo reassured her. "Gian helped me, too."

"Did he, Pablo?" Aimie asked, "Did the same thing happen to you?"

"Yes."

"You know," Aimie began anew, "today I remembered, I remembered my baby sister. My baby sister died while I held her hand in a hospital room. She was very sick, and I, I was so little myself. We were all alone then, and I didn't know what had happened."

"I'm sorry," Pablo interrupted, sensing how hard this was for his new friend to talk about.

"I didn't know," she began again as tears glistened from her childlike eyes. "I didn't know what happened until later when my mom came back in the room. I was so frightened, until today, until Gian helped me to see, that my little sister was in a better place, and that I wasn't alone in that room on that day, my sister was there with me and God."

"I know," Pablo tried his best to comfort her, "I know."

"Gian has an extraordinary gift," Aimie said, wiping her eyes after placing the tape player back on the table. Pablo proceeded to sit down beside her on the sofa, his eyes staring off into space.

Aimie, realizing how distant Pablo suddenly seemed, added, "I know how worried you are about him and your friends, but I'm sure that they are all right." She reached forward and kissed him on his cheek.

"Pablo, they are so lucky to have you in their lives."

"No, Aimie, I'm the lucky one."

"Tonight," she replied softly, aware of how concerned he was, "Tonight, you sang a song. A song that you wrote from your heart, Pablo, and everyone's heart belonged to you in that moment. That is your gift, your very special gift."

Pablo was stunned, too overcome to respond at first. He nervously moved toward her, and quietly reached for her lips with his. Aimie responded with a kiss in return.

"Pablo," his dad suddenly appeared in the room in a stir of activity that included Faith's parents, Nancee, and Budd, each anxious for answers. "Is Gian or Faith here?"

"No," came the quick but meek response from his son.

"Do you know where they are?" Budd asked them.

Pablo's face was answer enough, as was Aimie's as they separated, and each stood before them at a loss for words.

Everyone began to speak at once, so concerned about the whereabouts of Gian and Faith, Reverend Martin, and Monsignor Lilli. After the rally, the four of them seemed to vanish and no one knew where they were.

"This is crazy," Budd began, "Tonight is just plain crazy."

"Think, Pablo, please," his dad begged, "You know them best; do you have any idea where they might be."

"No, dad, I wish I did."

Everyone was still too nervous to sit, especially Faith's parents.

"She's all we have," Faith's mom whispered loud enough for all to hear.

"Look," Budd responded reassuringly, "Gian and the others will protect her. You don't have to worry about a thing."

"You must be Aimie, right?" Pablo's dad inquired as he faced her.

"Oh dad, I'm sorry. I forgot to—"

"Yes I am," Aimie interrupted.

"Oh, Aimie," Nancee exclaimed, "Have you called your parents to tell them you're all right? They must be worried about you."

"Oh, yes," Pablo's dad added, "You must call them. Here: Use our phone."

"No, that's all right," Aimie responded. "I shut my cell off during the concert. I'm sure they've left messages. I'll just go and call them, don't worry."

Aimie proceeded to stand and walk to the corner of the room, as the others spoke amongst themselves.

"Tonight was incredible," Budd began. "Just incredible." He then proceeded to take a candy bar out of his pocket, open it, and devour it in a matter of seconds.

"I don't know how you can eat at a time like this," Nancee chided her friend.

"I can eat at any time," Budd declared, as he removed a piece of gum from its wrapper, and tossed it into his mouth.

"You eat all the time," Nancee responded smiling. Everyone in the room seemed to smile a little in response.

"What?" Aimie's voice pierced the room with its concerned tone, and all turned to face her as she spoke into her cell phone. "All right, all right," she continued, "Yes, I will, yes, right now, okay. I love you, too. Bye."

"What is it Aimie?" Pablo quickly asked.

"Turn on the television to channel five, hurry!" she was able to blurt out as they all gathered in silence before the set, for it was Gian who appeared on that screen before them, ending his sermon on that stage at the concert. Immediately thereafter, a television newswoman took to the airwaves amidst the chaos with her startling commentary. She confidently stated that the search for Gian Terzo was expanding. She implied that she, herself would play a pivotal role in that search, asking anyone with any information at all to call or e-mail her as soon as possible.

"I have interviewed close to a hundred or so of the participants of this rally," she continued matter-of-factly, "and all of them stated in one way or another how deeply moved they were. I, myself, did experience something, too," she paused for a moment in an attempt to control her own emotion, "a personal transformation that was nothing short of miraculous. It seemed too real to be a forgery, too personal for mass hypnosis, too life altering to be anything short of, short of, I know this sounds crazy, but it's true. Just witness to my left here," she paused as the camera panned out to the front of St. Gerard's Place, where literally hundreds of people were gathered, as well as several news crews, before continuing, "The questions continue, and the search is on. If anyone has any information regarding the whereabouts of this man, please contact me at our station, as soon as possible."

"Thank you for that report," another newsman back at the station began as the feed from the rally disappeared behind him. "We have received new information regarding this event. In a statement issued by officials of this diocese of the Catholic Church, it states the diocese will begin their own investigation into this matter, and will release any and all information to the general public as it becomes available." The reporter turned to face the camera head on, as the camera focused its attention more acutely on him, "some have speculated that this is a desperate attempt for attention by a deeply troubled church."

Pablo quickly turned off the set, and everyone stood there, in silence at first, confused and concerned more than ever for their friends and family. They all knew in that moment that soon the news would spread, the questions would multiply, and they all could not help but be afraid.

Pablo's dad broke the silence. "I can't believe this, Pablo," he began quietly, "I mean, did you know about Gian? I mean, I always knew he was a special kid, but," he paused, his eyes filling with tears, "tonight he touched my heart. I felt him. I saw him. Tonight wasn't a hoax. Oh my God," he paused as he made the sign of the cross, "Tonight I witnessed a miracle."

Pablo ran over to hug his dad, for he had never seen him so emotional before, never.

"Yeah, well," Faith's dad now added, "and now my daughter's with him. My only daughter, you know, and I'm sick about it, 'cause people change, you know. They always destroy the things that they don't understand."

"Faith's all right," her mom quickly responded, in a different voice, "And besides, she's with Gian, and she wouldn't want to be anywhere else. You got to believe that God would keep them safe."

Pablo let go of his dad, as Faith's mom took hold of her husband's hand, and Aimie sat on a nearby chair. In only a few hours, life had become so complicated.

"Pablo, please tell us the truth. We need to know, my son, did you know about Gian?" his dad repeated.

Pablo sat down, as the others just stared at him, intent on his reply. "Yes," he quietly responded, "Yes, I did know about Gian, Dad, I did."

"My God!" Faith's dad exclaimed, "You mean my Faith knew, too? How long? How long? Please tell me."

"I really can't answer for Faith, Mr. Verita," Pablo quickly responded to his question, "I mean, we always sensed something was different about Gian, but a couple of days ago it all began for real."

"Oh God, help us to find them," Pablo's dad prayed openly, "And keep them safe."

"Look, we can't stand around here any more," Faith's dad, Mr. Verita commanded, "let's separate and start a search."

"I'm going to stay around here just in case they come back," Joachim, Pablo's dad replied. "I'll ask my friends at the parish if they've heard anything."

"Good idea," Mr. Verita agreed. "We'll all split up and search. Pablo, you go with Aimie in her car, and I'll go with my wife. Nancee, you go with Budd. We'll call each other with any news, you hear?" He almost shouted as they all rose to leave. Once outside they came to realize the harsh reality of the situation. There were so many lights, from all of the camera crews that it appeared like midday instead of midnight outside. They each hugged each other, as one by one, each departed into the crowds in search of their family.

Across town, Gian awoke in unfamiliar surroundings. "Where am I?" He thought as he lay there and surveyed his surroundings, too weak at first to speak or sit up, too confused to move. Finally, he could see Faith nearby, her head held down, as she appeared to be writing on a pad beneath her. She looked pale and tired, there in the dim light before him, and then he could no longer keep his eyes open, much less muster enough strength to speak.

"Oh, father," she quietly asked of someone nearby, "Do you think he will be okay? He is so weak and vulnerable."

Gian could hear his friend, Monsignor Lilli, respond in his familiar voice nearby, "Faith, we all need to pray for guidance and for comfort, and for understanding, for the burdens of God are great, and we all need to help Gian carry them."

"I'm so worried."

Sensing Faith's fear and concern, the monsignor stood and helped his friend to stand in return. "Come Faith, let us go into the kitchen. It smells as if the good Reverend Martin's sister must have cooked something for us. Please, come on. You'll feel better after you eat something. Gian is fine here. He is safe."

Gian could hear them both depart and finally was able to reopen his eyes, but again found that he was too weak to move or speak. He gazed around this unfamiliar room. "So, this must be Reverend Martin's sister's home. Why," he thought to himself, "am I here?"

The good reverend had opened the doors of his church in one of the worst neighborhoods in the city because of a vision he had had in a dream once. He told Gian that he could hear the voice of a stranger calling out to everyone. The voice of an angel, he would say, that would change the life of everyone he encountered and more. That voice, he once told Gian, was his. "You, Gian, are the reason I am here," he said, "It all began with you."

Gian could hear his good friend Marc's voice inside call out to him now, too, and he could not help but recall all of the stories he had told him, how he had fought every day with the memories of his fractured, tormented past, the Vietnam War and its aftermath, and how he strove every day to rise above it all, and help others.

When he was finally able to keep his eyes open, he struggled to sit up as the early morning Sun streamed in through the windows, and illuminated a paper lying next to him on the floor. He reached for it as he sat up and immediately recognized the writing it contained. He turned toward the window to acknowledge the birth of a new day before him. The Sun gradually filled the room with its warmth and its radiance, and Gian realized that he must have been sleeping for hours. He needed all of his strength, just to read the paper he held in his hands, as it began...

> Please don't take away tomorrow
> Then we will only have today
> Only minutes left to hold you
> Only minutes left to say
> Please don't go away
> Please don't take away tomorrow
> Because I love my life with you
> For it seems like only yesterday
> We found together
> What we could never find alone
> We took a chance on love
> And together we have grown
> A lifetime of dreams
> To dream upon a star

Once so very close
And now so very far
We found the sunlight
Amidst the sorrow
Danced on the moon
Forever tomorrows
So
Please don't take away tomorrow
Then we'll only have today
Only minutes left to hold you
Only moments left to say
Please don't ever go away
Like the flowers need the rain
The Sun to kiss them every day
Please
Don't leave me now
Don't let me go
I won't know how
I just don't know
I need you for forever
And one more day
A million tomorrows
Together
I pray
Don't take away tomorrow
Because I love my life with you
I need you for forever
And one more day
A million tomorrows
Together
Forever
I pray

As Gian looked up from the page, he could see that Faith had walked into the room. The glistening sunlight shone brilliantly on her face in that moment. It revealed the visage of an angel, the inner peace of a sleeping child, the overwhelming beauty of love itself. He could not take his eyes off of her. He could not breathe like he did before. He could not speak at first, for he did not know what to say. He was overwhelmed by Faith's ability to express herself in song. Feelings usually left unspoken, unwritten, were the focus of her creations. He struggled to stand, and, finally, approached her, softly, slowly. He stared into her incredible eyes and she into his. They both smiled, although her eyes filled with tears that now flowed down her beautiful cheeks. Her face revealed a portrait of worry.

When he reached her, he gently moved the hair away from her face and wiped away her tears. He kissed her softly on her lips, and whispered quietly into her ear. "We will always be together, Faith, for I will never leave you."

He gathered her up into his arms and held her close. Weak as they were, together they appeared strong again, renewed in spirit. Faith gently let go of him, but not before whispering, "Whatever happens, Gian, whatever may come, I want you to know that I love you and I'll never leave you." She leaned forward to kiss him as Monsignor Lilli entered the room, apparently hearing them stir.

"I'm sorry, I am so sorry," their friend uttered as he approached, recognizing that he had walked in during a very special time for the two of them. "Gian, we've been waiting and praying for you to awaken. We need to speak to you."

Just then Reverend Martin entered the room and, surveying the scene before him, spoke out in a concerned tone.

"Gian, I brought you here to my sister's house to avoid all the confusion after the festival. I brought you here to rest. No one will look for you here, and very few people know where you are. I felt this was the safest place for you. Do you understand, my friend? Do you agree?"

Gian was so confused at that point. More of the events of the preceding night began to overwhelm him, and he felt as if he was being invaded by them. Gian placed his hands on his face at that moment, apparently overwhelmed.

"Maybe you should sit, Gian," the monsignor responded as he helped his weakened friend to sit down. Faith sat near him, and held his hand, but in that moment, Gian did not even appear to acknowledge her presence.

"Gian," Reverend Martin asked, "How much do you remember about last night?"

Gian searched his mind for an answer as his recollections became clearer. He finally realized why his friends appeared so worried, and why he had been brought to a stranger's house.

"Gian, can you hear me? Do you understand?" Faith asked, concerned still about him.

"Yes, Faith, don't worry, I can hear you. I do remember, but I don't, I don't understand." He paused, and searched all of their faces for an answer to all of his questions about last night, and then he realized that they were all just as confused as he.

"I wish I had the answers you seek, Gian, but alas, I do not," the Monsignor began in a somber tone. "God's work is indeed baffling to us all, but know this my good friend, that His work is always special, always good. You don't have to see the Sun rise and set on a cloudy day to know that it has. It just does. We don't have to understand it all, we may never fully grasp it all. We can only help each other, to offer each other support and guidance, and most of all, love."

There was a silence then, unlike others before, a sacred silence.

"But Reverend Martin," Gian spoke, piercing the quiet, as he turned to face him, "You must know more about all of this. You must. You picked me from a crowd. You heard my voice. You knew I was coming. You must know what's next and why. You must."

The reverend's face glistened with sweat. His eyes were red and puffy from worry and lack of sleep, and yet he was able to smile as he responded to his friend's concerns. "I could only hear your voice, Gian, in a recurring dream. I could hear you speak," he responded with confidence, "And your words were so soothing to me. I knew that I would find you here in this city, and that is why I came, and that is why I searched for you." He paused, searching Gian's face for a response. "I do remember one thing, and one thing only, that a voice repeated over and over again in countless dreams. This voice haunts me still with the words, 'It will begin on the day that the sins of the father are forgiven.'"

"What does that mean?" Gian asked, more bewildered than before.

"I don't know, but it has begun." The good reverend replied, "And begun it has."

All of them were indeed unable to speak for a moment in response. They each had unanswered questions, and the uncertainty of the future seemed daunting.

"Listen Gian," the reverend reassuringly began again, his tone soothing, "I don't know how. I don't even know when. I just know, I just do, that all of this was meant to be, and it must be."

"When you follow a path," the monsignor politely interrupted, "less traveled, there is always more danger ahead, more uncertainty. But you will be guided to your destiny, Gian, as you have been guided so far. Just follow."

"I wish I could help you to understand better, my friend, but I fear I cannot," the good reverend advised. "For I do not fully understand myself. I can tell you that throughout history there have always been those chosen. In every religion throughout time there have been the chosen ones, the unlikeliest of warriors."

"Up from the most common, came the greatest of souls," Monsignor Lilli added.

"But I am not like any of these people that I've read about," Gian began, "I am invisible, so how am I to help others when I am so confused myself?" Gian finished his thought, and searched his soul for an answer.

"Gian, if you knew, you'd realize that the response of the chosen was always the same as yours," the monsignor responded.

"But I don't want this. I don't know what to do. I'm just so tired and so confused. I think, well, I'll just go home now, and maybe I'll feel better at home, back at work. Maybe some time needs to pass and I'll understand more."

"Gian, you can't go home," the reverend explained.

"What? Why not?" Gian pleaded to Faith as he turned to face her, "We could go to your house then, right Faith? We could, we could."

"Gian, you don't understand. After last night, Gerard's Place is surrounded by reporters," the monsignor explained.

"But why?" He asked in apparent denial.

"That TV news reporter. Do you remember her, Gian?" he asked.

"Yes, I remember her," he replied.

"Well, she broadcast your sermon, and she questioned people afterward, and at first it was only on the local news, but the news has spread statewide, and a few national talk shows are picking it up."

"Oh my God," Gian began, "my God, oh my God—"

"Believe me, Gian," the good reverend interrupted, "We have been watching the news all night, and I cannot believe the coverage. Some are in awe of what occurred last night, and others are afraid. They call you a healer. They call you a helper. Others proclaim that you are nothing but a fraud."

"It is safe for you to stay here for now, Gian, until we can feel comfortable with your leaving, until we have more answers," Monsignor Lilli concluded.

"I understand what you are saying and what you are doing, and, well, I do know that you are all worried about me. But I have to tell you all something that I feel, deep inside." Gian paused in reflection. "There is really no place to hide, and this is not the time. I have to go home. I have to answer all of the questions that I can. I have to go home."

"Oh, Gian," Faith began, "but you are still so weak and so confused."

"Faith, your family and our friends must be worried sick about us," he begged, "we can't worry them any more." He glanced into her frightened eyes, and reached out to touch her face. "If I could, I would run away with you forever today. But I can't. We can't. I cannot run away from this. We can't hide from the future. I know this. All of you do. You all know that I cannot."

"You are right," Marc spoke at last, "It is time to go home." His voice was somber and low. "When I was in Vietnam, a part of me wanted to leave. Some did, but I didn't want to live the rest of my life in hiding, a fugitive. I fought to live, and I earned the right to be here. I did not know if I would live or die, but I did not run, I did not hide, and neither should you, Gian."

"I guess you're both right," the monsignor added quietly.

"The road less traveled is always more troublesome, but you're right, my friends. You must continue on that road, Gian, you must," the reverend concluded.

"And I will make sure that you arrive safely, my friend, and that you stay safe once home," Marc exclaimed, "For somehow I feel that, this is my job, just mine."

"I hope," the reverend interjected, changing the subject, "that everyone will stay to eat a little of what my sister has been preparing. She cooked for all of us, and I hope you won't disappoint her."

"That is a good idea," monsignor added. "We'll all feel better after we eat a little."

"I'll join you in a little while," Gian replied, "I need to wash up a bit first."

Eventually they all sat down to eat, after the reverend introduced his sister, his brother-in-law, and their two children. The meal began with grace, and for an hour we enjoyed a beautiful time. We laughed with the children, and sang with them, too. It seems that they were newfound fans of Faith's music. For a short while everyone seemed to forget. For a little while things appeared normal, and all of them needed that.

When they finished, Gian and Faith thanked their hosts for being so gracious and kind, and for allowing them into their home, their family, and their lives. Monsignor and Marc soon followed with their own expression of gratitude, as they all departed the house. Once outside, Faith, Gian, the monsignor, the reverend, and Marc all managed to squeeze into the car that had brought them there, as they began the drive home. They each knew, during that short journey, that nothing would ever be the same. They each knew that life would be different, but none of them could ever have imagined by how much.

As the car approached the front of Gerard's Place, a few news reporters and cameramen began to set up for it. Once it was ascertained that the vehicle contained the object of their quest, several more reporters moved in. All of them inside the car could hear them shout Gian's name. The car's driver, Marc, was forced to stop as they swarmed all around the vehicle, like a swarm of bees, taking pictures, shouting, and asking questions.

"Oh my God!" Faith exclaimed. "I can't believe all of this, Gian, I never thought—"

"Don't worry, Faith, it will be all right. They just have questions," Reverend Martin answered, trying to reassure her.

"Look," Marc began, "The three of us will get out first and try to distract them. We'll try to explain, and if that doesn't work, then we'll just encircle you both, Gian and Faith, like bodyguards, and guide your way through to the house."

"Sounds like a good plan to me," Faith agreed.

With that, the doors of the car opened and none inside expected what happened next. Cameramen and news reporters began with a flood of questions and a barrage of lights. Faith and Gian quickly followed the rest of them out. Once outside, they each were overwhelmed by the crush of reporters and the incoherent questions they shouted. Gian grabbed onto Faith, and even together, they were trapped in a mass-media nightmare.

One reporter grabbed Gian's arm, and demanded an answer to his question.

"Look, Mr. Gian Terzo, ever since last night, reportedly thousands of dollars have been pledged to this parish and its homeless shelter. Is all of this some sort of publicity stunt?"

Gian struggled to continue forward, breaking free of his grip with Faith's help, as the lights of the cameras blinded him. What could he possibly say to these reporters to prove to them that he was not a fake, not a fraud, not a criminal, not an illusionist, as each of them now shouted out?

Faith and Gian tried to break free, but instead the reporters ensnared them, as they continued with their endless barrage of questions.

"Look, just answer a few questions and you can go. How did you pull off such an elaborate hoax, anyway?" the same arrogant reporter demanded as he forcefully took hold of Gian's wrist again. Only this time a scene he did not expect confronted him. For Gian and this reporter suddenly found themselves in a dark place. It was cold, and Gian could barely make out the two figures before him in this dirty alley that he found himself in. A young man lay still on the cold pavement, his upper body propped up next to a garbage can, while another screamed for help and repeatedly shook him. This pale fallen figure did not respond; his eyes were wide open but unresponsive. Gian noticed a tourniquet wrapped around this man's upper arm with a needle protruding from his forearm below it. His chest was not moving.

"Someone please help me, please!" The young man by his side cried out, as he turned and saw Gian standing near him. His sobs suddenly ceased, and he just stared at Gian in apparent shock. In an instant, it was over and Gian found himself staring into the same set of eyes from his dream. Suffocated by the crowd of reporters, he felt lost and confused, and suddenly so weak that he collapsed. The reporter, whose hand still gripped Gian's wrist, and who had shared Gian's vision, suddenly picked up this fragile figure of a man and carried him into the house.

Moments later Gian awoke and was confronted first by the reporter who had earlier harassed him. As their eyes met, yet again, he recognized him from the alleyway, and before he could speak, the reporter began.

"I carried you in. You're safe here," he quietly explained, his voice trembling. "I am so sorry that I doubted you. Please forgive me, please." With those words he quickly departed, and Gian could hear his voice once he was outside, yelling to the others to leave them alone. He began to shout over and over again, "Everyone just go home, tomorrow is another day, leave these poor people alone." With those words, the commotion outside seemed to die down. Gian looked about, recognized his apartment, and fell fast asleep.

He awakened a short time later, but the only thing he could hear clearly was the television. He could hear one call him a "fame seeker," and another say "this was his fifteen minutes." Others compared him to psychics who speak to the dead and tell fortunes. A few established that this was all orchestrated by the Roman Catholic Church "to revive what's left of a dying dynasty." Gian's name was constantly being invoked, and rarely in a positive manner.

"All I tried to do was offer some hope, some peace to people who need it. That's all," Gian uttered, startling all those present, for they were unaware that he was awake and worse, unaware that he could hear the newscasts.

"I just tried to help is all," he repeated as he sat up in a chair. Startled, Pablo bolted toward the TV and shut it off.

"What's wrong?" Aimie pleaded as she followed Pablo outside.

"Aimie, is it wrong for me to want things back to the way they were?" Pablo began, like a young child wishing for a bad story to end. "I'm losing my family. I feel like I'm losing everything. What if something happens to them? What if?"

Aimie rushed to his side and embraced him as she whispered into his ear, "Faith will always be your sister and Gian your brother, and your friends and family will always be. Nothing can change that."

"We're all worried, Pablo," Father Thom declared as he exited Gian's apartment, "but together we'll get through this." He then explained that Aimie's parents had just called and were outside the church waiting for her, and that she had to leave.

"I have to go," Aimie replied as she kissed Pablo gently on his cheek, "But I'll be back soon."

Pablo couldn't respond as he watched her leave.

"We have to go back inside now, follow me," Father Thom almost demanded, as he opened the door to Gian's place, and Pablo quietly followed.

"All of you have to leave immediately," he demanded of those present in the room. Gian, Pablo, Faith, Marc, Budd, and Nancee were stunned. "Gian needs to wash up, and eat, now get out all of you."

Everyone obeyed except for Faith and Marc.

"I'm staying, Father—just in case, for added protection," Marc replied in defiance.

"I'm not leaving either," Faith boldly stated.

"All right, all right," the arrogant priest accepted as he left the apartment.

"Maybe the mean guy is right, Gian. I think you'll feel better after you shower and change," Marc concluded.

"I think he's right," Faith agreed.

Gian gathered up some clothes from his drawers in an instant, and quietly made his way into the bathroom, closing the door behind him without a sound.

"We are going to have to be very strong for him now," Faith began.

"I am ready to do whatever I have to," Marc replied confidently.

"He needs us more than ever," Faith declared.

"I know."

"I will keep him safe, you have my word on that."

"I know you will try Marc, you are such a good friend, but I don't know if anyone can keep him safe."

"God can."

"I pray that you are right."

"I have to be."

"What do you think about all of this, Marc?" Faith pleaded.

"You know, Faith, I learned long ago not to try and figure this all out, you know, life and all. I just take it day by day, with God's help of course, most days, I can feel him close by."

"I believe," Faith almost whispered in response, her eyes suddenly filled with tears. Marc moved closer to his friend and hugged her there in the stillness of that small room, in the quiet of that moment, offering her shelter from her worry in his strong embrace.

"Who will keep you safe?" Faith was finally able to reply, as Gian reentered the room after a quick shower, and startled them both.

"Is something wrong?" he almost shouted, as he approached them.

"No, Gian, no," Faith exclaimed as she raced into his arms, "Everything is all right now that you are here."

"I hate to interrupt," Marc began, "But everyone is waiting for us at your house, Faith, and we don't want to worry them, besides I just looked outside and the streets look clear."

With those words, the three of them departed into the eerily damp and cool night. Marc walked ahead of Faith and Gian along the empty alleyway leading into the street. No one remained outside, it seemed, and a fog seeped in all around to darken the street lamps' glow. Innocently, Faith and Gian followed their friend across that abandoned street in the early evening. Unknowingly, they followed him into the future, each step taking them closer to their destiny.

CHAPTER 9

As they walked across the street just a few feet from Gerard's Place in the darkness of a fog-laden evening, a group of hooded men emerged from two parked cars ahead of them. One grabbed Faith and she began to scream. Another quickly struck Gian in the back with a bat. Stunned, he fell to the ground, unable to breathe. Four men cornered Marc, and were pounding him with their combined brute force, but somehow he managed to fend off his assailants and get free. He turned to pounce on Faith's attacker with such strength that in seconds he seemed to render him unconscious in a pool of his own blood.

Gian could barely see what was happening around him, as he struggled to stand and turn around. He witnessed one of the men grab hold of Faith, forcefully covering her mouth with his hand. Three of the others began to beat on Marc unmercifully, striking him with bats, until he fell silently to the ground, soon they each approached Gian wielding bats, and one of them produced a large, shiny knife from inside his jacket. Within seconds they began to pound on Gian with a combined force that easily overwhelmed him. Faith managed to free herself enough to scream, and Marc managed to get up onto his feet again unnoticed, struggling to regain enough strength to fight back.

Gian was now face to face with a knife that had already grazed his cheek in the struggle, when Marc sprang upon his attacker, knocking the knife on the ground as they both fell onto the cold, harsh pavement below. No sooner had they landed when another of the men struck Marc on the back of his head with such force that the bat broke in two pieces around him, and he fell lifelessly into a pool of blood emanating, it seemed, from everywhere. Faith managed to scream out again, and Gian turned toward her only to see her collapse into unconsciousness with tears streaming down her ashen face. A sudden blow to his back sent Gian down onto the ground beneath him, as his own blood dampened his body in the cold.

Three bodies lay upon the unforgiving asphalt of the inner city, two beaten and near death. Gian was able to turn over as one of his assailants, now unmasked, approached with a face so cold and angry that only evil could be seen. Somehow Gian became distracted as the glow of the luminous cross above St. Gerard's church drew him toward it, and he began to pray. He could see the figure of a man within the curtains of a second floor window, whom he recognized to be Father Thom, their eyes met in an instant, and in another he was gone. Gian gazed upward long enough to see that his attacker was only inches from his chest with a menacing knife so close to taking his life from him. He reached out to deflect it by grabbing his assailant's arm with just enough force to direct the knife toward his upper arm, and it pierced his clothing and skin. Easily pushed aside, Gian's assailant, with eyes of pure evil, now regained his stance and redirected his weapon at Gian. In the dark fog, upon the desolate streets of a frightened city, Gian prayed for his friends, and for his Faith, and he experienced firsthand what his mother must have, as she lay dying in a stranger's house, alone. He could hear his mother's voice cry out his name, and then, and then, he heard a gunshot ring out. He opened his eyes to see his attacker clutch his chest now filled with blood, and fall to the ground.

Gian looked about and found a lone gunman aiming his weapon at the others, and they all fled into the shadows. Gian recognized the face of this hero to be none other then that of the gang leader from the night before that had attacked him. This sole young man raced over toward where Faith lie, and picked up her body, and carried it toward her house.

Gian struggled to stand, his clothes torn. He was unaware of the extent of his injuries at that point, unaware that the dampness that he felt was that of his own blood on his upper arm, unaware that he could barely breathe, so totally unaware of death as it surrounded him and his fallen friend, Marc. Once upright the glow atop the church became overwhelming, and all he could do was follow it, as he slowly walked toward the church, and climbed the stairs to the front entrance. He peered upward once again, and could see Father Thom's face amidst the curtains above him, and he begged him to come and help them with his eyes, for he could not speak. He stumbled upon the church door, and found it locked.

Gian then attempted to open it with his remaining strength, but to no avail. From behind the door, he could hear all the latches and bolts come undone, as it quietly opened. He entered and uttered "Father Thom," but no one was there. No one answered.

He limped forward holding his arm and struggled to get air inside his lungs. He opened the back doors of the chapel to enter, and could see the statue of Mary before him aglow in a light that made her appear almost lifelike. He inched toward her. He made the sign of the cross with his bloodied hands, and fell to his knees in anguish, screaming out in pain, "Mother Mary help me so that I may help…." He stumbled forward, and collapsed just a few feet up the aisle in front of her. His desperate breaths were all that one could hear, as he blacked out on the bloodstained carpet below.

Gian awoke some time later immersed in a light so bright he kept opening and closing his eyes to adjust to its incredible force. He found himself on the carpeted floor, beneath the statue of Mary above him. He felt amazingly at peace, at home, and pain free. The light gradually faded as he peered toward the statue. Dazed, he could not believe what he saw, for it appeared that Mary's eyes were crying, and that her face was cut and bruised. Her upper arm was bloodied, and her clothes torn.

"I must be hallucinating," Gian thought as he quickly arose, as the memory of the tragedies of the night paralyzed him with fear. Fraught with worry for his Faith and for his dear friend Marc, he quickly turned to run out of the chapel to find them. As he approached the back doors, he found Father Thom there kneeling before him with his face peering at the ground, and his hand over his heart. Father lifted his head and his tearful eyes faced that of Gian's, as he proceeded to make the sign of the cross several times muttering to himself incoherently.

"Father Thom?" Gian asked, as he approached. "Are you all right? Do you need help?" There was no response. "What happened? Do you know? Please tell me. Is Faith all right? Is Marc still alive? Please answer me, Father, please!" He begged, but to no avail. Father seemed unharmed, yet he was unable to speak, so he proceeded past him and opened the door to leave for he had to find Faith. He had to help Marc.

As Gian exited, he heard father finally utter the same words over and over again, "Forgive me," he would say, "Please forgive me."

Feeling sorry for him, he turned back around and helped the trembling priest up and into a pew. He grabbed hold of his hand before he left and uttered one final time, "Please, Gian, forgive me." Father was apparently in a state of shock, but he knew he had to leave him and find his friends. He had to find Faith.

As Gian left the church that night he was filled with worry, but also at peace, a peace he had not felt before, serenity he had never known before. Once outside he could see two police cars with their lights flashing across the street and one ambulance. He could see a couple of his assailants now unmasked, and in handcuffs, being led into the police cars.

One of the men turned toward Gian, spotting him upon the church stairs, and his face grew pale and his voice shrill as he screamed out, "Oh my God, my God, look! He was stabbed, and he's not hurt. There are no bruises, no blood. It's not possible, my God, it's not possible!"

The policemen, unaware of what had occurred, just pushed the criminal forward into the car. "Don't you understand? He should be dead," he screamed out. The door slammed in his face as the two cars sped off, containing the assailants as each of them stared over at Gian in disbelief. One appeared to be crying.

Gian gazed down upon his body and realized that it was indeed unharmed, his clothes though, were torn and dishelved. But all he could think of was the health of his friend Marc, and his love Faith. He could see Marc's body being lifted into a waiting ambulance by two EMTs, and he quickly ran to his side. His heart was pounding as he approached his dear friend. Marc's neck was collared and his head bandaged, with blood seeping through. An IV was running into his arm, and he was intubated as one of the EMTs filled his lungs with air from an ambu bag. His eyes were swollen, his face bruised and bloodied, and Gian could barely bring himself to ask, "Is he going to make it?"

"He is seriously injured, and we need to get him to the hospital immediately," one of the crew responded, as he closed the back doors of the ambulance.

"Are you all right? Do you need assistance?" he questioned.

"No, I'm fine. Just take good care of my friend now, please, please go." Gian said before the ambulance departed.

Gian stood there alone in the middle of the street, and even though there were gatherings of people scattered about, and their mumblings he could hear around him, he felt alone, so totally alone in that instant. He was so full of fear as his thoughts and prayers went with them. His dear friend Marc was fighting for his life after trying to save Gian's and Faith's. Marc had saved so many lives before, and he struggled to save his own now. It was not fair. Life was so unfair. To lay down your life for your friend, they say, is the ultimate sacrifice, and in so doing your souls are forever joined, you are one, but these thoughts did not offer him any comfort.

Gian could hear Faith's voice screaming his name from across the street. At first he thought he was imagining it.

"Gian! Gian!" she screamed from her front porch as she exited her house and Pablo quickly followed. "You're all right! Thank God you are all right." Gian was overwhelmed by her voice, and stood there motionless in the middle of the street. She looked good there in the distance. 'Thank God she was okay,' he thought, 'thank God.'

Before he could move or speak, a large vehicle appeared out of nowhere. It sped up and screeched to a halt in front of him, blocking his path and obstructing his view. It was black with tinted windows, the largest SUV he had ever seen. Four large masked men poured out of it and onto him, and within a second Gian was thrown to the floor of this vehicle and it took off. He could hear Faith scream in the distance, as well as the shouts of spectators, but then nothing. Distant flashing lights appeared, and then disappeared. Gian attempted to move when someone jabbed his thigh with a needle and within moments, he collapsed into darkness.

Several minutes later, Faith, Pablo and Father Thom were being escorted by police to the station for questioning. The car ride was silent except for the sirens and a few muffled sobs. No one spoke at all. Sad, despondent faces with quiet sighs filled the backseat of the car this evening. At the police station the three were escorted into the building, shielding them from the throngs of news media already posted outside. Like zombies, they each walked into the building, seemingly oblivious to it all, as a dense fog settled in on this cloudy, dark night.

Inside they were taken to an interrogation room, and all three sat quietly at a table there. The silence was overwhelming, and short of a clock ticking away the time, nothing else was heard, not even a heartbeat. Within minutes a few officers entered the room, and each of them surveyed the muted scene. Pablo had positioned himself near Faith and quietly held her hand. Beads of perspiration covered Father Thom's forehead as his head fell forward, and the drops of sweat fell quietly to the table below him.

The picture presented was one of post-traumatic stress, the remnants of life remaining after a sudden tragedy. It is said that when an emotionally crippling event occurs, life appears to stand still for all affected. The Sun still rises and sets, the flowers still open and close, the butterflies still dance, and the birds still sing, but no one notices, for a horror has overwhelmed them. Tragedy supersedes all. It overwhelms the senses. It embalms the mind.

A group of well-dressed men sporting FBI badges entered the room, and conversed briefly with the officers already present. Afterwards the police officers left the room. At first the agents spoke to each other, and then they began to address Faith, Pablo, and Father Thom. No one was listening to them, therefore no one responded. One of them continued to question them. His olive complexion and black hair surrounded his deep, dark, penetrating eyes, which surveyed them like criminals. His words seemed to echo about the room like the muffled sounds one hears when wearing earmuffs.

"I am agent Roy Despirito of the Federal Bureau of Investigation," he spat at them, loud enough for each of them to finally hear him. Each of them turned toward him before he continued, now that he finally had their attention.

"We are here to investigate the kidnapping and disappearance of one Gian Terzo. I need your help. We need your help."

"The FBI," Pablo broke the silence, "They called in the FBI," he repeated, like a little kid might. "Faith, if anyone will find him, they will."

"Look everyone, I can't overstate this one fact enough. Every minute that passes is essential in a kidnapping. The sooner that I can ascertain all of the facts surrounding the abduction, the better."

"I don't understand, officer," Faith meekly questioned, "Was the van carrying Gian lost?"

"I'm afraid the answer is yes," the officer paused for a moment, his voice emotional for the first time. "Whoever kidnapped Mr. Terzo was a real professional. This was a well-planned act." He paused again, "Well planned," he repeated, his eyes averted.

"First they tried to kill him, and this time they almost did, and now, now they've kidnapped him," Faith tearlessly sobbed. "Why? Why him? He's never hurt anyone, officer, never. He's only tried to help." Pablo, sensing his sister's anguish, held her close.

"We need to know everything about the events of the past couple of days, everything," the agent began again, "The smallest detail might yield a clue." The agent turned to face Faith. "And you, Faith, need to help me understand Gian better. I need to get inside of his head, and only you can help me do that."

"Faith, he's right," Pablo began to speak quietly to his friend, and Faith composed herself, "You have to tell him as much as you can remember, please Faith. You must believe it's the right thing to do. You must believe that Gian will be all right."

"You're right," she responded as she sat down to retell a tale, most of which she wished would have never happened. Everyone listened intently as Faith recounted the events of the past few hours. No one interrupted her. No one could. It was all too surreal. She even recounted some of the events of the past few days. Father Thom quietly sat there, sighing at times in remembrance.

"Wait a minute," agent Despirito finally interrupted, "You said that Gian was stabbed at least once, and was beaten unconscious, and yet when he emerged from the church, he appeared unharmed. His clothes were torn and unbloodied. How? How is this possible, Faith?"

"Look, everyone there saw it happen," Pablo quickly, almost angrily retorted, "it just did. Don't you believe them?"

"I am just gathering the facts, trying to make sense of what has transpired. I need to know what happened inside that church."

"One man here knows the answer you need," Pablo volunteered.

"I know," Father Thom meekly admitted, as he raised his head up to face the officer, falling silent again.

"Well, father, I believe it's time for you to tell us your story," the agent proclaimed.

"I, I don't believe," Father Thom began again, before pausing.

"What, father? What are you saying to us? What don't you believe? What?" the agent impatiently asked.

"You won't believe me anyway, even though it's the truth. Very few will."

"Look father, just please tell us what happened tonight, and we'll take it from there." Moments of silence passed, empty silence.

"I was afraid," he began somberly, "I was so afraid, you see. I looked out from the window and I could see what was happening. I could hear Faith scream out, but I was too afraid to move." He paused as he closed his eyes to ponder his own fear, "Unless you're in a situation like that yourself, I guess you'll never know what you would do. I never thought I would be paralyzed. I prayed every minute for guidance, but I just continued to look out from the church window as if it were a movie scene and not reality. And when Gian finally managed to crawl up the church stairs bloodied and crying for help, I did nothing," he paused again to compose himself before continuing. "Gian looked up at me, maybe twice, and both times I failed him. I could not speak. I could not move. God forgive me." He sobbed at this point for a brief period. No one else spoke for a moment.

"Continue, father. I know how difficult this is for you, but I need to know exactly what happened," the agent queried.

"Faith is right. They're all right. Why don't you believe them?" He scolded the officer now. "Gian was beaten and knocked unconscious, and stabbed. I saw him bruised and bloodied as he crept up the stairs and I did not let him in." His tone continued softly from this point, "I just left the window and hid."

"Then how did an injured man get into a locked church? Did he have a key?" the agent impatiently continued.

"No," Father Thom meekly responded, "No, he did not."

"Monsignor Lilli was there?" Faith interrupted, confused.

"No, Faith, not Bishop Lilli," Father Thom paused, as if in prayer, before continuing. "No one else was in the church tonight but me. But those locks came undone and the door opened. I heard them." He paused again to make the sign of the cross, "And I gradually made my way down the stairs to see—"

"Oh my God," Faith uttered, interrupting briefly.

"Yes, Faith, you are right, my dear girl," father continued, "For when I reached the bottom of the stairs, no one else was there. Gian had apparently gone into the chapel, and I could see a pure light emanating from the openings in the doors. Amazed, I quietly made my way to the entrance and slowly opened one of the doors, enough to be blinded by the light that surrounded me. I stumbled in with my eyes closed, and fell to my knees, and I began to pray."

"This light," he continued, for no one else could speak, "was indescribable. So pure, so innocent, so beautiful, so warm," he paused again to open and close his eyes. "Finally, I was able to see the altar, and at first I thought I was seeing things, for the statue of Mary was missing. I continued to stare, and I could not see Gian or anything else. My focus was on the altar, and the missing statue." He stopped to look into each of their faces before continuing.

"As the light faded, Gian approached me and he, and he, my God, he was unharmed. And I could not speak nor move. He asked me if I was all right. Do you believe that? He asked *me* if *I* needed help. I shook my head no, and he left." Father Thom cried at this point, with tears from his eyes, tears of sorrow and despair. "He asked me for help, if I needed help," he paused again in between sobs, "I witnessed a miracle tonight, officer, I did. There is no other explanation but that."

"Father, please let us draw the conclusions," the agent replied in apparent disbelief.

Out of nowhere, the second agent approached our interrogator and with moist eyes, he began to speak loud enough for all present in the room to hear. "Roy, look, I've been in the church. The statue of Mary is there on that altar."

"See," the first agent interrupted, "See?"

"No, no. Let me continue, please," the second agent pleaded. "The statue, her robes are pierced on her upper arm, with what appears to be blood emanating from it, and her eyes are crying, what appears to be tears. And, and her arms are stained with blood. And her head, according to the sisters there, used to face upward and now she is looking down with bruises upon her face. He fell silent, as an eerie silence ensued.

"Oh my God, my God," Father Thom blurted out, "That is why I couldn't see her on the altar, for she wasn't there, you see. She was helping one of her children, you see. My God, forgive me. She was helping Gian."

The second agent now escorted Father Thom out of the room, as he continued to ramble on and on. The events of the past twenty-four hours proved too much for him in so many ways. Faith and Pablo could understand a little better, for the thin line between truth and fiction had begun to blur days earlier.

Another agent abruptly entered the room and began to speak at great length in relative quiet to agent Despirito before he exited just as mysteriously as he had entered.

"What's happened?" Pablo began, "Did they find Gian?"

"Please tell us that they found him all right," Faith pleaded.

"No, no, Gian is still missing but we are pursuing every lead."

"Well, what about the men that attacked us tonight. They might know something," Pablo exclaimed anxiously. Stunned, the agent did not respond immediately.

"Is something wrong? Please tell us," Faith nervously queried.

"Well," the agent began again, "the apparent leader of the group escaped. In all the confusion, he managed to disappear."

"What!" Pablo exclaimed, "How is that possible?"

"Look, your friend Gian has created utter chaos. That entire area of town had to be secured, and in all the confusion, he escaped."

"What about the other men?" Pablo asked.

"One is dead, and the others, well unfortunately they haven't helped. They either don't know anything or are refusing to cooperate."

"Then we're nowhere," Pablo quietly uttered.

"That's not true, believe me," the agent reassuringly replied, "There has never been a search like this one that I've ever been involved in. Local, state, and federal agents are involved. Have faith."

"Have faith. Gian used to say that a lot," Pablo recalled, "Marc, too."

"Have you any news of our friend Marc's condition?" Faith pleaded.

"Wait, wait just a minute, you two. Hold on here," the officer abruptly declared as the two of them stood up.

"Look, we're leaving and there is nothing you can do or say to stop us. So don't try," Pablo retorted.

"You're not safe out there. Don't you understand? Marc wasn't a target either and well, look at what happened to him."

"We don't care about our safety. Don't you understand that? Our friends needs us now," Faith replied.

"Please give me a few minutes to arrange this, then," the agent finally conceded, "You'll need transportation and extra security. Just hold on there for a few moments, okay?" They nodded in agreement as he left the room.

"Marc needs us, Pablo. I just know he does."

"He'll be all right, Faith. Don't worry. He has been through worse than this before. He is a strong man."

"I just don't know, Pablo. I just don't understand. I don't understand any of this."

"I know."

"I'm afraid, Pablo. I'm so afraid."

"I am too, Faith, but we must believe…"

"Believe," Faith interrupted, "Believe," she repeated.

Pablo hugged his friend, his mentor, his sister, and in each other's arms they felt a little comfort. Together they had been through so much, and together again, they hoped and prayed that they would get through this. So much had changed in such a short time, but one fact remained. Whatever happened from this moment on, this family would face it together, and together they would survive.

"Faith, I'll get you to the hospital, even if they won't take us. Don't worry. Somehow I'll drive you there."

"Pablo, please, enough has happened already." They each smiled a little in response.

The silence that remained exacerbated the loneliness the two of them felt, the emptiness of their lives without Gian and Marc. The emptiness they felt was audible in the silence. When the agent returned, cell phone in hand, all eyes were upon his pale, worried face.

"Your friend Marc," he coldly recounted, "is in critical condition in the intensive care unit at St. Vincent's hospital. He is unconscious after an operation to remove some accumulated blood in his brain." He paused and his tone became more somber, yet caring. "The doctors are not sure if he will ever regain consciousness. I am truly sorry."

"Do you mean that he is in a coma?" Pablo could barely speak the words, whose answer he did not want to hear.

"Yes," was his frank response.

"Oh God. I know that Gian could help if…" Faith uttered.

"We have to go and see him!" Pablo interrupted.

"I still have questions," the agent replied, "and besides, it isn't safe."

"Are we under arrest?" Pablo sarcastically asked.

"No," came the reply.

"Then we can leave at any time?" Pablo continued.

"Well, yes, but…"

"Then, agent Despirito, please understand that we must act, despite the risk," Faith explained. "Our friend Marc needs us. He is the one who saved us. He is fighting for his life because of us. He is one of us."

"Then we're leaving and we're going to leave now, with or without your help," Pablo responded and hastily stood up and grabbed hold of his sister. "Let's go, Faith. We have to go now, I'll drive."

"Pablo, if you drive us, we will get to the hospital all right, but not as visitors."

They both smiled again, as they separated, and the levity seemed to break down the doors of fear and worry that had surrounded them just moments earlier.

Agent Despirito was surprised by their change in tone. "Did you two hear already? All of the arrangements have been made. A couple of the local police officers will escort you both to the hospital."

"When?" Pablo nervously interrupted.

"Now," he replied, "They are already waiting for you both down the hall."

Faith and Pablo quickly exited with their federal escort leading the way. Ecstatic that they were finally on their way, they failed to say good-bye, for they were quickly brought out a back door and into an unmarked car before them. Once inside, they huddled close together as they departed, initially on the floor of the car, as the officers directed them to. After a few moments though, they sat up and gazed behind them toward the police station. They were amazed at the throng of news vans and reporters that had gathered in the front of the building.

"Oh my God, Faith," Pablo proclaimed as he witnessed the incredible scene behind him.

"You're right, Pablo, you don't know how right you are."

They both realized in the back of the car what they had only thought before. The world had changed for them. Their world was different now, uncertain, dangerous, and insane. They both knew the truth as they drove off together peering through the tinted glass windows that surrounded them. The truth was that nothing would ever be the same again, nothing at all.

CHAPTER 10

Across the city, in a place visited by only a chosen few, lay a figure of a man clad in a robe across a disheveled bed. The room surrounding him was rather small and dark and somber. The furniture it contained was sparse and old and worn. The sleeping figure was restless as it thrashed about intermittently in the darkness, at times silent, at others yelling incoherently. Perspiration flowed from a once innocent face now haunted by nightmares, a youthful face, now drowning in sweat. Dark circles surrounded the closed eyes. A small growth of beard dotted the once childlike face whose youthful glow now faded amongst the demons of his dreams.

There was another there in the shadows, seated near the door amidst the darkness. He was dressed in a long dark robe, motionless. He was almost invisible in the surroundings. Something he held in his hands seemed to attract the only light in the room, as it dangled from them. This object seemed aglow, lost here amongst the shadows, and the darkness of a nightmare.

A closer look at that restless figure on that small bed revealed that it contained a familiar face, a face at first unrecognizable in this darkness of worry and despair, a face that was clearly seen. It was that of Gian.

"Faith" came out of his mouth in sheer panic, as this figure quickly sat up on his bed. His piercing blue eyes now open, appeared frightened and lost. Those same eyes darted across the room for a few moments, adjusting to the dim light. They continued to search for a familiar sign, but none was to be found there in the empty silence of this small place. "What happened?" Gian uttered to himself as he grabbed his head, for it was pounding, and fell back onto the bed in pain and anguish.

He tried desperately to remember where he was and what had happened, but he could not. His head throbbed like it was about to explode, and barely out of the corner of his eye, he could finally see a figure approach before he passed out again before the cloaked figure of a mysterious stranger.

In his dreams, Gian was in a safe place. Life was good, and he was happy. A part of him did not want to awaken, that part of him that contained the child inside, that part of him that still believed in happy endings.

He awoke some time later, and still his head felt different, as if he had been drugged, but soon the intense pain subsided. His clothes and bedding were wet with perspiration, and slowly he sat up again, and attempted to survey his surroundings in the darkness. He had hoped that this was some sort of nightmare, but it was not. He was totally bewildered. He felt totally alone. He began to search the room for answers, and a part of him began to remember what another part of him tried desperately to forget.

A figure seated across the room now stirred, stood up, and approached him in the dim light. Startled, Gian began to scream, "Where am I? Where is this? Who are you? What has happened to me? Where is Faith?" Overwhelmed, he grabbed hold of his head again in his hands, his vision blurred, and he felt nauseous, disoriented, and dizzy. He continued to struggle to stay awake. He continued to fight to clear his mind.

"What's wrong with me?" he pleaded to this dark shadow at his side, for he still could not focus. "Am I drugged, huh? I've never felt like this before. Please tell me!"

There was no response from this mysterious stranger. Gian gazed down upon his body and realized that it was dressed in what appeared to be surgical scrubs with some sort of slippers on his feet. He felt as confused as a young mouse in a large maze, and just as frightened. He needed so many answers, and yet he was in no condition to fight, but a part of him knew that he needed to fight. He had to gather enough strength. He had to. "Is this what a prisoner of war feels like once awakened in his enemy's camp?" he thought. Alone and lost, he searched for answers, clues, ways to escape. A part of him is struggling to remember what happened, and how he came to be here in this place, and another part longs for everyone who loves him with every fiber of his being. Survivors of a tragedy are forever changed, he thought, in this puzzle of life in which we all live. All of the pieces may fit together in this puzzle one calls life on the outside, but on the inside the pieces just don't fit together like they used to. Somehow they're forever altered, and the finished product is forever changed.

The world can seem so at peace in the distance before a war, like the Earth so calm before a storm. Afterward, those still standing are labeled survivors, and no one seems to understand that these souls are forever changed. Gian felt like one of them now, here on this small bed in this unfamiliar place, a fractured soul, just a fragment of the man he used to be, tormented, and searching for yesterday.

The shadowy figure across the room now approached, and a burst of light streamed in as the door behind the stranger flew open, flooding the small space with light. Gian closed his eyes to adjust to the light, and reopened them. He could plainly see two men dressed in similar robes standing near his bed. One must have entered, and in his confusion he hadn't noticed. Instinctively, he stood up in an effort to defend himself, but he quickly realized that he was still too weak to stand on his own. He was about to fall back down if he did not struggle to steady himself, his body trembling beneath him.

"Gian," one of the men surprisingly declared his name as he rushed to his side. "We mean you no harm; do not be afraid." Gian stumbled about at first, unable to comprehend all of what was being said. He could not walk without stumbling.

"Gian, Gian," another voice close by now spoke. "Please listen to us, look at us," as the voice pleaded for recognition. "You are safe here. We do not want to hurt you."

"You don't want to hurt me," he repeated in a weakened voice.

He continued to struggle to regain his balance, his sanity, his freedom. His mind was an endless maze of confusion, as he tried to sort out what was happening, and what had happened. Flashes of memory stalked him filled with Faith's screams, and the awful pain of being hit repeatedly, and the agony of struggling to breathe. He fell back again upon the bed, overwhelmed by it all. At first he could neither open his eyes nor lift his head, but then he began to feel a little better and he reopened his eyes with renewed vigor.

"Gian," a voice asked, "are you all right?"

"Gian," another voice began, "Do not be afraid. We brought you here to keep you safe. Believe us when we tell you this. Your life is in danger. The outside world is too dangerous for you now. Please believe me."

"Don't you remember," another voice began, "don't you remember what happened to you last night. Try to remember, Gian. You must try."

Gian, with his cold hands cradling his perspiring face, was trying desperately to remember. His fragmented, tortured visions at first overwhelmed him, then suddenly he began to recollect more clearly the events of the preceding day, the carnival, the prayer, the attack. All of the questions, all of the concerns, all of the pain of the preceding night came crashing back, but he still had so many unanswered questions. Why was he unhurt? How could he be okay, if he was really stabbed? He sat up in his bed, his mind racing out of control, for he could not completely comprehend it all. He struggled to speak, but yet again could not, and within seconds he fell back down upon the bed into darkness. He dreamed again of her.

Faith sat there in the pew of the hospital chapel alone. She prayed in silence just as she had been doing for hours. She refused to go home until Marc opened his eyes. She prayed for Gian, for his safety and his safe return. She did not feel alone here in the chapel, surrounded by statues of Mary, and Jesus, and some of the saints. Since she had been a little girl, she prayed in St. Gerard's church across the street. Many times she would sneak in and talk to the statures like most girls talk to their dolls. She felt at home in any church, or chapel, for on many nights growing up, they were her only true family. When her parents would go out and leave her, or when they were too drunk to know, Faith would set up house in God's house. Mary was her mother, and Jesus, her brother, the others were friends or cousins or neighbors. Today she pleaded with her family to keep her friends alive, and she cried alone there in that chapel, like she had done so many times before, until she fell asleep in her Mother's arms.

"Faith, are you all right?" came the startled cry of her friend Nancee, as she approached her sleeping friend.

Startled, Faith sat up and wiped her eyes, and for a second, she did not know where she was. She turned to face her friend now and smiled, so as not to worry her further.

"Come on, Faith, you need to eat something. Pablo tells me that you haven't eaten in hours."

"Nancee, thanks for being here. I'm really glad to see you, but really, I'm not hungry."

"Look, girl, you aren't going to do anyone any good if you're too weak yourself and need a hospital bed," she softly scolded her friend as she approached her, and grabbed her by the arm.

"No, I can't, really I can't," came the feeble reply.

"Oh, yes you can," her friend insisted, pulling her up by her arm.

"I can't go, please Nancee, please, I can't, I just can't!" Faith exclaimed, and then she sat back down in her pew and began to cry.

"I'm sorry, really, I am," Nancee apologized, realizing how emotional her friend was.

Faith wiped away her tears and replied, "It isn't your fault, really. You haven't done anything wrong. It's me."

"What is it, Faith, what's got you so spooked?"

"Everything."

"I know that you're scared, we all are, but Faith, we are all so worried about you, Pablo, and your parents, everyone. We are all so worried about you."

"Oh dear God, I had no idea, I guess I didn't realize. I'm so sorry."

"Oh no, there you go again, apologizing, and making me feel more like a heel," Nancee responded, and then she sat down near her friend and gave her a quick hug.

"I'm sorry."

"Oh God, not again."

"Oh no, I mean, I'm…"

"Don't say another syllable, you hear."

They both laughed for a moment, for one precious moment.

"Do you honestly think that God wants you in here, minute by minute, hour by hour? Honestly, you're like one of those annoying kids in a toy store. He heard you, He knows already."

"I'm afraid to leave," Faith finally admitted in a sad little-girl voice. "I'm afraid that if I walk out that door, I'll lose everything, and I've already lost so much."

"You don't have to stay, Faith, God knows, He's heard you, please come with me."

"I just can't."

"All right, God, your daughter here, doesn't believe me, God knows, Oh damn," realizing what she just said, "Now I'm damned, oh well, what's new?" she continued, "Please give her a sign that it's okay for her to leave? God knows that," she paused for a moment, "Damn! Just give her a sign, please? So that we can get the hell out of here? Oh God,…damn,…I'm screwed."

The door to the chapel opened in that instant, and a very tired-looking Pablo burst in, as the two girls turned toward him, "You coming Faith?" he blurted out. "Come on, sis, take a break, even God rested on the sixth da—I mean, you know, on Sunday."

The two girls just laughed, as they stood up and walked down the aisle toward their dumbfounded friend.

"What, what is going on here?" Pablo was barely able to finish, when the two of them grabbed hold of each of his arms, as they continued on their way out of the chapel.

"Who woulda' thought, Pablo, God's messenger…" Nancee blurted out.

"What?" Pablo repeated.

"Just keep on walking Angel Gabriel," Nancee replied as they opened the chapel doors to exit. Faith turned around for just one moment to gaze upon Mary. As she left, her thoughts were of Gian, only of Gian.

When Gian reawakened, the glare from the hallway lights blinded him momentarily. The door to his room was open, and he quickly canvassed his surroundings. He found no one else present in the room with him. He sat up and this time his headache was gone, and he could focus better; his vision seemed normal. He wondered at first just how much time had elapsed since the night he was kidnapped and drugged, for it was all such a blur.

The room itself was quite small and sparsely decorated. It was windowless and dull, and dampness in the room led him to believe that he was housed in a rather old building. His gaze now focused upon a wall just behind him, and he was struck by what he found there, hanging upon it. It was the only object that adorned any wall in the room, and he could not take his eyes off of it. He opened and closed his eyes several times, but there it remained, such a familiar sight in such an unfamiliar place. It was a plain, rather lonely crucifix.

Two men suddenly entered the room and were apparently startled to find him awake and coherent. Gian stared at them, and realized that their dark robes were actually religious attire, the robes of a religious order he had seen before, but had forgotten. Why would these men kidnap me and bring me here? Were they really monks?

"Gian, please listen to me," one of the men began quietly as he approached. "Please listen," he continued as he sat down next to him on the bed.

"We mean you no harm. You are safe here," he repeated. "We brought you here to keep you safe. You must believe me. Do you understand?"

"No, I don't understand," Gian began, startling his captors. "I can't begin to understand. Where am I? Who are you? Why am I here?"

"Gian, look at me, and see that we are men of God. We only want to help you. We brought you here to help you. We are only here to help you. Look at me and you will see I am telling the truth."

Gian could not face him. Instead he rebelled again. "You dragged me into a car against my will. You stole me away from my friends who need me now more than ever. You drugged me, you hold me here against my will, and you say that you are men of God? God would not do these things."

"Sometimes we are forced to do things for the greater good that we do not condone. We are sorry for all the pain that we may have caused you, but we had no other choice. If you had stayed behind, you almost certainly would have been killed, as well as your friends and family."

"Why would someone try to kill me?" he asked painfully. "Why?"

"So many will try," was the response. "So many have tried."

Gian glanced over at the face of one of his captors and recognized his gentleness. His wrinkled countenance contained eyes that offered only comfort and concern and hope.

"Where am I?" Gian began pleading with the gentle warrior. "Why am I here?"

"You are still in the city. We brought you here to help you. Look at me and you will see that I am telling you the truth."

"Why won't he answer my questions?" Gian thought. "Could this just be a lie?"

"We have been waiting for you to awaken, Gian," another voice added, "praying, all of us, for you to awaken."

"If this is true, then why am I here with the two of you, in this prison cell. Why am I here? Where am I?"

"You, my dear friend, are at the cardinal's residence in our great city. This prison cell is my room," one of the men replied.

"The cardinal's residence?" Gian quickly replied. "Why am I here?"

"Because you are safe here, Gian."

Minutes must have passed as Gian collected his thoughts. He had so many more questions and so few answers. He began to retrace in his mind all of the events of the preceding night. He could feel the beating, the repeated stabbings, and yet he was unharmed. He could not see a mere mark on his body of any struggle. He remembered climbing the steps of the church. He remembered Father Thom peering at him from behind the window. Once inside the church though, some of his memory became a blur. How could he be all right? He thought. How much time had passed? Could he have been nursed back to health here? No, he remembered leaving the church unharmed and he did remember, oh God, he finally remembered what tragedy had befallen his good friend Marc. He recalled his abduction there in front of the church, in front of Faith. "My God," he thought as he finally remembered.

"Why would men of God kidnap me and keep me here against my will, drug me, and take me away from my friends when they need me most?" he asked them.

"Those answers are forthcoming, Gian, but not from me. I do not have those answers, but another will, and he is waiting for you; he is praying for you."

"A man of God would not take me away right in front of the woman I love, the woman who had just, well, seen a tragedy, and now must be worried sick about me. Is this what men of God do?" he asked sarcastically.

"No, of course not, under normal circumstances, but do you understand that your mere presence places the lives of all you love at risk?" the monk responded pleadingly. "Sometimes love means sacrifice." A quiet ensued as the clergyman's words struck Gian down like a sword.

Another monk entered the room with a tray of food in his arms and placed it down near Gian. "You haven't eaten for quite a while. Please eat, you will need your strength." The three of them quickly left the room and closed the door, but Gian could still hear them just outside. He ate while his mind raced with worry. He knew that he needed to maintain his strength for Faith. Shortly thereafter, the same monk came in to remove the tray, bearing clothes.

"I will escort you to a private bath, so that you may shower and change. I do believe you'll find these clothes fit." They exited the room, and walked past several monks, all of them staring at Gian. Once inside the private bath, Gian showered, shaved, and brushed his teeth. He couldn't believe how good simple things made him feel. The clothes left for him were comfortable and fit fairly well. Once dressed, he felt almost normal. This time alone, able to do normal, everyday things, allowed him to forget his problems, at least for a short while.

Gian exited the bath and was surprised to see that the corridor was empty. He quickly retraced his steps back to the room, entered, and found no one present. He sat down on a chair, and within minutes, the horrors of his assault flooded his mind: the kicks to his body, the stabbing of the knife, the pain. It was all too much. He could feel someone grab his arm and scream his name. He opened his eyes, at first disoriented, to find several monks surrounding him, one shaking his arm. He must have fallen asleep; it had all just been a nightmare.

"I don't know what's real anymore," he began at last. "Everything's so scattered," he continued while rubbing his fingers across his forehead. "I'm so confused."

"This is normal," a gentle monk's voice responded. "You have been through so much."

"Where was everyone earlier?"

"In prayer," was the meek response. "We all prayed for you, Gian, and your friends, and we prayed for answers for us all."

"But I must pray, too, father. I need to," he pleaded.

"You will have plenty of time later to pray," was the response, "but now someone awaits, someone who can help you, someone who knows some of the answers you seek."

"How is Marc? Do any of you know? I need to pray for Marc, please. I have to pray for my friend," he pleaded.

"You must follow me now, Gian," the gentle brother quietly interrupted, "You must."

"I must help my friends, don't you understand? I must have answers."

"I do understand," was the reply, "and that is why you must come with us now. Father has been patiently waiting for you for some time. He has some of the answers you seek; that is why you are here," he repeated.

"Father, father, the cardinal wants to speak to me, then please, take me to him. I must speak with him also!"

Gian quickly arose and followed these two religious men out the door and down long corridors. He could not concentrate on anything but the cardinal. Maybe he held some of the answers. Yes, he could help him. They finally arrived into some inner sanctuary, hidden deep within this religious house. This sanctuary was a rather large room decorated with elaborate chairs and tables, ornate religious paintings adorned the walls. It was an oddly circular room with high ceilings and only one entrance. Gian was asked to sit and wait in one of the chairs, which he did, transfixed by his surroundings. He felt eerily at peace in this room, surrounded by likenesses of Jesus and Mary, Buddha and Mohammed, Moses and Abraham. Once the cardinal entered, the monks quickly departed. Gian could not believe that this man, so plainly dressed, was indeed the cardinal, but he recognized him immediately. He was a rather large man with a robust face; rare wrinkles lined his brow despite his advanced age. He stood there as Gian sat staring at him. As the cardinal approached, Gian quickly stood and smiled. With his hand, the cardinal beckoned for him to sit again, as he proceeded to sit in a chair nearby.

"Father, please help me, for I must go," Gian immediately asked, to the cardinal's surprise. The cardinal seemed to be praying, for he, at first, did not respond.

"Father," Gian began again in earnest, "Please help me, for only you can. Please."

The cardinal's prayers continued, only now audibly.

"Why am I here, father? Why? Why is this happening to me and my friends?" Gian pleaded. "Please answer me, father, please. I need your help."

The cardinal took one of his hands into his as he completed a prayer in a language unfamiliar to Gian, then finally, he spoke.

"I wish I could help you, Gian, in the way that you want me to. I wish I could answer all of your questions. I wish I could, but some questions cannot be answered, my friend. Some questions no one can answer." A pause ensued, a silent minute wherein Gian's thoughts raced, and he became even more disturbed.

"I want to reassure you, my young man, that we are only here to help you in any way that we can. You must believe me, Gian; we are only here to help." With that, he let go of his hand, and awaited a response.

"Dear father, you must know what is happening to me. You must, and why?" Gian pleaded.

The cardinal proceeded to stand and walk toward the portrait of Jesus where he again began to pray. Gian began to sense that this man knew less than he, and his heart began to pound out of fear, out of desperation. If he couldn't help him, then who, he thought, could help him?

Once finished praying, the cardinal stood nearby as he responded once again to Gian's inquiry.

"There is someone here, Gian, who can help you; someone who has been patiently waiting for you."

Gian's thoughts raced to his dear friend Marc, as he envisioned him lying lifeless on an ambulance stretcher. His thoughts were of Marc, and the tragedy that had befallen him that evening because of him. Marc had always placed the interests of others before his own, sometimes to a fault. Once Gian had asked him why, why he cared so much, why he worked so hard, why he fought so hard for those he did not know? Why would he give some of his meager salary to Father Thom to help strangers? His answer shocked Gian. Marc explained that during the war he had to hurt the innocent, sometimes kill the most innocent of all. "That is war," then repeated, "That is war." He explained the promise he made to God there in hell on Earth, that if he survived, he would spend the rest of his days helping to make the world a better place. He said he would help the innocent if he could, all the days of his life. He was one of the few who kept their promise.

Suddenly Gian was startled by the appearance of several monks dressed in elaborate clothes, and behind them all, the Pope. At first he could not believe his eyes as he entered. Could it really be him, he thought? He knew that the Pope was here in the city, but could it really be him, here in person? Dressed in a plain white tunic, he appeared smaller than he had imagined, older, frailer. He seemed to require the assistance of others as he slowly approached, his eyes filled with tears, his hands trembling. It was indeed the Pope, and he was here with Gian, but why?

As Gian gazed upon his countenance, it was as if he could see all of the sorrow he had seen etched within his wrinkles and contained within his eyes. As the Pope slowly approached with the assistance of others, it seemed as though he carried the burdens of a troubled world atop his shoulders. The cardinal quickly departed, and Gian was too overwhelmed to stand, too weak to move. This gentle, fragile symbol of a fragmented and fading empire now leaned forward to kiss Gian's forehead, and then sat down next to him out of breath. There within his reach was one of the world's true leaders. Gian could sense his fragility, his tremendous faith, his inner peace, his hidden power. He struggled to stand and to speak, but could not, and this gentle man beckoned him to remain seated, as they each quietly gazed upon the other.

One could see great humanity within his eyes, a serenity of spirit, and a true peace as this man of God stared at Gian for the first few moments. Gian felt protected for the first time in a long while, safe, as if his father was finally here to hold him after he had awakened from a nightmare. The others in the room had since departed, and once alone Gian could sense a familiarity of spirit. It was as if on some level that they each knew each other very well, as if their souls had recognized one another, as if this moment was predestined. Their eyes seemed to glisten with hope.

Gian thought of this fragile man's papacy, of his greatness. His religious life seemed to flash before Gian's eyes, especially the Pope's recent announcement to the world that he would indeed convene a religious summit unlike any other before, a religious summit where every religious leader could attend. This summit, he had stated, was for all the religious leaders to come together to seek a common ground, to show people of the world that despite their differences, religious men and women could come together in peace to celebrate their similarities. He wanted to unite all religions under one constitution, signed by all attendees, and its first rule was that no one should ever persecute, or take the life of another, based solely upon their religious beliefs.

His papacy strove to end religious persecution, to end all war, all hatred. He preached that one's religion was not a reason to hate and be hated, kill and be killed, but a reason to accept and be accepted, love and be loved. He wanted to show the world that humankind is all one. He believed that all religions held at their core the basic tenets of kindness and charity, love, and hope. The most controversial point, and most believed, the real reason behind the Pope's assassination attempt years earlier, was his belief that one religion could not claim the rights to heaven or the afterlife. For this leaders of his own church soundly criticized him. He was dismissed by many as a fanatic; others dismissed him as a senile dreamer. Some in the Catholic faith felt that he had undermined their religion, and should step down. Most in the church today have accepted this man, for they too dream of a more unified world in such a chaotic time, though a few continue to question his motives. Some openly speculate that this theory was just an elaborate ploy to create a new religion with him as its founder. These same few felt that such a summit would already fragment an already fractured church. It did not help that the press could not be censored, preventing them from reporting the Pope's fragile condition, such that at times people saw him as a confused old man, too old to command world attention and respect. They questioned his competency, his authority, and ultimately his church.

As Gian continued to gaze upon this clergyman as one would look upon a true hero, his Holiness turned away for a moment, as if the world in that moment seemed too heavy a burden for this great man to carry alone.

At last he spoke and his words confused Gian. "I wish to be alone with my son." As he uttered these words in a frail voice, Gian searched the room for another. To his surprise just inside the doors stood another, watching them from afar. He was dressed in a dark brown tunic with simple sandals on his feet. His black hair streaked with gray revealed a man who, past middle age, seemed to hold much authority, as he remained there at the door despite the request to leave. In apparent defiance, he just stood still.

"I am speaking to you, Father Saddujj," the Pope continued. Stunned, this man did not move nor speak.

"Did you not hear me, kind father?" the Pope asked quietly.

"But Father, we do not know this man. I feel I should stay," the monk finally, adamantly, declared.

"You are wrong," the Pope replied calmly, "I do know this boy, father. He is a child of God, and he will not harm me. Now please, leave us, and I thank you for your concern."

The father quietly opened the door, and stood there again, as if reluctant to leave.

"Please close the door behind you, dear friend; I will call you when our meeting is over."

Father Saddujj reluctantly departed, but not before he gazed upon Gian with his eyes, as if warning him to behave or else.

At last they were alone. Gian had almost forgotten how he came to be there. He was still haunted by so many questions, so many concerns, and here he sat with the leader of over one billion followers. At last, he felt that he could help him to understand.

"The Catholic church is bleeding Father," Gian spoke the words he had been dying to say.

"The world is bleeding, my son," came the sad response. A few moments of silence ensued.

"Gian," the fragile Pope began in a soft but familiar voice, his English slightly accented, "I have been waiting for you." He paused for a few moments and closed his eyes to pray, as he grasped the rosary in his pocket, and mumbled under his breath.

Gian was totally bewildered. This great man whom he just met could not possibly be speaking of him, he thought. Perhaps he was indeed too old. The Pope's eyes opened, and his gaze was suddenly that of a simple man who had finally found his way after wandering lost in the woods.

"Believe me, son, I have been waiting for you," he repeated as his moist eyes clouded his view and his voice trembled with humility and age. "I have been praying for you to come. I was praying to live long enough to finally see you, here at last, before me. You see, dear Gian, I have seen you in my dreams; heard you speak as I slept. I've marveled at your words, and was stunned by your power. Long before I met you, I envisioned your future."

A silent pause ensued, a perplexing silence. This elderly man of God began a fumbling search for something deep within his pockets. Once found, he removed a folded paper, opened it, and gazed alternately at the paper and then at Gian, as tears began to flow down his cheeks, silent tears, contagious tears, for now even Gian was moved. The paper was gently handed over to Gian, and once in his possession, his eyes could not believe what it contained. It was a colored sketch of him, as if it were drawn today, but it was not, according to the date at the bottom, below the artist's name. It was drawn years earlier. "How could this fragile piece of paper, worn by age, contain a current sketch of me?" Gian asked himself.

"You see, my son Gian, I had an artist draw that over ten years ago from a recurrent vision of you I had in my dreams, and since then I have traveled far in my search for you. I have searched the crowds for your face. I have asked religious leaders from around the world if they had seen you, and…" This fragile man paused to sigh deeply before continuing. "A few told me that they had seen you, too."

Gian could not speak, overwhelmed by it all.

"We have been searching for you, Gian, praying to find you safe. Recently, we had almost given up hope. Ten years is a long time, a very long time."

Gian realized that he couldn't respond. He could barely comprehend what the man was saying. How can a portrait drawn ten years ago depict him as he looked today? How is this possible? How is any of this possible?

Finally, Gian was able to stand up, and he felt compelled to approach this great man, and embrace him as he wept quietly in his arms. Gian felt so much with this religious leader in his arms, so much power, so much pain, so much love, so much grief, so much prayer, so much peace. Gian held onto him for some time before he let go. He sat down beside him, overwhelmed.

"One of my brethren contacted me from the United States," continued the Pope, "the cardinal himself recognized you from my sketch and called me. I immediately came, hoping that, indeed, I had finally found you." He paused to gather enough strength to continue. "I knew when I saw your face on TV and heard your voice, that it was indeed you, and I knew then that you were in danger and that I must find you and bring you here to keep you safe." He paused again before continuing in a softer voice. "Now all can see what I have known for years; and a few others, they can see, too." He mumbled almost incoherently.

Gian could not contain himself any more, and finally he spoke in a soft and quiet voice, as gentle as a child's, "What can they see, Father?" he began, his breath audible. "Please help me to see."

"Oh my dear Gian, my dear son, you have it all wrong. It is you that will help me to see. It is you that will help the world to see."

Confused more than before, Gian sat there, beholden to a man whose glory preceded him, whose love was universal, whose words reached millions, and yet, who praised him, Gian, a lowly janitor.

"Oh, Father, please, I am just a simple man with many questions."

"You see, Gian, it has always been a simple man or woman that God has chosen. From the beginning of the written word, we have read about them in almost every religious text throughout the world," he paused and gazed toward Gian as he continued. "You, my son, are far from a simple man, Gian, far from a simple man."

Confused, Gian waited for more, hungered for more answers.

"Recently, my dear son, people hear the simple words of God but they do not listen. They read His words but do not comprehend them, or worse, they distort them. They rewrite His teachings, and a few of these men and women now lead many astray. A few hold the world's attention, a few have damaged the very basis of so many of the world's good religions. They exploit the basic tenets of faith for their own selfish, and evil purposes. A few cause so much pain and division, so much harm. Every religious man or woman should strive every day to better themselves, and the world around them, and so many fail. Even within our own church there is chaos. Listen to me, Gian, we are all human, we make mistakes, but mistakes that harm others, especially the innocent, require immediate attention, immediate investigation, and immediate remediation if true harm has occurred. People need to believe in us, Gian, in everyone who pretends to be a man of God." A quiet pause ensued as the fragile man of faith grabbed ahold of his rosary and the crucifix it contained with his trembling hands.

"I am but an elderly man whose words are easily forgotten, but you..." He struggled to stand, and proceeded to walk toward Gian. Once he stood there before him, the Pope placed one of his outstretched, fragile hands over Gian's beating heart as he continued to speak to him.

"You, dear Gian, hold here, deep within your soul, the power to unite us all. You are a living testament to His very existence. You are the beginning, the rainbow we have been searching for in this storm, the dawn of a new day in our modern world. You are a fragile bird of peace, a humble messenger of faith, a single, strong ray of hope. Don't you see that we are all just wounded birds away from our nest hoping for someone to bring us home, someone to reach out and tell us that everything will be okay? You are that someone, my son." He paused to remove his hand from Gian's chest, and swayed slightly, as if too weak to stand any more. Gian immediately stood up and helped the great man to sit, before he sat down next to him.

"You see, Gian, as I was about to say, you are our guide, our strength, our bridge to salvation."

Gian had so many questions and finally he began to speak, and at last the words came forth, at last. "Why me, Father?" he began quietly.

"Only our Father knows the answer, Gian. Trust in Him."

"How can I help anyone when I could not even help my friend, Marc?"

"Gian, your journey is just beginning, your path uncharted, your future is tomorrow. Anything is possible, even that."

"How will I know what to do, what to say? How can I be strong enough?"

"He will guide you as He has guided you so far. Listen to your heart, my son."

"Whom can I trust?"

"Oh, Gian, there are so many who this very day would pay anything, risk everything to harm you. They are everywhere, as evil is, and you cannot avoid them, for they are everyone and no one just the same, strangers and friends alike."

"Then how can I continue? How?"

"My son, evil has already found you, and once already our Mother healed its wound upon you. But understand, Gian, and be careful, very careful, for life is so very fragile, so very, very fragile."

This learned man seemed to speak in riddles, and Gian was still so very concerned, so very concerned. "I'm worried, Father. I can't help but worry."

"Gian, I had a couple of my security guards follow you last night. It was my attempt to keep you safe, but alas, someone here, someone of position here, called them back last night just before the attack. Only a chosen few knew the code used to summon them, so you see, even amongst my closest friends lives a traitor. That is why I sent some of them back on that secret mission to apprehend you, and I am so very sorry, Gian, so very sorry for the pain that it has caused your friends, but I felt like I had no choice. There seemed to be no other way."

"Do my friends know where I am? Does Faith know I am safe?"

"No, it would be too dangerous to tell them. Eventually, perhaps in a few years though, you will be able to."

"What if I choose my family, my friends, my life? What if I just run away and wait for this to be over?"

"Gian, you must understand and you must accept. A few have seen you in their dreams, like I have, and they travel now to see you. The world knows your name. The world has seen your face."

At first overwhelmed by these words, Gian listened for more advice. Like a flower bends toward the Sun for life, like a butterfly searches for an endless field of flowers, Gian was drawn to this religious man. He offered him safety, guidance and advice. He sat in awe of every religious person who risked their lives every day throughout the world, without the benefit of miracles, to spread the way of God through their kind words, their generous deeds, and charitable acts. They, who sacrifice their lives and the comfort of their homes, their friends and family for an even greater goal. These brave souls risk their lives every day in silence. Some even die in silence to spread the very words Gian now feared. They have traveled the very path Gian now needed to travel alone, with nothing except for the guidance of their prayer and their deep faith and trust in God. Gian's thoughts were interrupted by an attempt made to speak from his weakened host nearby.

"You know, Gian, that you are God's fragile messenger, his wounded bird, sent to accomplish an enormous task. You have been chosen like those before you to convey his powerful messages of hope, of love, and of eternal life. That is why you must, you *must* come..." He paused, unable or unwilling to complete his thought.

"What is it, Father? Where do I need to go? What do I need to do? Please tell me."

"Soon, Gian, soon," the great man replied, "for now you must realize that evil also knows your name. It has seen your face and heard your voice, and felt your power, your very existence. You are a threat to so many, my son, so many who conspire to destroy you, and you must be strong and have faith and pray. Pray for guidance and peace. Gian, my son, they have found you, and they will not stop until they destroy you." He paused to take in deep breaths before continuing. "We will all help you in your quest, just as the Virgin Mary healed you. We will all support you and pray for you and protect you."

"The Virgin Mary, dear Father?" Gian responded to another riddle.

"When you were brought here, Gian, you were unharmed, no cuts, no bruises, no pain, no blood. Do you not remember what happened that night, my son?"

Gian was stunned by the question, gazed downward, and re-inspected his body. His mind wandered back to that awful night, and he could indeed remember the beatings, the stabbing, the blood, and the pain. He did remember entering the church and the chapel within it. He remembered the beautiful statue of Mary on the altar, welcoming him in, and an incredible feeling of peace and love, but that is all.

"You are right, Father, for I do not remember what happened in the chapel. Please, Father, help me to remember."

"Gian," he began quietly but forcefully, "you see only what you want to see. You remember only what you want to remember. Sometimes that which is too difficult to remember, we choose not to. The truth sometimes is too difficult to face, so we hide from it, as you are hiding now. The world has seen the truth, Gian, the truth that you have forgotten."

"What, dear Father, what are you saying? What truth? Help me to remember," he pleaded.

"A lone reporter arrived just as you were walking toward the church. He captured you, Gian, struggling up the church stairs in the dim lights of a city, all could clearly see your torn clothes, all could plainly see your blood, and hear your pain as the church doors opened, seemingly by themselves, and you entered. Minutes later, this same reporter captured your exit, and then everyone became a witness to a miracle, my son, for you exited the church unharmed, no blood, no pain, no explanation. Moments later, this news reporter ran inside the chapel before the police arrived to stop him, and he videotaped for the world to see what is now considered a miracle. He videotaped the statue of Mary upon the altar of St. Gerard's in great detail. Quietly, he taped and all we can hear are the sobs of the videographer, for there, upon that tape, is seen, the bruises on Our Lady's face, the tears upon her cheeks, the blood that stained her robes where it was apparently torn by a knife in the very place where you were stabbed, Gian. And now the world has seen this video, my son, and the whole world is searching for you. The whole world is searching their souls to believe in what you cannot remember."

At first Gian seemed unable to remember what the Pope was saying, but then he remembered. He remembered it all. "I remember, Father," Gian almost shouted, "I remember, I do remember that which I can remember, before I fell asleep in Our Mother's grace."

"Do you understand the power that is your gift to the world, Gian?" The Pope paused as he struggled, it seemed, to continue, struggled for the right words. "Miracles happen all around you. This is your gift, Gian. It is just one of many I have seen in my dreams. You must believe in these gifts, my son, and in the power of those things we cannot understand. This is your gift to us. Do not try to understand it, but recognize it for what it is, accept it, and others that will follow, and know, dear son, that God is with you."

"It doesn't seem real, Father. This can't be real."

With that, the church's elder statesman arose and opened a cabinet nearby to reveal a small television set within. He took its remote and, turning it on, Gian recognized the picture it contained. It was a picture of him. Within minutes, a videotape of that evening played and he could plainly see the statue of Mary as the Pope had described. Once ended, a reporter stood there across the street from the church, and Gian was amazed by all of the people and all of the activity there. The Pope then changed channels, and so many of them contained the same events, so many of them spoke of him. The Pope turned the set off, and sat down again, exhausted.

"Allow yourself to remember, Gian, my son. Allow yourself to remember it all; you cannot hide any longer from the truth, and only you know the truth."

Gian closed his eyes and recalled in vivid detail all of the events of his life leading up to this very day, this very time. He could feel for the first time the healing touch of a mother he had not felt for so long. Overwhelmed, he could finally speak again to his new friend, but in such a feeble voice. "I remember," Gian uttered with tears in his eyes, "I remember."

"You need to remember."

"Who am I, Father?" Gian tearfully asked, "What am I?"

"You are human, Gian," the Pope almost whispered to this confused young man by his side, "A fragile soul whom God has chosen to spread His word."

With those words, this fragile pope recognized the awesome burdens he had just placed upon Gian's all too human shoulders. He helped him to lie down upon a sofa nearby, and prayed as he fell asleep. Gian could feel him close by for a time, watching over him. He could feel his spirit strengthening his as Gian continued onward in his dreams until he could no longer sense his presence there beside him. Asleep, he could remember Faith. He could see her brilliant eyes, her wondrous smile, her beautiful hair, and he began to smile, too. He could feel her soft and loving arms around him, and then just as quickly as she had come, she disappeared, and he was alone again, so very alone. Gian dreamed of his mother next, and to him it felt so good to see her again, to feel her again as she took him into her arms, and embraced him as only a mother could. She held him, as only a mother can hold her only child, and he felt safe. He felt safe here in his dreams. He finally felt safe, and he did not want to leave.

When Gian did awaken, he was disoriented at first. He was in unfamiliar surroundings, his clothes wrinkled, and he could feel the growth of a small beard upon his face. He felt thirst and hunger. He could not think clearly at first. He was in yet another small bedroom in the cardinal's residence, and he was alone. A tray of food with water lay nearby on a table, and he quickly ate and drank to relieve his body's need. Once finished, he found clothes nearby, fresh and clean clothes, so he quickly made his way into the adjacent bathroom to shower and to change. When he reentered the bedroom, he felt empowered to go forward. His confusion had ended and his strength seemed to return. He finally seemed able to contemplate his future. He felt strong enough to face the world ahead of him, and he knew what he must do.

Gian walked over to a window and proceeded to open the blinds. It was so dark outside; this could not be the same night, he thought. How many nights had he slept through? How many days? It was eerily quiet, and he could see but a few feet in the distance. He was able to see a small but glorious star in the black sky above him, a ray of hope in a dark atmosphere of emptiness.

He suddenly became aware of the presence of another person behind him. He turned and in the dim light of the small lamps within the room, he recognized the figure as that of Father Saddujj. He was indeed the Pope's first assistant. His face appeared more aged now, more fraught with worry than before, his eyes were dull, and his mouth bore a permanent frown, a light perspiration upon his eyebrows was evident upon his fractured face. His breathing was audibly rapid and shallow.

"I am Father Saddujj," the priest proclaimed nervously as he proceeded to sit in a chair nearby and beckoned Gian to sit, too. "I am so sorry to have startled you, but we have been waiting for you to awaken for so long, and I can see," he declared as he gazed about the room, "that you have eaten and changed. Good."

"Where is His Holiness? And where am I?" Gian asked.

"The Pope asked us to move you here after you had fallen asleep," he responded blankly. "This is one of the larger rooms usually reserved for honored guests of the cardinal."

"And where is he now?"

"He is in the chapel, deep in prayer. He often prays for hours at a time. He is at home in prayer. He prays for guidance and strength. He prays for peace and understanding."

"How, how long have I been asleep, father?"

"Over twenty-four hours. I wanted to awaken you, but his holiness forbade it. After your meeting, he prayed for a short time, then he himself slept for a while, but not before he ordered me to watch over you and keep you safe, for he is well aware, as we are, that one amongst us has already betrayed him, one who threatened your security and, ultimately, your life."

"I needed to sleep. I don't understand it, but lately I cannot help myself. I don't know why."

"I could not disturb you, even though I've been waiting to speak to you, praying to speak to you, actually."

Sensing concern, Gian immediately responded, "What is it, father? Is something wrong? Did something happen while I slept?"

"No, no" was the cold and quick response. "You are safe."

"I need to see the Pope again, I need to. Please show me the way to the chapel, please!" Gian immediately arose from his chair, anxious to leave, but a very disturbed Father Saddujj quietly blocked his path.

"I have spoken to Faith," he declared, as Gian froze in his tracks, unable to speak clearly, for Saddujj had mentioned a name that clearly overpowered him. Gian's thoughts were filled with worry and concern, and yet a part of him felt overwhelming joy and relief and love. Faith, he couldn't wait to see her again. He could not wait to hold her again, so close that it would be impossible to let go. Faith, he had never missed her as much as he did now, and he needed to hear more. Faith: For a moment, he felt like he couldn't breathe; his heart stopped, just for a moment.

"You've spoken to Faith?" Gian asked in disbelief.

"Yes," was Saddujj's simple response.

"Today?"

"Yes."

"Is she all right?"

"Yes."

"Does she know that I'm all right? Did you tell her that I am all right, so she doesn't worry about me anymore?"

"Yes."

"Is she here? Father, is she here? Did you bring her here to see me, to keep her safe?"

"No, Gian, she is not here," he replied quickly, "and she doesn't know where you are, just that you are safe and among friends."

"Why would she believe you? She doesn't know you."

"At first she did not, but I was finally able to convince her, and she cried for you, Gian, tears of joy."

"Oh, my poor Faith," Gian responded wearily. "I must have put her through hell with worry, and my friends too. I am so glad that you called her, father, so glad you called."

Gian stood there for a moment, awash in thoughts of her. He had allowed her into his life and now could only they go forward together. Poor Faith, he thought, she was now a part of him, forever, a part of him, and the chaos that his life had become.

"What did you tell her?"

"Very little."

"Does she know who I'm with? Does she know who you are?"

"No."

"Why not, father?"

"I fear for your safety. It was a breach already for me to have called her. No one knows of this call, no one."

"Then why would you call her and tell her nothing?"

"I called to tell her that you are safe. I know how much you care for her, and she for you. She believed me, Gian."

"What did she say?"

"She told me to tell you that she loves you, and that she always will, no matter what."

Gian could not reply.

"She said that she spends most of her day in the ICU at St. Vincent's Hospital, watching over your friend, Marc."

"Is he going to be all right?"

"She did not say, Gian."

"Is he still in a coma?"

"I believe so."

"Did she sound okay, or was she worried? Did she sound all right?"

"Yes, she was glad that I called, and of course, I swore her to secrecy. I told her that your life would be threatened if anyone found out about my call, anyone at all."

"She must be so worried about me."

"She is better now, Gian, now that I have spoken to her."

"I have to go and see her, father," he began. "I cannot stay here any longer. I need to see her and explain to her all that has happened. I need her. I cannot stay here any longer. I can't."

"Calm down, Gian, I do understand, believe me, I do. That is why I called her despite orders not to do so. That is why I am telling you this even though I know that if you were to tell another, I would be severely reprimanded."

"Then you must let me speak to her. You must allow me to visit her or for her to come and see me."

"It is not safe for her to come here; she is being watched closely, very closely. It is not safe for you here any longer Gian. That is why we are going to the Vatican as soon as possible."

"The Vatican, the Vatican, *the Vatican in Rome*," Gian repeated nervously and in utter disbelief. "The Pope did not mention relocating to the Vatican to me, father. Oh no, I cannot go now, not without Faith. I cannot leave, not before seeing Marc for myself. He saved my life and I cannot run away from him when he needs me most. He is fighting for his life now." Gian paused as his eyes filled with tears at the mere thought of leaving the country, of leaving his friends, of leaving Faith, perhaps forever.

"I do not matter, father," Gian continued," My life won't matter if I spent the rest of it alone, if I abandoned my friends in their time of need, if I ran away."

"Believe me, Gian, you will be much safer there. Once there, you will not be alone. Things will be different."

"I need to see Marc…I have to see him."

"It would be too risky for you to go to the hospital. Father would never approve."

"Oh, no, no!" Gian exclaimed as he rushed to the door. "I must see the Pope at once. He will understand."

Father Saddujj quickly blocked his egress with his body. Startled, Gian stopped just before him in the room.

"I can take you to her," he began in a whisper, "But you must calm down. You must lower your voice and listen."

"What? What did you say?" Gian responded in disbelief. Father Saddujj's words echoed loudly in his mind. His thoughts began to race: Did Father Saddujj say that he would take me to Faith? Can I truly trust him to keep his word? Would Father Saddujj really risk everything to take me to her? I know that he is my only hope, my only chance of seeing her again; the only chance for me to see Marc. No matter the risk to me, I know I have to take it. Now, would I? Could I? A part of me does not trust this priest, but so far, he has only tried to help. The Pope believed in him, so now I should, too. He is my only chance to fulfill a dream of mine: to see Faith again and to see Marc.

"I can take you to her," the father repeated. Sensing disbelief on Gian's face, he added, "But you must calm down. You must lower your voice, and you must listen."

"I understand," Gian quietly but quickly replied, eagerly awaiting his plans to leave. He could feel the anxiety sweep over his body; his hands were aflutter with random movements. A part of Gian could not believe him, but he had to believe. He was his only hope.

"I swore to my good father to protect you at any cost. But you are clearly pained by your separation from your friends and loved ones. We have only a short time, a very short period of time to go to the hospital and return."

"Let's go, then," Gian interrupted, "please, let's go."

"I could go alone," the rather nervous father paused awaiting Gian's response.

"No, I have to go with you. Faith would never abandon her friends. Not now, not without me. And I have to see Marc. I must."

"This may be too risky," he nervously added.

"I will take full responsibility for this, father, I will. If we fail, it will be my failure, so please, let's go now."

"I need to make a few phone calls, so wait here until I return." He left the room momentarily and Gian could hear his muffled voice speaking on the phone outside. His thoughts were only of Faith and Marc and the others. He could not believe that he would be reunited with them in a short time. He prayed that God would keep them safe until he arrived and he prayed that he was making the right decision for all of them.

The father quickly returned to the room, panting and began to speak so rapidly that Gian had difficulty understanding him.

"Lie down upon the bed quickly, for they are coming. Don't you understand? They're coming."

Gian stood there motionless, bewildered by the actions of an almost hysterical man. He now began to push Gian forward toward the bed.

"Don't you understand? You must get into the bed."

Gian lay down upon the bed, as the priest nervously arranged the blankets. In a lower tone, he explained. "The brothers are coming. I told them that I could not arouse you, and that I was concerned something was wrong. Once they arrive, I will do all the talking, Do you understand me, Gian?"

Gian did not respond.

"Do you understand, Gian?"

"Yes," he finally responded.

Within moments, the door to the room opened and the brothers rushed in. Gian could hear them approach the bed.

"I don't know what's wrong," Father Saddujj began, "But I cannot wake him up. Perhaps he is sick, very sick. He has been under so much stress for such a long time, please, help me."

Gian could feel the hand of one of the monks pick up his arm to check his pulse.

"Oh my God, his pulse is rapid" Gian heard a strange voice exclaim.

"Quickly," Father Saddujj explained. "Please go and get help. Do not dial 9-1-1, for you will place his life in jeopardy; find brother Gardner, and bring me the emergency kit, hurry, now please, you must go now. I'll take care of Gian; please go." The men apparently obeyed their superior for Gian could hear them quickly exit.

After a few moments, Father Saddujj barked for Gian to get up and ordered him to follow him out of the room.

Together they quickly exited the room and raced down several corridors, Gian nervously in pursuit before exiting out a back door into a dark alley. Father Saddujj could barely see, so he momentarily stood still to adjust to the sudden lack of light. They could hear the noises of a dark urban night around them, the distant screams of sirens, the loud radios, the all too real cries of small children.

"Come on, we must go now," was the order Gian could hear clearly in the distance. He struggled to follow, and panting, he arrived alongside a dark SUV across the way. Father Saddujj nervously opened the front door with a set of keys from his pocket and then quickly opened a rear door and ordered Gian to get in and lay down on the floor. Gian obliged and within seconds they took off at great speed for what appeared to be miles. Gian could only think about the others. He knew he was doing the right thing. He knew that he had to do this.

Gian could hear Father Saddujj dialing on his cell phone. "Yes...where? We'll be there in about five minutes...Yes, I understand," were the only words spoken before the monk nervously closed the phone. Gian wondered momentarily about who he had enlisted to help him, but quickly thought about what was soon to be. In just a few minutes, he would be reunited with his friends. He could think of nothing else.

The car came to a screeching halt, and Gian was thrown forward onto the backs of the front seats. Within seconds the back door was open and he could see a visibly nervous priest before him, his face red with perspiration dripping upon his shirt.

"Gian," he barked, "We have to change cars here. They'll find us in this car, so come on, we must go, and we must go now." Gian could not help but notice how nervous his accomplice was, as his hands fidgeted about his sides, and his fingers opened and closed in rapid succession.

Gian quickly exited and surveyed the surroundings. He was surprised by what he saw. He did not recognize the area at all. This was a part of town that appeared nearly abandoned. He could see a few old buildings about, though none with recognizable names. They were on a poorly lit street, and he could not place it. Surely this wasn't close to the hospital? he thought to himself.

It was quiet, too quiet. Father Saddujj, now agitated, pushed him along toward another parked vehicle nearby on the street. It was an old van of some sort with out-of-state license plates. He scrambled to the ground now on his hands and knees as he reached for something behind the left front tire, and arose with car keys dangling in his shaking hands. He nervously opened the rear door and barked for Gian to get in and get down. He obliged and the door was slammed closed behind him. Gian could hear the father fumbling with the keys outside and then he could hear them drop to the ground as his driver mumbled.

Why is he so nervous when we are so close? Gian thought. Perhaps he was having second thoughts. I'm sure his superiors, especially the Pope, would have many questions. Maybe the Pope himself was helping him. I doubt it though. The pope seemed adamant about keeping me safe there at the cardinal's residence.

In the darkness, suddenly Gian could hear whispers, someone calling out his name. At first he thought he was dreaming, but the whispers became louder, and it was the voice of a woman. He could hear it. It sounded like Faith. Gian opened the rear door to exit, at the same moment he could hear Father Saddujj open the driver's side door to enter. Once outside, the voice became louder, and seemed to be coming from a small factory across the street. Gian ran toward it and once in front of it, he turned back around to see if Father Saddujj was following him. He could see him, fumbling with the set of keys in the front seat of the van, apparently unaware of his exit. What if he left without me? Gian thought. He yelled to him as he began to start up the van, for it had stalled a couple of times, and he did not hear him. Gian yelled out again, and this time Father Saddujj quickly turned to face him as the engine finally started.

Next came the sound of a loud, very powerful explosion, and Gian was knocked to the ground in its wake. He must have been knocked unconscious for a few moments, for when he awoke, he did not remember where he was. He sat up and then stood in the tremendous glow of an enormous fireball ahead of him where Father Saddujj and the vehicle had once been. Gian fell to his knees and made the sign of the cross. He was both horrified and alone. He could not comprehend what just happened. He could no longer recognize anything familiar. Everything was a blur. He was physically and emotionally traumatized.

How could this have happened? Gian asked himself, Father Saddujj was dead and I was supposed to be, too! Whoever helped Father Saddujj must have betrayed him, or maybe this priest planned the entire escape, and like many before him, would sacrifice his own life to kill me, Gian surmised. He thought back to the priest's face as the car had started, and could sense the panic, the anger. In that moment Gian knew that he might never know the answers.

Gian stood up and, except for a headache, he seemed all right. The whispers ceased and he could only see a few homeless people approaching in the distance. Half-hidden faces scattered about, too afraid to help out of fear for their own safety. It was all too real. The night was not part of a bad dream. The past few days had been a new reality for Gian. He could finally see why the Pope was so afraid for him. The Pope couldn't trust anyone, and neither could Gian now. Here he was, alone and surrounded by strangers. He had thought he was so close to seeing Faith and his friends and now he was so far. A part of him worried if he would ever see them again. A part of him knew that all of them would be safer without him in their lives. But he could never imagine his life without them in it. When he had first arrived here in this city, he was so totally alone. Now he had a family, and he needed them. He needed them desperately.

As the intensity of the blaze faded a bit, Gian could see the light of a beautiful star that adorned a small white building a block or so away from him. Somehow he knew that that was where he needed to go, and he quickly walked toward the building. He could hear the mutterings of a few street people as he passed.

"It's you, isn't it?" He could hear a voice call out as he passed an alley.

"Who's there?" Gian asked.

"It is really you," he could hear a female's voice respond in the distance.

"I called out to you, you know, when I first saw you, you know," was another reply heard in the dark.

"Who are you?" he asked. "Let me see you."

"No, it is enough for me to see you and hear your voice. I must go now. I must go home."

"Please wait, I want to thank you," Gian pleaded into the darkness.

"I know what I have to do. I have to go home now. I asked God to send me a sign, and He did. He sent you and I saved your life, and now you've saved mine."

Gian could barely see a thin figure of a woman in the distance, the glimmer of her young face in the alley.

"Please don't go," he pleaded.

"Thank you, Gian," was the response, as the figure disappeared into the darkness.

"No, thank you, and may God bless you," Gian responded, hoping she heard him, as he began again his search for a star. Something told him to follow it, and he obeyed. As he approached, the star's bright light seemed to fade, and he could see that the star and the white building it sat upon were worn and faded, neglected and poorly kept. This building was completely surrounded by a fence, and the gate of this fence loomed several feet high. As he neared it, he realized that it seemed impossible to enter, and around him, was nowhere and no one.

He was about to use an old call box to gain access when he noticed that the gate was indeed open, so he entered the property uninvited. Gian was so desperate for any help at this point that he didn't care. Besides, he felt a sense of peace once inside the gate that he had not felt in days. He felt safe.

He approached the building amidst the shrubs and trees surrounding it, and noted writings above the front door. It was an old synagogue, he realized, as he proceeded to knock. Within seconds an outside light turned on, and he could hear a series of inside locks open. He waited for someone to open the door. Nothing. He turned the knob and proceeded to go in, expecting someone to greet him. There was no one there. Shocked, he surveyed the hallway and, again, no one. He walked through the empty corridors until he came upon the house of worship. He found a pew and sat down, relieved to be safe and able to rest for a while and collect his thoughts. This house seemed a safe haven for this stranger in a storm.

"So much has happened to me and I need a plan," Gian thought aloud. "I had to find a phone, but who would I call? The Pope? Monsignor Lilli? Reverend Martin? Whomever I called I would certainly place in jeopardy. But why?"

Suddenly his body ached for sleep. Gian then lay down upon the pew, and in the quiet and peace of his newfound haven, he fell asleep.

"Who are you? What do you want?" a man's voice bellowed, and Gian, startled awake, sat up to see who was confronting him. "Who are you? I asked you," he continued, as Gian gazed upon his face in the darkness. Gian could sense the anger and the fear of the loud figure before him, so he began to speak quickly and quietly.

"I must have fallen asleep, sir. I'm sorry that I startled you. Are you the kind man who opened the door and let me in?" he asked while rubbing the sleep from his eyes.

"Stay where you are. Do you hear me? Do not move" was the stern reply as the lights of the house of worship were lit one by one. Gian could see a rather small man in front of him, middle aged, one would guess, with a large stick in one hand, a cell phone in the other.

"Don't move," he demanded. "Don't move. I did not open the front gate or the door. No one did. You must have broken in, and I'm calling the police."

"No, please," Gian responded quickly. "I mean you no harm, you must believe me. The gate outside was open and someone unlocked the door for me. I am not a burglar. I just needed a place to rest."

"Just sit there and don't say another word. Don't move, do you hear me? That outside gate is never open. It is electronically controlled, and this inside door has several locks and all of them were bolted. I know because I closed that door myself."

"Please, sir, you must believe me," Gian interrupted. "Someone did let me in. Please believe me. Is anyone else here? Maybe you could ask them."

"I said don't move, and don't say another word until the police arrive, do you hear me?" came the angry response. Gian did not know what to do, and the police would surely arrest him, and all of those questions about father Saddujj and—

"Do not use that phone," a commanding voice was heard. Recognizing the voice, the man quickly put down the cell phone and replied.

"Rabbi, please do not come any closer, please. This man is dangerous. He is here to rob us, or worse. Please stay back."

"Put down that bat and the phone. Can't you see that this man is harmless? Can't you see how frightened and alone he is? Can't you see that he is not a criminal?" A quiet man entered the inner sanctuary and proceeded toward the other man in front. As he walked, it was obvious that his gait was unsteady, his body trembled, his bald head revealed only a wisp of white hair, his face was that of an elderly and kind man.

"Rabbi, please allow me to call the police," the first man pleaded.

"Kind rabbi," Gian innocently interrupted, "perhaps you can tell your friend that you are the one who opened the gate for me, and unlocked the door."

"Sir, I did not, for we two were together in the back, and we are the only ones here" was the reply.

"That's not possible. Someone let me in. You must believe me, I did not break in."

"See, rabbi, he continues to lie. I must call the police. They will certainly find out the truth," the distraught man pleaded.

"Believe me, rabbi, I am telling you the truth."

"I do believe you, young man; I do not know why, but I do."

"Believe him? Why? No one else is here, no one. And the doors were surely locked," the agitated man continued. "I will show you, rabbi, that he is lying. I have proof." The short man approached Gian wielding the stick. "Come with me into the back room, the video surveillance cameras outside and in, will surely prove that you are lying, and that you are a criminal of the worst kind. Now place your hands above your head and follow me, do you hear? Move!"

Gian got out of the pew in front of the man, knowing that he would learn the truth that someone allowed him to enter and that he was not a criminal. He followed closely behind as they entered another small room. Contained within the room were a few television screens, one revealing the outside gate, another the front door from the outside, and another the corridor on the inside.

"I will rewind the tapes and we will see who is lying." The agitated man began to work, as the rabbi entered the room.

As the elderly man approached, his brown eyes twinkled and a faint smile appeared upon his wrinkled face.

"Why do you believe me, sir?" Gian asked.

"There is a calmness about you that I sense, a tranquil peace. I felt it as I entered the room earlier. I feel it now."

"I'm ready!" came the reply from the clearly agitated man still holding onto that stick.

The first camera was at the outside gate, which was clearly open as Gian approached in the dark night and entered the property. A silence ensued as the man quickly began the tape on the second set. Gian approached the outside door and knocked, within seconds, the light came on and he entered peacefully.

"How can this be!" the nervous man fumbled to play the third video.

The third screen played, and the corridor could be clearly seen within the darkness. One could hear the bolts and the door open, but no one was there in the corridor until Gian entered it—No one at all.

The agitated man immediately dropped his stick, and fell to his knees in prayer in Yiddish.

The rabbi approached the accused and grabbed hold of each of his arms and placed them at his side.

"I'm sorry that we doubted you."

"But who opened the door?" Gian softly asked.

"You see, my dear friends, you have forgotten that we three are indeed not alone here. This is God's house, you see. We are merely its keeper, and it is He who opened the gate, turned on the light, and opened the door to let you in. God is the one who allowed your entrance into His house, and welcomed you, and gave you rest. My young son, you see, it is our Father who welcomed you home!"

"God forgive me," the other man pleaded. "God forgive me, and you, young man, please forgive me, too, please?"

The rabbi embraced Gian and whispered in his ear, "Your journey is just beginning, and may it be a safe one." Gian felt weak, nearly faint. The other man, sensing his weakness quickly approached, and grabbed hold of his arm and shoulder. He could not keep his eyes open any longer, and he quickly fell asleep.

Gian awoke just a short time later and quickly arose out of the pew, to find that he was alone. He called out in a feeble voice but there was no response. It was eerily quiet. On a small table lay a glass of juice and a sandwich, which Gian proceeded to devour. It was as if he had not eaten in days. Gian then found a bathroom and was able to wash up. Out of nowhere he recalled the explosion and in that moment, tears of perspiration beaded upon his brow. He quickly exited the bathroom and began to search frantically inside this house of worship for the rabbi and his friend. He could not find them anywhere.

"Where are they? Could something have happened to them, too?" Gian thought aloud, confused, concerned, and alone, so totally alone. He frantically ran outside into the front yard and called out for them. Again there was no response. He ran to the front gate and peered out into the street. He so needed to find someone, anyone, for he was so tired of being alone, and he was frightened. He didn't know why, but he was. It was rather dark and damp, but eerily peaceful and serene. Broken glass lined the street curb, and the smell of smoke and gasoline lingered in the air. A few stray dogs passed as they pursued each other up the street. Gian could hear something else amidst the dogs barking, something more distant, more alarming. He opened the front gate, and walked out onto the sidewalk, and peered down the street toward the noise. It was the sounds of someone sobbing, the anguished cries of a stranger. "Could it be the rabbi? Did something happen to them?" Gian said.

Gian began to walk up the street and the sobs intensified. They were definitely a man's cries for help. He picked up his pace and could clearly see a young man ahead of him in the pale light emanating from a street lamp overhead, sobbing, below him was the motionless body of another. As Gian approached, he could see that the figure on the ground was that of a young girl, no more than eighteen. The man was actually a young boy, also no more than a teenager. His clothes were ragged, his sneakers worn. The unkemp hair atop his head was streaked with blonde. His face was pale, almost ashen, his eyes puffy and distant. He did not even hear Gian approach, for his sobs were constant. The young woman at his feet was pale and almost lifeless. He held her head in his lap. Her clothes were worn, a dark top barely covered her stomach, and a butterfly tattoo could be seen on her stomach in all of its brilliant color. Her blue jeans were faded and she wore sandals that seemed a little too big for her feet. This young man's sobs echoed in the distance heard by no one who would dare help, in an urban city where pain was so familiar, no one listened. No one cared.

This young girl had the pale complexion of a fallen angel, her face filled with pain, her lips almost gray. Sensing his approach, the sobbing ceased and the young man looked up at Gian with gray eyes and stared almost through Gian. Gian was thrust into a world he barely recognized. It was so unusually quiet on the normally chaotic streets of a dying part of this great city. The moon's light was forceful as the stars hid in its brilliance, and clouds were approaching. It seemed as if these three souls were alone in the universe, alone but together, and together they would travel through a world that had resulted in this tragedy. Gian wondered how two young people could find themselves here, so alone, one of them fighting for her young life.

Gian knelt down beside this young man and reached out to grasp this young girl's hand to feel her pulse, when it began. Gian glimpsed two small children crying in a small, cluttered apartment, as a disheveled mother was led away in handcuffs. The young boy and girl cried out for their mother. He could see them each sobbing in their beds in various group homes and foster homes, sometimes together, mostly apart. The silent sobs of children forgotten, lives lost in a system where some cared, but others did not. He could hear their cries for help. He witnessed their loneliness and isolation. When they were together these two clung to each other, because each of them saw the other as their only hope. He could feel the young girl's spiraling descent into a world of smoking, alcohol, and finally, drugs. She was losing a battle, losing her only lifeline, her only bloodline, her only family, her only friend: her twin brother. The last time they had been together at a court hearing lawyers argued in a room next door—young lawyers plodding through the motions of caring, but nothing more. The system was broken, and everyone knew it, but no one cared enough to change it, no one.

This time the young man had decided to run with his sister, to run away together, for he could see that she could not survive another group home; she would never see her eighteenth birthday. So they ran, and it was so easy for them to run away—too easy. No one really looked for them. The lawyers just moved on to the next case after filing their reports into a backlogged system of failures, just a few more sheets of paper to store in buildings filled with broken dreams, forgotten promises, and failure.

Gian could see these two homeless souls, searching in a desperate city for food, friendship, and for any sign that things were about to change for the better. Their clothes became even more worn. They carried their meager possessions in backpacks as they traveled. Hiding in the shadows, spending rare nights in shelters but mostly on the streets or in abandoned buildings, for fear of being caught and returned to a system where their tattered lives would almost certainly be destroyed. Anything was better than a group home; they knew it. Anything was better than a foster home for them, too old to be given a fair chance with the few in the system who truly cared, too old to find a home.

Gian felt their despair. One of them clung to the hope of a better future. He could still see the faint light of a real future; the other seemed trapped in darkness. They were arguing in front of an abandoned home this very evening, he pleading with his sister to leave, pleading with her to come away with him again. He knew that if she entered that home with the little money that she had, she would get high again. She had been sober till now.

"Please don't go in there, sis', please, don't. If you do, I'll lose even you, and you are all I have. You've made it this far, please not tonight. Give me one more night, and maybe, just maybe, you'll see."

Trembling, pale, and distraught, the young girl exclaimed, "You don't get it, do you? I'm dying, we're dying, and I need this to survive. I need this."

"You'll die if you go in there, I just know it."

"I died years ago," she replied quietly. "No one will miss me."

"I'll miss you. You are all that I have. Please, don't go. If you die, I'll die with you."

"Look, I'm not going to die. I'd never leave you; I just need some help." She grabbed his arm and shook him with all her might. In his weakened condition, he stumbled and fell onto the cold pavement and struck his head and collapsed. At first she tried to awaken him, with tears streaming down her face. She checked his pulse, and she waited for some sign that he would be all right. She sobbed until he began to move his legs and his arms again, until he opened his eyes a bit, and then she left. She left him there, she thought, for just a short time. She left him to escape again. She desperately needed to escape, just one more time.

Moments later she fled the building, calling out for her brother before collapsing there on the sidewalk. The young man ran to his sister, picked her up in his arms, and carried her to the place where Gian found them. He laid her down, too weak to carry her anymore, too weak to help her again, too weak to run for help. As she lay there dying, no one noticed. They were two more nameless, faceless tragedies in a city filled with tragedy. At first he held her in his arms on that sidewalk and prayed, prayed for the first time in years. He prayed aloud until he was too weak to hold her, too weak to pray, and that is when Gian found them on that cold sidewalk, forgotten and lost in a forgotten part of the city. He held both of their hands there on the cold city sidewalk, three people alone, who had traveled so far. They had traveled so far apart this night; they had traveled so far to find themselves here. Gian had tears in his eyes as he gazed upon this human tragedy, as he found myself lost within it, too lost to speak. He knelt down again beside the fallen child and placed her head within her hands as he brushed away her hair from her innocent young face. He held her there like her mother should have, and called out for help.

"I have no one now, no one," was the faint whisper heard from the mouth of a brother whose love seemed not enough, whose strength was not enough to save his sister.

"One day," Gian began, "so long ago, your sister made a choice to take a path so many choose to follow, a downhill path toward this end. The further down the path you travel, the harder the uphill climb to a different life becomes, but it is never impossible to turn around at any point before the end is reached. So many are here to help her up, but only she could have stopped to turn around, only she can make that choice to stop and turn around."

"I am alone," came the weakened response.

"You are not alone," Gian replied. "I am here with you. You prayed and we found each other, and together we can carry your sister home."

A few moments later, the forgotten angel in Gian's arms opened her eyes and began to cough and then to vomit onto the pavement below. Gian struggled to lift her up, and with her brother's aid, the two of them were able to raise her to her feet. Supported by their combined strength, they stood and then began to walk down the empty street, uphill, toward the stars. Gian did not even know their names, for names did not seem to matter now. Together those three, would hopefully triumph where two had failed before.

Within seconds a taxi seemingly appeared out of nowhere. Taxis were seldom seen on these streets, especially at that hour, but there it was beside them, and out came a turbaned, rather dark-skinned young man to assist them. He was wearing light, loose fitting clothing with sandals on his feet, and he had the energy that they so desperately needed.

"I found you, you see, I found you," were the accented words that rambled forth as he approached.

"Do you know us?" Gian asked, frightened that perhaps he had recognized him.

"No, no, no," he replied, "not really. I just knew that I had to come here tonight. I knew that I could help. I could hear you calling me." The stranger paused as he stood there, just staring at the three of them.

"Come on, get in. I'll take you to the hospital," the man continued, as he helped them carry the young lady into the back seat of the cab, and her brother quickly sat next to her.

"We have no money," Gian simply stated, standing there on the street, as the cab driver closed the back door.

"You sir, you sit in the front seat with me. I don't need any money."

Minutes later they arrived at the hospital emergency room, and the Good Samaritan jumped out to get a guard's assistance to help place the girl onto a stretcher. Once inside, Gian explained to the receptionist that Gerard's Place would pay for any and all treatment that was necessary. Gian also explained that the two were indeed residents at Gerard's Place, and once they were well, they would return to live there again. He handed the woman an official card for the residence.

"Sir," the middle-aged woman replied, "these two are mere teenagers, and I have to report them to the appropriate authorities."

With that, the young man reached into his pocket and out of a worn wallet came forth two photo IDs showing them both to be eighteen years old today. They were both eighteen years old just that morning.

"Fine, then," was the response, "I will do as you ask."

"Just call Gerard's Place when you are ready to come home," Gian stated to his new friend as he wrote down the name, address, and phone number on a sheet of paper and handed it to him. "When you call, just tell them that Gian sent you, and if need be, you could both stay in my apartment for now, and for as long as you both need."

"Thank you," came the weak reply from a young man on his birthday. With that, a nurse asked him to sit down on a wheelchair, for he too needed to be examined. She began to wheel him back in the emergency room when he suddenly arose and ran toward Gian and embraced him with all of the strength that he could muster.

"Thank you, Gian," he sobbed into Gian's ear, "thank you for helping me and my sister. Thank you for allowing us to believe again." With that, he let go, and walked toward the wheelchair and sat down. Gian stood there in the lights of that emergency room filled with hope, renewed hope. He knew that this was a new beginning this evening, a new beginning for them all.

"Where are we to go now?" my taxi cab driver asked interrupting the silence.

"Did you ask me something, sir?" Gian questioned.

"Yes, I want to know where we are going now," he repeated.

"Why do you want to help me?"

"Because I must," was the quick response.

"But why? You don't even know me."

"Here is where I am right and you are not. I do know who you are. I have been looking for you for two days. I told her, my wife, that I would find you, and I did. It is God's planet, you know. It is His place for us to meet, and now I am here only to help."

Gian stood there in total disbelief at first, so grateful to this stranger, but fearful. He did not know whom to trust. If he did trust him, would he be putting his life in jeopardy by asking him to drive to St. Vincent's? What choice did he have?

"It is best for both of us if you leave now. You have helped me enough already. You helped save two lives tonight. Your work is done. Thank you."

"Oh, no, I will not leave you now. My life and yours are now one."

"You do not understand, kind sir. My life is in danger. I was almost killed tonight. I cannot allow you to place your life in jeopardy too."

"My life is now with you. God allowed me to find you, me, a lonely taxicab driver in a city of millions. It is His wish, and I am here to help."

"I do not think you understand."

"But I do understand. I knew that day when I saw you on TV. I told my wife that I would find you, and I would help you, and now here we are, and she will never believe me."

"That is so kind of you, but I cannot ask you to help me. I cannot."

"Please understand that I do this because I need to, just like what you are doing you need to do. I cannot explain it any better. English is hard for me."

"I understand."

"What is your name?"

"My name is not special: Gian."

"Everyone's name is special."

"My name in English is Hero. I like that name, so call me Hero, Gian, okay?"

"Okay, Hero."

"Now where are we going?"

Gian somehow knew that his new friend would not leave him, but he hated to ask for his help even one more time.

He would be putting this stranger's life in jeopardy, or maybe his own.

"People are trying to hurt me, Hero, and they don't care if they hurt you, too."

"I will not leave, sir, I cannot."

"Yes you can, everyone has a choice."

"You did not. God chose you, and now he choose me. So please let me help you."

"Okay, okay," Gian reluctantly agreed.

Hero responded with a great smile and tears welled up in his eyes. "Okay, then, let us go, for time, she is passing us by."

"What about your job?"

"Don't worry about my job, Gian. It is safe with you."

"Do you know where St. Vincent's Hospital is?"

This question seemed to shock the relative stranger: his eyes widened and he appeared saddened and amazed. Tears filled his eyes, and at first he could not speak.

"Is something wrong, Hero?"

"No, no, Gian. St. Vincent's Hospital is where we need to go, don't you see, so we will go." With that, he led the way to his taxi cab and once inside, Gian was finally on his way to Faith and Marc and his friends.

The clouds above seemed far away, as the moon's glow began to fade a bit in the late night sky. Once inside Gian gazed about the cab, and there in the front was a photo of the driver with his large family. The car exited the area in silence, each of the occupants apparently deep in thought. Gian was too preoccupied with what had happened, and with what was to come. The past few days had been filled with so much heartache and pain. He began to realize in that moment, with Hero at his side, that there are certain journeys in life that one has to make. He realized that some things in life are meant to happen, and afterwards, well, that is the choice one has. Does one try to do what one believes is the right thing, or does one turn and run away. Hero chose to stay.

As the taxi approached an isolated bridge ahead, a figure standing on its edge looking out over the water was apparent. As the car crossed over, this figure became clearer; a man was indeed out on the edge of the bridge in the darkness overlooking the large deep and mean river below it. The cab came to a screeching halt as the driver pulled to the side, and then turned off the engine, leaving the headlights on.

"Here is where you can be, Gian, you see. That is why I am here, too, to help you to help, now go."

"What?" Bewildered at first, Gian turned to face his newfound taxicab friend.

"You are a god man and that is why I help you, and that is why we here," was the simple reply.

"A what?" Gian could barely discern what Hero had called him, accented as it was.

"A god man," came the quick answer, "now go."

"What? Just because you believe me to be a good man, doesn't mean that you can leave me here in the middle of nowhere. I don't understand, I thought you were going to drive me to the hospital, please."

"Gian look outside, through the glass," Hero began, realizing that his passenger was unaware of the man on the ledge. "See, this is why we are here, right now, you are a man of God, Gian, please go and help, please go, for you are a god man."

Gian opened the taxicab door and got out into the quiet, rather dark night. He could hear the water rushing beneath, and could feel a cool breeze about his body, as he approached near where the stranger was. His clothes revealed that the figure was indeed a young man, his feet clad in white sneakers. He called out to him to stop as this young man continued his ascent out over the beams and cables that separated him from the fierce water far below.

"Stop, please stop!" he yelled up to him, fearful that he was only a few steps away from his untimely death.

This young man turned to face Gian briefly in the dimness, and the jumper's eyes widened and his lips trembled and his face became so pale in the moonlight, it was as if he had seen a ghost. At first he did not move; he did not speak, and his eyes glistened with tears as he stared down momentarily. For a moment, the Earth seemed to stand perfectly still. Even the rumblings of the turbulent water below ceased.

"No, no, not you. It can't be you," this young man uttered in disbelief as he continued to stare down toward the only other figure on that lonely bridge.

"It can't be you. It can't be," he repeated as he turned to look up at the night sky, and then again at the fierce river below.

"Yes, yes, it's me. It is me," Gian responded, not knowing exactly to whom he was speaking.

"Oh my God, it is you, it is really you. Why you? I just don't understand," the sad figure painfully sobbed in the quiet of an early morning.

"I am here to help you, you see. That is why I'm here."

"He helps," Hero replied as he exited the cab, a witness to this sad scene, "He only helps."

"You cannot help me anymore, not even you, not after what I've done, not now, not ever. I don't deserve your help."

"Everyone deserves a second chance; anyone can make a mistake."

"I don't deserve it," was the cold reply.

"I am here only because you do," Gian answered quietly. Stunned, the young man turned to face him for an extended period of time, as if he had been afraid to face him before, and his face became vaguely familiar, yet he could not place it. He was a man in his early twenties, no more, his clothes drenched in perspiration and covered with stains.

"They forced me to do it. I had no choice. They threatened to kill me if I didn't do it. Do you understand?"

"Whatever it is, I am here to help."

"I killed a man tonight, you know, and you…and you know that, you can't help me!" was the startling response. Gian stood there in silence, at a loss for words, shocked by what was so coldly stated.

"They said they would kill me and my family. I had no choice, but no one will believe me; no one can forgive me."

"If you come down, there is a chance for forgiveness, a chance to explain to your family why you did what you did, a chance to explain to the police what happened and to tell them who was really behind the murder."

"I tried to kill you," The young man sobbed.

Stunned, Gian could neither respond nor place the voice. He could not see this young man's face clearly.

"You see, no one can help me," he uttered before recommencing his climb to the top.

"No, please stop!" Gian screamed out as he pursued him, "I don't know who you are, please stop and turn around, so that I can see your face, please."

The distraught man stopped, and turned to face Gian, his frame lit by a nearby bridge light.

Gian finally recognized the face, a face that he had seen twice before, and he could not believe it. Hero was right. This was not a chance encounter, and Gian was confused. This was the man who had attacked him days earlier, until the vision changed his mind. The same young man who appeared out of nowhere and saved his life the next night, when he shot his attacker dead, there in the empty streets in front of Gerard's place.

"I killed a man, and I never done anything like that before."

"You saved my life."

"I killed a kid that I know, I killed him."

"I'm sorry."

"I don't know who I am anymore."

"I know that you need help. I know better than anyone else that you needed help along time ago, and no one came. I know that recently you came back to help me, and I am here to help you now."

"Really? Really man? You're not lying to me, are you?" Gian could see a young man there in the shadows, but his face and voice he recognized only from his vision, as that of the frightened little boy locked in a closet. Silence ensued as the turbulence of the waves below the dark bridge surged forward.

"I am here for one reason only. I didn't know it at first, but I am here to help you. Why else would I have come? I am here to hold your hand and help you down, to open that door that locks you in, the door that you helped open when you saved my life. You let the light into that dark closet. You let the light back into your soul. You chose life, and now there's hope. Without it, there is nothing."

The young man began to sob openly at the top of the bridge, and for a while his sobs were the only sounds present. After a few moments, he began his descent. Soon he grabbed hold of Gian's outstretched hand, and together they climbed down out of the darkness and into the light.

"Can you ever forgive me?" the shell of a man asked in anguish, as he slumped forward on this ice-cold bridge. Gian walked over to him and held him, whispering in his ear, "Yes, and now you must begin to forgive yourself."

Sirens in the distance were rapidly approaching and Gian knew that they must leave.

"I have to leave before the police arrive. Wait here for them, and tell them your story. I will help you."

In the stillness Gian and Hero departed into the taxicab toward their future. For a few moments there was only silence as Gian gazed into the sideview mirror as the police approached and apprehended the young man he had left behind. His road seem predestined, his path predetermined. He could only think of the future, of what lie ahead, for the past was nevermore.

"You see," the taxicab driver interrupted the silence. "You see, you were meant to come here tonight, Gian, and I was meant to bring you. You are a god man and I am your friend."

Gian gazed out about the streets before him, and saw the rare faces of humanity all about, leading a so-called normal life, unaware, and a part of him longed to be one of them.

"Did you not hear me, Gian," Hero began again. "Can't you see what a simple man like me can, that you were meant to be, you are meant to be."

They continued onward in silence. As they rapidly approached Gian's neighborhood they made their way to St. Vincent's.

"Gian, is something wrong?" Hero again tried to break the silence, as a new day began around them, and the Sun rose in the distance.

"You cannot change everything, Gian. You can only do what you can," he continued. "That is all you can do."

The cab driver could see a woman starting to walk across the street in the distance holding a child in each hand as she proceeded to cross. Once in the street, a car angrily turned the corner, and erratically veered to and fro at an incredible pace toward the poor woman and her children, now frozen in their tracks.

"Hero, you've got to stop that car."

Within a moment, the car came to an abrupt stop just in front of the stunned family. The out of control vehicle swerved toward the sidewalk, nearly missed the cab, and crashed into a street post nearby.

Hero ran out to check on the poor woman and her children there beside the curb. They were unharmed, and one of the children was crying. Gian remained in the vehicle staring out into space. He did not move at all.

The taxi driver then ran over to the vehicle whose front end had crashed into the steel post of the streetlight, and managed to open the car door and assist the driver out of the vehicle. The driver appeared unhurt, except for some bruises on his face from the deployed air bag. After a short time it became obvious that the driver was under the influence of alcohol.

Gian was startled by the touch of someone's hand upon his shoulder. It was Grace, a local woman who helped out at Gerard's Place as a volunteer. Gian recognized her immediately.

"Gian," she began tearfully, "Thank you for saving my life, and my children's lives," she continued despite the tears, "Thank you, be strong, we need you."

Sirens surrounded the area as Hero returned to the vehicle. "This is a night I'll never forget," he proclaimed as Gian gazed out at St. Gerard's Church, and its illuminated cross, as thoughts of more innocent times flooded his mind. Gian grabbed hold of Grace's hand before they departed, looked up into her grateful eyes, and smiled. He winked at the children before he had to let go.

It seemed like a lifetime had passed in just a few days. Overwhelmed, Gian continued to stare at a neighborhood that had become his home, only now he felt like a stranger, a total stranger.

"Is something wrong?" Hero questioned his passenger, sensing something amiss.

No response was forthcoming, not even a glance. Worried, Hero pulled over to the curb and stopped the cab.

"Gian, are you okay?" he asked of his new friend.

Two men appeared close by as they were walking along on the sidewalk in the quiet, early morning light. One of them quickly recognized the car's passenger and called out his name with palpable relief, startling the cab driver.

"Gian!" Bishop Lilli yelled out as he approached the passenger side of the vehicle. Hero jumped out of the cab, for he had recognized the two men from the TV News as the bishop and Father Thom.

"Sir," he began, "Please take my place, he needs you."

"Who are you, and what is wrong with Gian?" the bishop responded, somewhat alarmed that his friend had not responded to his name.

"I am Hero, a simple cab driver who try very hard to help, but I don't know, he is in shock."

"Did anything happen tonight? Is he hurt?"

"Ah, many things happened, strange and wonderful sad things, but no, he is not hurt."

"I see," the bishop responded, sensing the concern in this stranger's voice, and his innocence, "Don't worry, I can help."

Bishop Lilli entered the vehicle, and once inside he was shattered by the appearance of his good friend. Gian was unresponsive to his presence, his face pale and drawn, his eyes distant, and a slight beard was scattered about his face aging him more than his youth. He reached out to grasp his hand, and held it tight within his own, overcome by emotion; at first he could not even speak. He prayed for guidance and strength, and he prayed for Gian.

"Gian, my son," he began in a wavering voice, "for a while I thought you were dead, after the Pope called about the explosion, and for a while all of my hopes died, too. I am so happy to see you, and so thankful that God has kept you safe."

Gian remained unresponsive.

"The journey God asks of us," he almost whispered to his friend, "is never an easy one. It is one of sacrifice and sometimes pain."

Tears welled up in Gian's eyes in response, his sad and still distant eyes.

"You are not alone on this journey, my son, for I am with you and your friends and Faith, and thanks to the media most of the world is with you."

Gian turned to face his trusted friend and father and, finally, he returned the grasp of his friend's hand.

"And most of all," the bishop continued, "God is with you, and His family. If you search your soul you will see Him. You will feel Him. You will hear Him, my son, for He is always with you, always."

After a moment, Gian opened his lips to speak, and at first, no words were audible and then, finally he spoke.

"Thank you, Father."

Father Thom approached Bishop Lilli and spoke to him through the open window, whispering softly into his ear, "Yes, yes, you are right," was all one could hear as the sound of distant sirens neared.

"Gian," Bishop Lilli proclaimed, "We must leave at once. We will come with you to the hospital as your friend Hero has explained to us. You will need our help to enter the building, for the press surrounds it. Your friends await your arrival, my son."

With those words the Bishop exited the vehicle, as Hero resumed his seat behind the wheel, and Gian smiled when he saw his friend, and Hero couldn't help but smile in return. Father Thom and the bishop quickly entered in the rear, and within moments they began their journey to the hospital.

"Tonight," Hero proclaimed, finally breaking the silence as they approached the hospital, "Tonight is, is a...tonight is a maracle."

"A miracle?" Father Thom asked.

"Yes, yes, that too," Hero smiled.

"Go around back," Bishop Lilli began, "I used to come here often, and I know all of the security guards well. They are all my friends."

Swarms of news reporters encircled the building like bees around a hive, and yet no one seemed to notice the cab turn and head toward the rear of the building. Once there, Bishop Lilli and Hero exited the vehicle to speak to the security guard stationed there.

Father Thom's voice pierced the silence of the occupied cab, "Can you ever forgive me?" he began, his voice trembling, "For I cannot forgive myself."

Gian turned to face the distraught priest behind him, and smiled, "Dear father, you are stronger than you've ever been. I can feel it. God has forgiven you and so have I." Father Thom wept in response.

Hero approached the vehicle out of breath, "Come, Gian, please, you must come at once."

They quickly exited the cab and approached the back entrance to the hospital, where Bishop Lilli and the security guard stood. Suddenly a group of reporters appeared out of nowhere, and called out Bishop Lilli and Father Thom's names. Gian was thrust into the building, apparently undetected, and the security guard and Hero blocked their view, as the barrage of questions began.

Once safely inside Gian quickly disappeared into a nearby stairwell, and made his ascent alone. "God is with you. He is always with you," Monsignor Lilli's words echoed in his mind, and suddenly the darkness lifted that had surrounded this solitary figure upon his journey of discovery. He opened the door as the light poured in from the hospital floor ahead of him, and smiled, for he knew that he was not alone, and he knew that he would never be alone again.

CHAPTER 11

Gian quietly opened the door as he quickly entered each floor. He read the posted signs while he waited to find the adult intensive care unit. It was so early in the morning, few people were about, and finally, as he entered the fourth floor, the sign clearly read AICU with an arrow pointing to the right. He could not believe that he was there, and he quickly approached the doors to the ICU. A desk centrally located at that point had only one nurse at it, and she was busy on the phone, unaware of his passing. Gian glanced quickly through the narrow glass panels of each ICU door, hoping to find his friend. The fourth room was his, for when he gazed inward, he could plainly see him there, so silently he entered Marc's room and closed the door. He had finally arrived.

Gian could hear the sounds of his friend's heartbeat on the monitor beside him, and a part of him was afraid to bear witness to this tragedy. He could hear the machines and the blips of his friend's heartbeat about the room. He turned and found his friend Marc on a lonely bed—his savior, in this small, dark room surrounded by machines and attached to IVs. No one was there with him, no one. He was alone in his battle for life, his head bandaged, his eyelids black and blue. He appeared so lifeless there alone on the bed that Gian could not feel his presence. Gian could always sense Marc around Gerard's Place; his soul was large and all encompassing. He could not sense it here. He could not find it here. He was too late to talk to his friend. He was too late.

Tears welled up in his eyes, making it even more difficult to see, there in the glimpses of sunlight that barely entered on this early morning. He walked forward ever so slowly and sat down near his bed. He gently grasped his friend's hand in his own, hoping for a sign. None came. He stood up and bent over his body and grasped his friend's shoulders with his hands as tears flowed down his cheeks, and silently fell upon the dark floor below, but there was no response. Marc did not open his eyes. He did not move a muscle. Gian could not even reach for his hand and hold it. He was too late. He began to question why this would happen. How could this have happened to such a good and selfless man who had overcome so much adversity in his life? He had suffered so, and yet overcome so much.

Gian could sense that his friend had disappeared, and he felt so terribly alone, so very alone. He sat back down on that cold chair beside his trusted friend and disappeared; he had become invisible, as if he no longer existed. He was suddenly a little boy again, crying alone in his old bedroom, holding a picture of his beloved dog, Ocean, in his hand, and here is where his confusion began.

The door to his old bedroom suddenly opened. Gian was a young boy, alone, crying over the loss of his best friend, Ocean. He looked up, and one could see that sorrow had permeated his soul. Devastated at the loss of his best friend, his constant companion. He felt as if a part of him had died that day, too. The door opened again and this time his mom walked in, and, seeing her son there, her heart was broken. His mom sat on his bed and pulled the sad little boy up onto her lap and held him so tight, as only she could. There is nothing that heals better than the caring arms of a loving parent.

She began to speak to him in her soft, reassuring voice, "Where there is life, there is always hope, Gian," she began. "Where there is life, there is always hope," she repeated before kissing him upon his forehead.

"I love you, my beautiful son, Gian," she began again, "because you care so much, because you love so much. You love with your whole heart and nothing less. I am so blessed to have you as my son, and Ocean was blessed to have you as a friend. Let us both pray together. Let us pray our special, simple prayer. "Dear God, light my path, so that I may see Your way more clearly."" The lost little boy could hear his mom recite a prayer he had long since forgotten. He could hear her voice so clearly. He could sense her strength and her belief in God, and sense the conviction in her impassioned plea.

She placed her young son on a chair nearby, and gazed upon him with her loving eyes, only now Gian was fully grown, no longer a child, but an adult who for a while was just as lost and alone and sad as the little boy on that fateful day oh so very long ago. Her hand reached out to clasp his, as Gian began to recite the prayer his mother had just retaught him. "Dear God, light my path, so that I may see Your way more clearly."

Startled at the sounds of machines overhead, Gian opened his eyes to find Marc there by his side, his hand still clutching his friend's, his body just as lifeless.

"You said that you would protect me, Marc, and you did. But I failed to protect you. You risked everything for me, everything. And all I can say is thank you, my friend. I love you. And remember always what I had forgotten, where there is life, there is hope. And I pray and I hope now that life will bless you with its presence."

Remarkably, Gian felt a presence there in that room, a presence that he had not felt before and the room itself appeared more alive, more bright, and he almost cried out when he felt his friend's hand firmly in his, tighten within his grasp. He immediately looked upon his good friend's face, and there he could finally see that his eyes were open. He closed his eyes, fearing this was all but a dream, but he could still feel his friend's grip tighten around his outstretched hand. Gian reopened his eyes, and with tears flowing, there in the miracle of that moment, he stood up to see that Marc was indeed awake, and that this was not a dream. In that moment Marc attempted to smile and then to speak, setting off a series of alarms. He managed to say his friend's name, "Gian," before he closed his eyes again, and Gian stood there sobbing. Two nurses hurried into the room, and were shocked by the sight before them.

"Oh my God!" one of them screamed out, "My God, look, his eyes are open and he is moving. They said he was nearly brain dead." The other nurse rapidly approached the bedside and encountering Gian there, screamed out, "Who are you!? What are you doing here? How did you get in here?" She proceeded to push him out of her way, to tend to her patient, but not before continuing her angry assault. "If you do not answer me immediately, I will call for security at once. Do you hear me?" Overcome by it all, Gian was finally able to mumble in response, "He opened his eyes, he held my hand."

"That is it!" the angry nurse yelled out. "I am calling security at once. You'll just have to explain it all to them." She proceeded to rush out of the room, and Gian quickly followed, fearing that if security responded he would never find Faith, but not before he glanced back at his dear friend, Marc. Gian's tearful eyes met his, and Marc managed to utter his friend's name aloud, taking the one nurse still present in the room by surprise. "Gian," Marc coughed out, "Gian, thank you."

The remaining nurse, with tears flowing down her cheeks, exclaimed, "Gian!" in response as she made the sign of the cross before he closed the door behind him. The other nurse was on the phone with hospital security, as Gian raced out into the corridor in a desperate attempt to escape before they arrived. Thankfully, the hallway was empty, for his mind was filled with the joyful words of his dear friend, Marc, as he raced for safety.

The elevator at the end of the corridor arrived with a ring, and the voices of men inside on walkie-talkies, security men, could plainly be heard from behind the closed doors. Gian quickly dashed into the nearest room and quietly closed the door behind him. He could hear the sound of footsteps rush past and down the corridor, and he breathed again at last, at least for the moment.

The sunlight of a new day was beginning to filter in all around. Gian stood there frozen behind the closed hospital door, immersed in thought and deep reflection at what had just occurred. A part of him needed to jump up and down in joy, but he couldn't. His heart was still so heavy and his soul ached. The Sun seemed to catch up to his face as it rose blinding him in its radiance. Before him he could plainly see the face of a pale little angel lying on a bed. An innocent angel, a child appeared, and at first he thought her a dream. Her thin and fragile face contained a glimpse of heaven. She was just old enough to ride on a merry-go-round. Gian remained transfixed by the mere sight of her. How could such a small angel be here alone?

He approached the bed, and he could see the IV fluids at her side. He could see the oxygen tubing in her nose, upon her pale and perspired face. Her closed dark eyes spoke of a doll she could not hold, a picture she could not see.

Suddenly, voices from just outside the door awakened him from his trance, and shook him back into reality. He ran to hide behind a partially drawn curtain just beyond the bed, as the door opened, and he could hear the footsteps of a few people as they entered the room. He was, in this moment, so unbelievably vulnerable again, and so he prayed for strength and guidance, and he prayed for the little angel at his side.

"I don't understand how this could have happened," a sobbing woman's voice broke the silence, her English a bit difficult to understand. "For a few hours you said she was cured and now this."

"The antibiotic seemed to be working, and then, well, she seemed to worsen," a man's voice responded in a subdued tone, "You know that we are doing all we can for her, and now we must wait."

"But my little girl has only hours to live. Look, she is not strong enough to open her eyes or speak anymore. She is barely breathing. She is dying." Overt sobbing was overheard on this early morning on this incredible day, but no one seemed to be listening.

"Please let us go outside and wait for your husband," the doctor continued, "I need to speak to him." Gian could hear the door to the room open and close, and from outside he could hear a police officer identify himself and ask if they had seen a man there in a photo that morning. They quickly responded in the negative and it was quiet once again.

Gian emerged from behind the curtain, and he could hear the labored respirations of his bedridden angel. As he approached her bedside, he could not take his eyes off of her. She was so beautiful and so small, he thought, so very young to die, too young to suffer so much.

He reached out to grab her fragile hand, and then sat down beside her in a chair by her bed. He whispered, "Angel, angel, please angel," almost incoherently, as he closed his eyes to sleep. "I am your angel," he managed to say before he drifted away, before he could feel this little angel return his grasp.

The door to this hospital room opened, and three figures entered into its early morning light, three figures frozen by the sight they beheld. The little girl was awake in her bed; her hand still in a sleeping stranger's beside her in a chair."

"Mom, Dad," she began in her pleasant little girl voice full of energy and hope, "Shh, you'll wake him, my angel." Sobs filled the room in response as the three gently approached the bed, and marveled at the little girl, and pondered the pale sleeping male figure at her side.

"Who?" the girl's mother was finally able to whisper in response.

"He said he was my angel, mom, my angel, my very own angel."

Finally the father who had been unable to speak spoke a word he had been struggling to say, "Gian."

"Gian?" the other doctor repeated almost in disbelief that this pale, thin, bearded, disheveled man before him was indeed the young man the whole world seemed to be searching for.

"Yes, it is him," the girl's father continued as tears fell upon his cheeks, "He is my god man," Hero spoke as his wife ran to her little girl's side and hugged and kissed her.

"Mommy why are you crying?" her daughter asked, arousing her sleeping angel by her side as all eyes focused upon him.

Gian opened his tired eyelids and searched the room quickly in alternating worry and wonder, after a short while he spoke, "Hero," was all he could say.

"I told my wife," Hero began fighting back the tears, "That I would find you; I told her that you were a man of God. I knew that I had to find you, I just knew."

"Oh my God in heaven," Hero's wife began, "It is really you, that man from television, the man of miracles. Oh my God, you were right. You were right all along, thank God you found him, thank God."

Overhearing the commotion, a security guard burst forth into the room, almost knocking down the doctor before him as he entered. Once inside, he surveyed the room, and quickly set his gaze upon Gian. "You!" he shouted, as he spoke into his radio to call for backup. Hero suddenly subdued the security officer and yelled out, "Go! Gian go!" he continued, "And may God be with you." The doctor in the room also helped to restrain the guard as Gian quickly made his way to the door.

"Thank you," a joyful mom spoke.

"Good-bye Angel," her daughter interrupted her and spoke, just as her angel closed the door behind him.

Once in the corridor Gian ran toward the exit door and froze when he found it locked. He struggled to open it and it finally yielded as he raced down a flight of stairs and opened the door on the flight below panting for air. He surveyed the empty corridor before him and found a door marked "Chapel" on his right. He immediately rushed toward it and disappeared quietly into it, hoping to find a safe haven, a place to collect his thoughts and pray for guidance.

Once inside, He stood in the back of the small chapel, lit only by the sunlight streaming through the elaborate cross window near the altar. His eyes gradually adjusted, and he could see the figure of a woman ahead, standing in front of the altar unaware of his entrance. He stood there in silence for a few moments as he studied this young woman from behind. Her hair was as brilliant as Faith's, her body as beautiful. "Could it be her?" he wondered or was his tired mind playing tricks? He could not help but whisper one word from his lips to break the silence, "Faith."

The young woman partially lifted up her head in response and slightly turned, and then again bowed down in prayer. "It was not her," he thought. It wasn't her. Gian stood there, unable to speak and then he felt that he had to speak, only this time in a stronger voice. This time he would risk everything to know for sure if God had led him to his beloved Faith.

"Faith," he began again, "I am so sorry for all of the pain that I have caused you, and all of the worry, can you ever forgive me?"

The young woman nervously stood there at first, and then she slowly turned, and there before her eyes he stood, her Gian, just a shadow of the young man that she so deeply loved, and Gian could plainly see his love, his beautiful Faith, at last. She stood there in the radiance of the early morning Sun behind her, as if she were an angel. Their eyes filled with tears, in the shadow of an altar that contained a statue of Mary holding her crucified son, as the glow from the cross window illuminated the chapel so brightly.

Neither one of them could speak in that moment. Neither one of them could believe the sight each beheld, for at last they had found each other. They had finally found each other at last. It seemed as if they had not seen each other in forever. At times each of them had wondered if they would ever see the other again, and here, at last they each stood, just a few feet from one another, in God's little house, alone at last.

Gian walked slowly at first up the aisle, and then walked faster toward his Faith, stopping just inches away from her. He stared into her beautiful eyes and gazed upon her incredible face. The world around them appeared to stand still. It was quiet, so quiet that it almost seemed like no one else existed. Gian reached up with his hands to feel her hair and to touch her face, and he began to wipe away her tears as they silently fell down her incredible cheeks. "My angel," he thought, "is really here. This isn't a dream, this is real."

His face drew nearer to hers as if drawn by a force all of its own. His lips touched hers in that moment, and they kissed like never before. A kiss where two bodies became one, where two lost souls unite at last. Neither one of them wanted it to end, but when it did, Gian took his beloved into his arms and held her so close that he could feel her heart pounding inside her chest, and she could feel his. He let go long enough to look into her face once again, and he kissed her in the incredible sunlight that encircled them, and he worried that if he stopped, if he spoke, this moment would be lost forever.

In these moments together, they each realized how far the other had come, how much had changed. They each realized how fortunate they were to be alive, and how thankful they were to have found each other again. In those moments together, their love for each other grew stronger. Together they knew that they would always be, for no one could ever stand in their way.

Faith's angelic voice broke the silence at last. "I love you, Gian," she spoke ever so softly, and with such emotion her voice seemed to almost sing, "I prayed so much for this moment. I prayed to see you again, to touch you again, and my prayers have been answered."

"I am so sorry, Faith, so sorry for not telling you everything, so sorry for everything that has happened to you. I am so very sorry Faith, my dear, beautiful, innocent Faith. I am so very sorry."

Gian realized in that moment that their relationship had changed. He realized for the first time that their lives had been altered forever. They were never to be as innocent as they were before, life would never be as innocent as it once was. Both of them had grown up so much in the past few days. Both of them had changed. The life they would now lead was not the one they had planned for so long together. Their lives were never to be the same again.

"You don't have any reason to be sorry, Gian," Faith quietly but sadly responded.

"I love you, Faith, but I'm so worried. I don't understand what is happening to me, and I am afraid, so afraid. Sometimes I wish I could go back, and life would be normal again, but I cannot. I am so afraid, Faith, so afraid for you."

Faith could not help but to stare at her love, for he was almost unrecognizable. His face was tragically pale, his eyes only a fraction as bright, his body frail, but his spirit seemed stronger than ever.

"These past few days, Gian, have taught me so much. How fragile our lives are, how precious our time together is. It taught me how all of us, Pablo and Marc and everyone at St. Gerard's, are inseparable, all part of a bigger whole. Together we can be strong enough, only together."

"Oh but Faith, if only I could change—" Gian began, but Faith immediately interrupted.

"Gian, I wouldn't change anything about you. I wouldn't want to change anything that has ever happened to you in your life, for it has made you the man that you are today. People are beginning to see in you what I have known since the very first day that I met you, what I have felt since that very first day. Your life has made you who you are. These past few days have changed us both, and we are stronger because of it. I love you, Gian, for the boy that you were, for the young man that you are, and for the man that you will become."

At first Gian was too overwhelmed to respond, too overcome. He suddenly realized what he needed to do, what he desperately needed to say. He stepped back ever so slightly and began to undo the gold chain that he wore around his neck. Behind the crucifix hung objects that he had placed there days earlier. A gold ring that his mother had given him. He removed the gold ring from his chain and stood there, facing his beautiful Faith upon the glorious altar in God's house illuminated by His warm Sun. His eyes began to well with tears, and his voice trembled a bit as he began to speak.

"I wasn't truly alive until I met you, Faith. You are my heart. You are my soul. You are my life."

He proceeded to kneel down upon one knee before her, and before God, in that quiet little chapel on this miraculous morning. It felt like the two of them had suddenly traveled to a place where only true love can enter, that very special place where time stands still, and the Sun never sets on an endless, incredible summer day. He gently took her left hand in his, as he gazed into her incredible eyes.

"My grandmother gave my mom a very special gift before she died, and my mother gave it to me. She told me of this great love my grandfather and my grandmother had for one another, and she hoped and prayed that someday I would find a love as strong, and that I would give this special ring to her to wear forever." He paused as he began to slip his grandmother's ring onto her finger.

"I love you, Faith, and I will always love you. I cannot imagine living my life without you. Will you marry me, Faith? Will you marry me forever?"

Faith's eyes met his and her face never looked so radiant. She gazed downward and her trembling right hand reached out to touch his cheek. "Yes, Gian, I will marry you, forever."

Gian immediately stood and gathered her up into his arms, and then he kissed her, in a kiss that seemed to unite their two separate souls into one. The sunlight filtered in around them, surrounding them in its glow, enveloping them in its warmth, seemingly protecting God's house from any evil.

The chapel door burst open. The two of them immediately turned to look in fear behind them.

"Oh, there you are Faith," the familiar voice of their friend Pablo exclaimed as he ran into the chapel. "Gian, is that..." and within seconds he tripped over his own feet, stumbled over the last pew and went head over heels into the pew itself. Gian and Faith both scrambled to the rear of the chapel, and by the time they arrived, Pablo was again on his feet, rubbing his tousled hair as it fell scattered about his head. His face was aglow, and a broad smile formed across it.

Gian seemed to see his friend for the first time in a new light. His face still resembled that of a child's, but he was grown up, and in the past few days their friendship had turned into a brotherhood. He felt a new bond with Pablo. He never knew what it was like to have a brother growing up, but now he finally knew, for the two of them had formed a bond that transcended friendship, a bond of true brotherhood. Gian was so happy to see him standing there in all of his clumsy innocence, that he forgot that Pablo had just interrupted the most important moment of his life. A part of him was so happy to see his friend; the part that needed to share this joyous moment.

Overwhelmed by the mere sight of his friends together, Pablo could not contain himself as he thrust himself forward in his friend's Gian's direction, tripping over his sneaker laces, and landing right into his arms. "Damn," he uttered as he fell forward. Gian quickly helped to place him back into the upright position almost laughing, for Faith had been laughing for some time.

Pablo leaned forward to bear hug his friend and yelled out, "I'm so glad you are all right!" His bright blue eyes glistened with the advent of tears. His voice trembled a bit, like a child's does when too excited for mere words.

"I prayed for you, Gian, to be all right, and to come home, so that we could be a family together." With that, Faith joined the two of them in an embrace. The three of them were a family, together.

Moments later, as they stood there at the rear of the chapel, Pablo began, in a rushed voice as if he were only five years old, "It all makes sense. I ran in here to tell Faith that Marc had made a complete recovery, and here you are. Marc is weak, but he is talking, and the doctors are very optimistic."

"Oh my God," Faith exclaimed, "That's the best news," she paused overwhelmed by emotion, holding back tears. "A few hours ago they were talking about brain damage and permanent placement in a home…"

"Faith, he is fine," Pablo interrupted. "Our prayers are answered. He's fine."

Pablo paused to gaze upon his dear friend and then smile as she reciprocated. He continued, "And a little girl down the hall, a very sick little girl, is suddenly better, too. She is talking of angels and the entire hospital is talking of miracles, and then I find you." He spoke as he turned to face Gian.

"Then this is a day of miracles," Faith interjected. "There have been so many miracles today."

"Yeah, ain't it funny that a man was there with Marc and with the little girl," he paused. "I should have known, Gian, that it was you."

"I didn't," Gian began clumsily, "I really didn't."

"Oh sure, sure," Pablo retorted, "there must be another young man dressed like you walking around this place performing miracles."

"I do not perform miracles, Pablo."

"Yeah, yeah, you just happen to be there when miracles happen, right?"

"Yeah, that's it," he replied anxiously, "You're right."

"Does it matter?" Faith interrupted, "Does it matter how the miracles happened. What's most important is that they have. Marc is better and that little girl and her family, and we're all together again, like a family, and…and, oh Pablo, Gian just asked me to marry him and I said yes."

"What!" Pablo exclaimed as his head jerked back and forth between the two of them, as if reassuring himself that this indeed was no joke.

"See," Faith exclaimed, pointing to her ring.

"And I want you to be my best man, brother," Gian quietly asked Pablo.

Pablo turned toward him, his boyish face overcome by joy, and he suddenly bear hugged him, almost knocking him over. "Sure, bro', I'd, I'd love to be your best man." Quickly he turned toward Faith, whose tears were flowing upon her blouse, and within seconds he held his sister in his arms, picking her up off the floor at times, screaming, "Congratulations, sis'!"

"Together forever, we three," Faith explained, "we're family."

"Yep," Pablo responded as he let go of her and turned again toward Gian. "And what a crazy family we are, but what a great family."

They were both so happy that Pablo was there in that chapel to share this special moment with them, it seemed so perfect, until another figure entered the chapel from the rear, quietly at first, observing them, before finally speaking. For a few moments, the three of them seemed to have forgotten all of the danger they had left behind, for a few moments at least, they were happy.

"Gian, Faith, and Pablo," Bishop Lilli's voice echoed out toward them, as each of them seemed to startle and quickly turn around to face him. "It is so good to see you three together again," he continued as he walked toward them, "but I have news."

"What is it, father?" Gian began.

"Oh Gian, it is so good to see you reunited with your friends," he quietly stated before he grasped his hand firmly and continued. "But we must leave, and we must leave now."

"I don't understand," Faith pleaded, "But why?"

Distracted it seemed at first, he just smiled, "I could sense you were the one, Gian, even before the news came about Marc and Hero's girl, but now my dear children, we must leave, for this hospital is swarming with reporters, and police, and even the FBI. Come, I know a quick way out, but we must leave at once. Please believe me, we must go."

"Okay, father," Gian replied, "I understand, we're ready."

"Gian, here," the bishop paused handing him a small shopping bag. "I almost forgot; I brought you a change of clothes." Gian opened the bag and without a word, quickly entered a confessional to change.

"Are you sure we are going to make it out of here, father?" Faith quietly asked, her voice quivering with fear.

"I am not sure of anything, Faith, but I do know that God will guide us, just as He has before."

"I don't understand, father," Pablo innocently asked, "all Gian has done is good, all that he has said is good, so why then, why?" He couldn't seem to finish the question.

"Pablo," the bishop began in a tone similar to that of a teacher speaking to a small child, "Life is not as black and white as you think. The world doesn't always make sense. Religion, you see, is a very powerful force for good in the world, but also a very powerful evil. Gian is becoming powerful, and power threatens so many, and power can be so dangerous."

"I still don't understand, monsignor," Pablo again questioned. "Gian has only helped people, that's all. Where's the harm in that, father? Where?"

"Oh Pablo, my son, Jesus' words and deeds killed him, and Martin Luther King's words, and John the Baptist's deeds, and well, the innocent die every day, murdered sometimes only because of their innocence."

"I understand, father," Pablo responded in earnest. "I don't want to understand, but I do."

Gian emerged from the confessional as Faith ran up to hug him before the four of them quietly exited the chapel following Monsignor Lilli. Gian quickly turned again to face the altar before he quietly exited. He quickly turned to face the altar before he closed the door, just for a moment, just a moment to take a mental photograph of the place where he had asked his Faith to be his bride, a mental photograph so that he would never forget.

Once everyone was in the corridor Gian caught up to his friend Monsignor Lilli, and quietly they made their way down an open fire escape door. Pablo was the last to enter, and no one seemed to notice that he was stuck there, mumbling to himself at the top of the stairs. On the first landing there in the shadows Gian, and Faith with Monsignor Lilli close behind, encountered a security guard coming up the stairs toward them. He immediately pulled out a gun and grabbed hold of Gian, pointing the gun to his head. No one spoke. It happened so quickly. It was as if all of their hearts stopped beating at once, when suddenly they could hear Pablo jerk away from the door just up from them with such force that he fell down the steps in an instant, directly upon Gian's assailant, knocking the gun out of his hand, and amazingly, the security guard unconscious.

Pablo quickly got up and started apologizing, explaining that his shirt had gotten caught in the door, and the door opened from the outside, and that he had to rip his shirt to get loose, "And I'm so sorry, oh my God, I'm so sorry, did I hurt someone? Did I?"

Faith ran over to hug her little brother, and then everyone hugged Pablo, after they checked the body. "We have to go, come on, we must go!" he exclaimed.

"What?" Pablo asked. "We can't leave this man here like this?"

"Pablo, he tried to kill Gian. See this gun?" Faith bent down to retrieve the gun from the floor. "He had it pointed at Gian's head and, he was…," she could not continue.

"You saved my life, Pablo, probably all of our lives, my friend. If it wasn't for your incredible ability to cause total chaos out of nothing, I would be dead right now, you see, God works in mysterious ways, my brother, and I thank God for you."

"What? I don't believe it. He was going to…Oh my God, Gian, my God, Faith, what if I didn't…" Pablo could barely speak.

"We are all right, thanks to you, Pablo, "Faith now hugged him close, "Thanks to you."

"Please everyone, we must go, please," the monsignor begged them to follow him quietly down the stairs, which they did, down several staircases to an exit down at the bottom. Monsignor quietly opened the door and the blinding sunlight entered, as each of them nervously searched outside for anyone.

"Come on, follow me, quickly now," the good monsignor beckoned his friends forward toward a police car just outside the door. He opened the back door of the vehicle, and asked the three of them quietly to enter, quickly closed the door behind them, and then he entered the front of the vehicle.

"Let's go," the monsignor commanded, as he closed the door behind him.

The driver was the officer that had patrolled St. Gerard's and the local neighborhood on a regular basis for the past fifteen years. He was a very good friend of Monsignor Lilli's and most of the others, too. The police car took off in an instant, as the police radio alerted cars in the vicinity to the incident that had just taken place inside. They described the hired gun dressed as a phony security guard on the stairwell in possession of a stolen gun. They alerted every police officer to be on high alert, to check everyone's badges, and to report any suspicious activity.

"Is everyone all right?" the officer asked as the car continued on its way without apparent detection.

"Yes," Monsignor Lilli quickly responded, "we are all all right, and thanks to you, we will reach our destination."

"I don't understand, Gian," Pablo began, "how someone, a stranger, can take away a life, just like that. For what reason? Money? I just don't know."

"I don't understand it either, Pablo," he responded, "But maybe someday life will be cherished by everyone, and no one will ever take another's away."

"I love you two," Faith quietly declared. "I just needed to say it, and I needed to say it now."

The car stopped suddenly, and Gian could see that they were behind Reverend Martin's church. Gian and Faith both recognized it immediately. It seemed odd that they would be brought here to the very place where all of the chaos began, the very church where their lives had changed forever, and their innocence was lost on that rainy day, oh so few nights ago.

"I still don't know if this is the safest place for us," the monsignor began in a somewhat worried tone of voice, "But everywhere else is being watched, or is swarmed by reporters or police, and the Reverend Martin is inside, and he is expecting us, and he assured me that we would be safe for now. I pray that he is right." The monsignor then opened his door as the car stopped, and each of them quickly exited the vehicle with him, except for their officer friend, who stood guard. Within seconds they entered the rear of the church, and were quickly followed by officer Simon, their trusted driver and friend, after he had parked the vehicle safely away from the church.

"I think we are safe for now," Simon declared from behind them, "at least for now."

"I hope so," Faith responded. "We need a safe place. We need time to think, we need time."

"Gian," Monsignor Lilli called out suddenly, "Gian, do not be afraid, for God is all around you. He is with you."

Gian uttered "Thank you," before he was ushered further into the church, and the five of them began to trek toward the inner chapel sanctuary to encounter Reverend Martin.

As they entered, they were shocked to find Father Thom there, and Budd, Nancee, and Aimie, Faith's parents and Pablo's dad, and a couple of residents of Gerard's Place, including Bernadette. Overwhelmed, they each hugged each other in a rare moment of pure joy. The Reverend Martin with some of his family, soon joined in as well, as did a few of his congregants, and for a short while it seemed a glorious extended family reunion of sorts. Amid the chaos, Gian searched for Faith and she, it seemed, was searching for him. When their eyes met, it was as if no one else existed. No one else could be heard. Gian rushed to her, and they embraced there by the altar where it all began, Gian holding her close, as if he never wanted to let her go.

"You promised me, Gian," she whispered in his ear.

"I know, Faith," he replied, as he paused to stare into her beautiful eyes. "Forever, Faith," he continued.

"You promised me forever once, Gian, what seems like a long time ago, as we ran in the rain toward this very place," she recalled.

"We will always have each other, Faith."

"Forever."

"Forever."

"You promise," she whispered.

"I promise you forever," he replied, and they kissed there by the altar as the clamor around them finally ceased.

"I have an announcement to make," Pablo began, as everyone turned to face him, all of their friends, and their family.

"You see, Gian has asked Faith to marry him today, just an hour ago, in the hospital chapel." He paused as the assembly began to cry, and gasp, and finally applaud. "Wait, wait, I haven't told you the best part yet," Pablo yelled above the conversation. "I am to be their best man, a brother, and now a...a best man. I can't believe it."

Pablo's father ran up to hug his son as the entire group applauded in unison, and Aimie began, "You've grown up overnight." she concluded, as she interrupted Pablo's father, and congratulated Pablo herself with a brief kiss.

Pablo responded with a quick kiss on her lips, as the Reverend Martin now interrupted the festivities with a message of his own.

"Dear family and friends, I want you all to know that this is not a mere coincidence that we find ourselves here today, just as it was not a mere coincidence lo those nights ago when these two rain-soaked souls entered my small church to begin their journey. I dreamt of Gian's arrival. I waited for him, and prayed for him to come. None of that was by chance; none of this is either. Look around you and you will see all of the people, Faith and Gian, who love you. Now we find ourselves in God's house on this beautiful day with three, count us, three religious men, and we are told that Gian has asked his love, Faith, to marry him. And I ask you all, why can't we marry them today, here in this church, with all of you and, I know, God's blessings?"

Everyone was stunned and overjoyed by the announcement. "That is a wonderful idea, Reverend. Well, Faith, what do you think? I know a woman wants her wedding day to be special..." Gian began.

"This day couldn't be more special. Of course, I'd love to marry you today, Gian, it will be perfect." She paused though, and concern etched her face, "But I don't have a ring to place on your finger, Gian."

"Yes, you do," he replied as he removed another ring from the chain he wore around his neck. "This ring was my grandfather's, Faith," he stated to her and to everyone present, "And you are wearing my grandmother's. These rings were a testament to their love, and now they are a testament to ours, for I had them inscribed."

Faith removed her ring and tearfully read her inscription. "I will love you," she stated, as she continued reading once she had looked into Gian's ring, "Forever."

Faith kissed her fiancée at that moment as their family and friends applauded, and they knew then that this moment, this wedding, was meant to be.

"One more thing," Faith interrupted everyone, "I want to ask you, Nancee, to be my maid of honor. Do you accept?"

Nancee bounded out of the group, and ran up to the altar, and hugged her friend tight, before screaming "Yes!" in response.

Sensing all of this commotion, Officer Simon now reentered the building and approached Monsignor Lilli.

"What is going on here, father?" he asked.

"A joyous event, my friend, Faith and Gian are going to be married here today, but I am glad that you have come, for you must perform one more special deed for me today, and only you can do it, with God's help."

"What is it monsignor?" he replied in earnest, "For I will do anything to help you and Gian."

"You are such a brave man, such a good friend," the monsignor exclaimed as he proceeded to sit down.

"You are so weak, monsignor, you look so pale. Are you sure you are all right?"

"Yes, Simon, I am just old, that's all." He paused to catch his breath as the officer sat down next to him. He fumbled in his pocket for an envelope and proceeded to hand it to the officer.

"You must take this letter to the Pope, at the cardinal's residence. It is imperative that he read it and respond. It is too dangerous to call him, and I am sure that the residence is surrounded. You are the only one who could enter. Here, just show the brothers my rosary beads." He reached into another pocket to retrieve them and hand them to the officer, "And they will allow you an audience with the Pope."

"Remember," he continued after just a short pause, "you must give this letter only to the Pope."

"I understand, monsignor, and I will not let you down."

"I know," came the feeble reply, "But remember, you must wait there for a response, and come back as quickly as possible."

"I will, I promise you I will," the officer and friend replied and departed without anyone's knowledge but the monsignor's.

The Reverend Martin was preparing to speak again, and everyone quieted down to listen. "We all have a lot to do in such a short time. My congregants will escort you to the rear rooms, where there are wedding dresses, suits, and tuxedoes at your disposal. These are all gifts from our congregation to those less fortunate than themselves, and many wonderful people, have been married here in splendor, and now you two. Some of my fellow worshipers, please go out and buy some flowers and food and beverages for this great occasion, but be careful and be quick, and do not tell anyone about this, please, no one at all."

"I cannot believe this is happening," Faith's mom exclaimed. "I can't believe my little girl is going to be married here today."

"And soon we'll have a son too," Faith's dad added, "A son as special as our first son, Pablo. We welcome you to our family."

"We must start the preparations, please," Reverend Martin interrupted. "Time is so very short." The wedding party was escorted to the back rooms, and within minutes each of them had picked out that which each would wear for the event. It was a crazy kind of chaos at first, enough to make them all forget their troubles for a short while, a wonderful madness. For a few minutes, life appeared almost normal.

Inside of one of the back rooms Pablo and Gian found themselves alone. After finding tuxedoes that fit, they just sat down together. It was quiet there, and they needed some quiet.

"I did all I could that night," Pablo began nervously.

"What night?" Gian asked.

"I can't get it out of my mind, Gian. I have nightmares about it."

"What, Pablo? What night?" he asked concerned and confused.

"The night we were attacked; I struggled to get free, but I don't think I tried hard enough," Pablo quietly and emotionally continued. "I was afraid, I was so afraid. I saw him punch you and punch you again and again, and I couldn't do anything. I was too afraid to do anything."

Gian walked over to his friend now, and placed his hand on his shoulder.

"I am so sorry, Gian," Pablo barely spoke those words before standing up to face Gian.

Gian took Pablo's hand and placed it on his body and instructed him to feel for any scars. "Do you feel any stab wound, Pablo? Do you see any scars? You did all you could that night, and so did I. I was powerless to help you and Faith, too. I could still see her face, so frightened she was, her mouth covered."

Gian paused and looked into his little brother's frightened eyes. "It was meant to be, Pablo, neither one of us could have stopped it. You could have been killed. By some miracle, I'm fine; we're all fine and happy. Happy to be here, happy to be alive, so happy to be marrying Faith, and so happy that you are my best man, my best friend, and my brother. And remember always that I owe you my life."

"And I owe you mine," Pablo answered.

Faith found them there, hugging each other when she entered the room, and joined in the hug.

"We've been through so much together, and we have so much more ahead of us; together we are strong, and we can get through this," she added.

"Well, it helps that wonder boy over here seems to be bulletproof," Pablo smiled at Gian then winked.

"You're wrong, I'm only knifeproof," he retorted as the three of them laughed or else they would have to cry. None of them were prepared for what had happened, and none of them could be prepared for what was to come. Gian could hear Budd calling for them to come into the other room. They each walked out, knowing that they could not take anything for granted anymore.

Once inside another back room that Budd had beckoned them into, they found Reverend Martin, Bishop Lilli, and Officer Simon there. The monsignor was holding a letter in his trembling hands.

All of them entered cautiously, nervously looking at their friend. "Sit down," the good monsignor instructed them. "This letter is from the Pope. He opens by thanking God for keeping you safe, and he believes that we are indeed safe here for now. He has sent some extra security personnel to guard and watch the premises from the outside. He writes that he will pick up you and Faith, Gian, and whomever else need come, tomorrow night, for he has made special arrangements to travel to the Vatican tomorrow night. He feels that for now, the Vatican is the safest place for you and for everyone you love. He ends the letter by asking you, Gian, to pray for him, as he prays for us, and his last words are, 'May God's will be done.'"

"The wedding is on," Pablo began," and then we're off to the Vatican."

"I cannot believe," Faith began, "that the Pope is asking us to pray for him."

"We are all connected, my dear Faith," the monsignor responded. "We are all brothers and sisters, sons and daughters of one ever-loving God, and our dear shepherd, our fragile father, needs our prayers, too. We must pray for peace and understanding, compassion and love, for if we pray for all of these, then pain will only be found in history books."

"You are right, father," Faith replied and then kissed him on his forehead. "I am going to get ready now. I love you all," she declared as she exited.

Gian asked to go to the chapel to pray and some of his friends followed. They knelt there in front of the altar and prayed. Gian prayed for his dear friend, the Pope, and he prayed like he had never done before. He looked around and found that he was indeed so fortunate to have a family such as this. He had thought he was alone in the world, oh so very long ago, when he had arrived here, just a child, it seems now, a lost child looking for a home, and now he had found it, here today. Home, he was finally at home, and he could feel his mother nearby, and he could sense that she was smiling, for she knew it, too. Her son had finally found his home.

CHAPTER 12

The chapel was transformed. There were lit candles at every pew and scattered about the altar, and several assortments of beautiful colored flowers decorated the room throughout. It smelled like a beautiful summer garden, the perfect place for a wedding. Everyone had worked so hard to make this day a special one. A serene tranquility seemed to fill the air, a sense of joy and peace.

Gian was dressed in a black tuxedo, as was Pablo. Budd managed to find a blue jacket, bow tie, and shirt that fit, although they were snug. He looked great, nonetheless. A small group had gathered, both friends and family alike, to celebrate a new beginning, a new life together for Gian and Faith.

Reverend Martin, dressed in his handsome wedding attire, entered, followed quickly by Monsignor Lilli and Father Thom. The good reverend approached each man present at the altar, and gave each a great bear hug before shaking his hand.

"I was honored by your presence in my church that rainy night what seems like a lifetime ago, "he began, "And I will be honored to marry you two here in my church today."

"I am grateful, reverend," Gian responded, "so grateful to you and your family, we both are, and for all you have done for us. I can only say thank you."

"There is no need to thank me, Gian, for we all must thank the Lord for making this possible," he replied, whereupon he began his ascent to the altar where he joined the other two who would help him unite them both in holy Matrimony. Monsignor Lilli was kneeling down on the altar, deep in prayer, and soon Father Thom knelt, too.

Faith's father entered, announcing to all that Faith was ready. Budd took his place at the organ, and he began to play the traditional wedding march. The entire church's congregation, small as it was, stood in response. Nancee entered first in a simple silk gown, her face beaming with joy. As the music played, she walked up the aisle, smiling, and graciously took her place near the altar.

Next, Faith entered arm in arm with her newly suited dad, and at first Gian could not see her, for the Sun shone so brightly upon them both that it was difficult to see her clearly. As the music continued, Faith began her walk up the aisle, and once she stepped out of the Sun's brilliance, all seemed to gasp at her radiant beauty. Gian could not take his eyes off of her, her brilliant hazel eyes and her incredible face still visible despite the small, transparent veil she wore. Her white dress was simple, yet elegant, and she wore it like a princess on the happiest day of her life. The faint sobs of the assembled congregation were audible, especially those of Faith's mom seated in the first pew. Gian's eyes were transfixed. For the moment, no one else existed. For him, this was a dream come true, this was heaven on Earth, a true sign of his love for Faith.

Faith approached the altar as she smiled through the tears of joy on her face. She could not believe how handsome Gian looked in his tuxedo. She thanked God, as she neared her fiancée, for everything that He had given her and especially for Gian. She could not imagine her life without him. Her mind raced through all of the joyful memories the past few years contained as she gazed into her beloved's eyes. To her this was a fairy tale; she was finally Cinderella.

Now at Gian's side in front of the altar, together they turned to face the religious trio, each glancing at the other with smiles that could light up the heavens on the darkest night. There were many tears of joy as the ceremony began. A rainbow of color seemed to encircle everyone. Everyone present felt truly blessed. Life was just beginning for this couple; it was indeed a rebirth. Two lives, joined as one; it was indeed a miracle.

Before the vows were exchanged, each of the religious men spoke in turn.

Father Thom began, "I am so truly, truly honored to be here today to share in this sacred event with all of you. I pray that these two souls soon to be joined together in holy matrimony, my friends, Faith and Gian, will enjoy a future filled with happiness and peace."

Reverend Martin then spoke, "It seems a lifetime ago that my doors opened here in God's house, on that rainy night, and the two of you walked in and sat down in those pews," pointing to the rear of the church, "with your clothes dripping wet and looking for shelter." He paused, at first seemingly unable to continue, as tears welled up in his pink eyes. "Gian and Faith, your love for each other was self-evident then, and it transformed us all on that incredible night. I know deep within my heart, deep within my soul that your love will become an example for generations to come. That true love can overcome any obstacle, that true love can survive any evil, that true love is eternal, and therefore, I wish for you both only that which God can give, peace and happiness, good health, and a life together forever in love, inseparable for eternity."

Monsignor Lilli was next to speak, but before he did, he approached both Gian and Faith and kissed them once on each cheek. His body seemed to tremble a bit as he did so, and then he shook the hands of Pablo and Budd and Faith's dad, and proceeded to kiss Nancee and Faith's mom. He was always the gentleman, always the superior officer, always in a class by himself. He returned to the altar with moist eyes and a joyful heart.

"Faith, I have known you since your baptism, and in your beautiful eyes on that joyous occasion, I could see your magnificent soul. Every day that you sing in our church, everyone there can see it, too. With your voice and through your songs and your kind and gentle manner, you give hope to the hopeless, and joy to all who have come to know you. Your life is a gift to all who are fortunate enough to have you as a friend." He paused and turned to Gian.

"Gian, from our very first encounter, I saw in you that which makes you so special. The fact that you cannot see it, or still cannot perceive it, contributes to your strength. For every joyous memory that you have given, for every miracle of hope that you have performed, for every word of wisdom that you have shared, for every tear that you have shed, you are a symbol of hope for us all. It is in your weakness that you are strong. It is in your innocence that you are brave. It is through your gentle touch, your chosen words, your quiet manner that you alone can alter the course of humanity as we know it." He paused again and looked lovingly upon the couple before him.

"Together today with God's blessing, you two will become a force for good stronger than any evil. Together you are most powerful." He paused again, looking up at the congregation present. "I wish for each of you, and I wish for both of you, that which you already have in abundance, an eternal love for one another that will last forever."

Monsignor Lilli paused, and then beckoned Pablo forward with a gesture of his arm, as he continued to speak. "A very special member of our family would like to come up, and share with you his very special gift, one that he has written for two very special people on this joyous occasion. Pablo, please come up and perform for us now."

Pablo awkwardly walked up to the altar and sat behind the organ. He did not speak, nor did he look upon any of those present as he did so. Maybe he could not. Everyone who knew him was so proud of him in that moment, and

Gian and especially Faith were, too. As he began to play, all eyes were upon him, all ears eager to listen to a gift from a brother to his sister and her new husband.

What finds you wherever you are
What holds you close when you are far
What guides you when you are alone
What sustains you when all is gone
What strengthens you when you are weak
What nurtures you from your very first breath
What binds you when you are apart
What fills you with its incredible heart
Love
And it is here today
Love
And it is here to stay
May it never leave
May it never fade
May you feel it
Always
At your side
For true love
Lasts forever
Love breathes for you when you cannot
Love cries for you when you will not
Love finds you when you are lost
Love forgives you at any cost
Love brings the sunlight in your darkest hour
Love brings the stars on your darkest night
Love embraces you when no one can
Love comforts you with an outstretched hand
Love warms your soul on your coldest day
Love touches your heart as only it may
Love knows when you are lost

And helps you find your way
For it is love
And love is here today
For it is love
And love is here to stay
May it never leave
May it never fade
May you feel it
Always
At your side
For true love lasts forever
Forever Gian
Forever Faith
Forever together
In love

Everyone was quiet, as Pablo finished the music at the end of his very special gift. Everyone present could feel the love this young man felt for these two, and in that moment, he shared it with the world. Pablo's dad stood up and began to applaud with tears of pride streaming down his face, and soon all present stood up and applauded with him. At that moment, on this special day, one could feel the presence of something few alive have ever felt. One could sense it fill the room at that very moment as Pablo proceeded toward Gian and Faith, it was there for all present to enjoy, an indescribable feeling, and just as quickly it was gone. Pablo hugged each of them before he took his place in the pew.

After a few verses from the Bible had been read—one by Nancee to her friends—it was time to exchange the wedding vows. Gian's grandmother's ring became his wife's, his grandfather's his own. As they each placed a ring on each other's finger, they shared their thoughts with the entire church family.

"Gian, I love you, and I will love you more each day, and I will never love you less."

"Faith, my Faith forever, I love you Faith, forever."

They kissed for the first time as husband and wife. Everyone there, all of their family, could share in a very sacred joy on this special day. One by one, Gian and Faith hugged and kissed each member of their family, and for a time the world's troubles seemed so far away. It seemed no evil could enter on this sacred day. That evening seemed to last forever. The food and beverages were served in the back of the chapel, and occasionally Budd would take to the organ for some music, and everyone would dance.

Near the end of the party, Monsignor Lilli called everyone to attention. "Everyone, everyone, my friends, please," he innocently pleaded with those present to listen. "God has blessed us all on this incredible day, and we shall be eternally grateful. May He now bless Faith and Gian and all of us present. May He guide us down life's path, help us on our journey, and never leave us." He paused, and looked over at Gian. "It is time to say goodnight to a beautiful day. May the joy of this day last forever in our hearts."

Reverend Martin approached the monsignor and began to speak. "Thank you for being here and thank you two," he gazed toward the newly married couple, "for allowing us into your family. My wife and I have prepared a room for you both, Gian and Faith, a special room in the rear usually reserved for those we marry here who do not have the money to stay elsewhere. It is your special room tonight, and do not fear for Officer Simon and Pablo and Budd and I will stand watch to keep you both safe."

Gian and Faith began to thank everyone present, and one by one they silently left. The reverend's wife then escorted the couple to a room, isolated from the rest, in the very back of the building. Within it, there was a large bedroom suite, lit with candles and lined with flowers. The newlyweds entered as Gian carried Faith in, and once alone, they became one in love. Two separate souls now united for eternity. They each knew that no matter what happened from this night on, they would always be together. They each knew it in their hearts. They saw it in each other's eyes, they felt it in each other's arms, and as they fell asleep in each other's embrace, they felt it even in their dreams.

CHAPTER 13

Faith awoke early the next morning. It was barely light outside when she quietly dressed so as not to make any noise. Once outside the room, she followed the scent of coffee into a small vestibule where she found Reverend Martin and Monsignor Lilli quietly talking to each other around a small table. The room resembled a small break room with a compact refrigerator, a tiny stove, a microwave and a television set. A few chairs were scattered about, and a couple of cupboards were on the wall next to a glass crucifix that sparkled in the sunlight of a new day. The two men were sipping coffee when she entered, and just as abruptly, their conversation ended. Monsignor Lilli arose from his chair and exclaimed, "Good morning, Faith! Have a seat," as he pulled another chair up to the table. "Why are you up so early, dear girl?" Reverend Martin poured a cup of coffee, and placed it in front of her as she sat.

"Good morning, Faith," he cheerfully stated, as they both now stared at their silent friend as she poured milk into her cup.

"Is something wrong, Faith?" the good monsignor again asked. This time concern was evident in his tone.

"Did something happen, Faith? Please, tell us," Reverend Martin queried her.

Faith just stared into her coffee cup, her eyes distant and deep in thought.

"Faith, please answer us, please tell us what's wrong," the usually quiet monsignor begged his friend.

"Oh, no, no," was the quick reply as Faith finally listened to her concerned friends' voice. "Oh, I am so sorry, fathers, I was just thinking, that's all."

"Are you sure you are all right? You can tell us anything, you know, anything at all, and it can't leave this room. Maybe we can help," the reverend responded as he reached out to touch her hand.

"No, really, yesterday was the most wonderful, the most beautiful, the most memorable twenty-four hours. It was more than I could have ever imagined. It was a dream come true, a fairy tale…" She could not finish as her thoughts seemed to overpower her. She raised her coffee mug to her lips to drink.

"Faith, I sense there's something you are not telling us. Something troubles you, my young friend; please, tell us what it is," her old friend asked.

"Oh, no, nothing monsignor, really. I think I'm just overwhelmed by it all, you know, with everything that has happened these past few days, and then yesterday, well, you know."

"Oh, yes, you both have been through a lot these past few days. Too much, I think, for two youngsters like yourselves—too much, too much for anyone," the good reverend repeated, as he lowered his eyes in thought.

"You and Gian are about to start a new life, Faith, and together you two will always be. You will be strong together," the reverend finished before praying for guidance.

"Oh, Faith, amidst the darkness," monsignor added, "Amidst the darkness there will always be light," he explained.

With that Reverend Martin's wife entered the room with two bags of groceries, and the two men immediately stood up to help.

"Good morning, Faith," she exclaimed, as she began to remove the groceries from the bags. "I'm going to be making breakfast soon."

"I am so lucky to have all of you in my life'" Faith said. "*We* are so lucky to have you in our lives, I mean."

"You don't have to thank us, believe me, we are all the lucky ones," the reverend's wife declared.

"I think I need to freshen up a bit," Faith announced as she stood up to leave.

"Oh, sure," the reverend's busy wife responded, "Surely go, but please come back soon for breakfast."

Faith began to make her exit when Monsignor Lilli whispered in her ear as she passed. "Are you sure you are all right?" he asked, still believing something amiss.

"You are such a wonderful man," she responded before making her exit into the hallway. Faith found her way into the chapel, and it was still so beautiful, she immediately sat down in the front pew and began to sob quietly. In the darkness of the pew behind her, someone was stirring, and Faith immediately quieted down. Pablo's head popped up, and after he rubbed his eyes and witnessed his dearest friend and sister before him, he immediately stood up and made his way toward her. Faith was relieved.

"Is anyone else here?" she asked as she surveyed the dark room about her.

"No," Pablo quickly responded. "Officer Simon is outside and Budd, well, he went out to buy more groceries." Arriving at his sister's side, he immediately sat down next to her. Faith could barely contain herself, for Pablo was and always would be her closest friend, her dearest confidante, and her crazy brother, all in one.

"I love you, Pablo," she began as she hugged her little brother. "Thank God for you, thank God you are here," she barely uttered before sobbing again in his arms. The two of them sat there, holding onto each other for a few minutes without even saying a word.

"Please tell me, Faith, what is wrong?" Pablo finally was able to ask when her sobbing ceased.

"Oh, Pablo," Faith began with her head still on his shoulder, "I am so worried, so worried about Gian. I don't understand what is happening to him, and I am so afraid, so very afraid, that something awful is going to happen, and I'll lose him forever," she paused for a second to catch her breath and then added, "Is that selfish of me, Pablo?"

"No, of course not, Faith," Pablo quietly stated the truth in his friend's ear.

"You don't understand, Pablo, a part of me wishes that none of this was happening, a part of me longs for a quiet and normal life with Gian. A part of me wants to wake up from this reality and leave it all behind. How is that not selfish?"

"It is human," Pablo responded. "You're just being human. You want what anyone would want in your situation, Faith. You could never be selfish."

"But how long will this last, Pablo, and what if something happened, and I were to lose Gian forever?"

At first Pablo didn't respond. He just stared at his worried sister for a short time, his blue eyes saddened by her heartbreaking words.

"Faith," he began quietly, "do you remember what I was like when we first met? I was alone. My dad loved me, but he's never around. I was so completely alone in a new place and I was afraid, so very afraid. Then I met you and we became friends and then family. When I had a problem, I spoke to you. When I couldn't sleep, I'd crawl into your bedroom window and sleep with you. My whole life changed because of you. But from that very first day I was worried,

worried that any day you might leave me, like...like my mother did. For the longest time I used to run up to your door or crawl into your window with my heart pounding, not knowing if you would be there, not knowing if you would still care. And then...and then I realized that I had to be grateful for you, every minute of every day that we did spend together. Because you never know what tomorrow will bring, and I knew no matter what, that we loved each other, and in our hearts we would always be together, one minute at a time, one day at a time. I thank God for you every day."

Faith, with tears in her eyes, was too emotional to speak at first, so she just reached out and hugged her little brother hard.

"When did you grow up, Pablo? When did you become such a great man, my little brother?" Faith finally whispered into his ear.

Faith and Pablo embraced for another minute in that chapel that very special morning. It was a moment neither one of them would ever forget. It was a moment shared, a memory made, a lesson learned. One must enjoy every minute of his or her life, for no one truly knows what lies ahead tomorrow.

"Hey, what is going on in here?" Budd exclaimed as he closed the back door to the church and laid the bags of groceries down on a pew. "I couldn't wake this guy up to help me, but here you two are now, like a couple of love birds."

They all began to laugh as Budd approached them and then congratulated Faith again, so happy was he to see her. "Why all the tears?" he asked as he wiped one away from her cheek.

"Just a brother-sister moment the day after a big event, that's all," Faith answered.

"Oh, I get it, growing up and all," he mumbled as he returned to pick up the groceries and then made his way to the small kitchen room. "Well, don't let me interrupt," he laughed as he left the room. Sitting there in the church as the Sun's early morning rays filled the room was a miracle in itself, the quiet before the storm.

"Pablo, you will always be a special part of my life, a special part of me forever," Faith said to her young brother.

"I know," Pablo responded as he grabbed hold of her hand. "I know that now Faith; we are all a family."

"We are more than a family, Pablo, we love each other even more. We care about each other more. Some families don't have that, but ours does. We are a heart family, together forever in love till death and beyond."

"You are definitely a poet, a great poet."

"When did you grow up to be such a special man, my little boy," Faith replied as she tousled his already tousled blonde mane.

A scream was let out in a room far away, a familiar voice, screaming a familiar name left all in the church in fear. They could hear Gian screaming for Faith as they rushed to his aid, so afraid for him. When they arrived, they found Gian sitting up in his bed, his eyes open wide, his face and body wet with perspiration as he screamed again and again, "Faith, no, God no, God no, Faith, Faith!" He sat there apparently unaware of anyone's presence. Seconds later, Monsignor Lilli and Reverend Martin entered with Budd nervously following behind.

"He's having a nightmare," Monsignor Lilli yelled. "He's still in his nightmare; he needs you, Faith, to wake him up."

Faith immediately sat on the bed and grabbed hold of Gian with all of her might as she spoke out, "Gian, I'm here. Gian, I'm here. I'll always be here, Gian. I'm so sorry that I left you alone, I'm so sorry. I'll never leave you alone again, never."

In that moment and with those words, the light in the room gradually reappeared, and the darkness faded. Gian could finally feel Faith's body next to his, hear her voice, and see her face. He couldn't remember what had frightened him so, but he did recall how dark it was, how very dark. He returned Faith's embrace and whispered in her ear how much he loved her.

The others departed quietly as he repeated those words over and over again, and then he held her close, and kissed her.

Neither of them could stop holding each other, kissing each other, loving each other. They loved each other that morning as if it were their last time together. They were completely lost in one another, as if no one else existed. Nothing else existed. They each wanted this time together to last forever.

Afterward they both fell asleep, locked in each other's arms. A sudden knocking on their bedroom door aroused them, and reality came knocking, unannounced and uninvited. The familiar voice of Monsignor Lilli gently called their names from behind the door. They each both quickly sat up in bed, and Faith was first to answer. Gian and Faith could hear him explain that they needed to join him in the kitchen, for there was something very important that he needed to discuss with them.

Faith turned to Gian and tried her best to convince him to go, for he seemed reluctant to leave at first. "We must shower and change. We have to go, Gian, we have to."

Reluctantly, Gian agreed. He knew she was right. A part of him never wanted to leave that room; a part of him knew he had to. He couldn't say anything in that moment. No mere words would ever be enough. He stood up and kissed his new wife, and then gathered up some clothes, and disappeared into the bathroom. In a few minutes he was done and Faith went in.

When Faith reentered the room, she seemed renewed, not just in dress but in spirit. She was so utterly beautiful. She came and sat down next to Gian on the bed and grabbed hold of his wrist.

"Are you all right, Gian?"

"I'm fine. I'll always be fine with you at my side."

"I didn't mean to leave you alone."

"It's not your fault, none of this is your fault."

"I need you, Gian."

"I need you, too, Faith." He spoke, but he couldn't take his eyes off of her.

"Faith, I am so sorry," he began, "So sorry for everything that has hurt you."

"Don't be sorry, Gian, don't ever be sorry. We are together, and we will continue this journey together."

"I don't think this will ever end," Gian sadly continued, "I thought that maybe, well…that maybe we were at the end of our journey, Faith, but…but that nightmare, well, I just don't think it will ever be over."

"Don't worry, Gian. Whatever happens, this is where I want to be, with you. We can get through anything together."

"Faith, I just wanted to live a normal life like other people you know? I just wanted to be normal. I wanted to buy a house, and maybe have some kids, with none of the bad stuff. It would've been great: no alcohol, no drugs, no missing dads. I just wanted to have a normal life."

"We can have a family Gian, and as long as we are together we'll be okay."

Gian just looked into Faith's eyes, and he could still see her innocence, her optimism, he could still feel her sincerity, but he was overcome by worry. "When I was little, I used to wish that when I blew out those birthday candles, my dad would come home, and we would be a family again. My mom wouldn't have had to work so hard and maybe, just maybe," He paused as tears formed in his eyes, "Well, maybe I, um…I feel like, um…maybe, if my mom didn't have to work so hard to help me through school, well…maybe she'd be alive today."

Faith was speechless, overwhelmed by pain, but she had to respond through her own tears; she needed to be strong.

"Gian, you are who you are because of everything you've seen, because of everything you've felt. You are the most kind, the most honest, the most compassionate man, and now the world is beginning to see that, too."

"You make me feel like somehow everything will be all right."

"It will be."

"These past few days I have seen so much, felt so much. I just hope that I will always do the right thing."

"Trust in God to guide you, trust in Him to guide us."

"You see? I just don't know what I'd do without you."

"Well you'll never have to worry about that."

"I pray that you are right."

"I am so sure of that, as I am that the Sun will rise again even after the worst storm, and that you'll wake up, even from your worst nightmare, and you'll see the Sun rise, just like you see it today."

"You are my sunlight, Faith."

"And you are mine, Gian."

"Faith, you make me feel like somehow everything is all going to be all right, somehow."

"Faith, Gian," Pablo's voice could be heard from behind the door. "Can you hear me?"

"Come in, Pablo," Faith replied. They both stood as Pablo opened the door and entered. They each hugged each other there in the large bedroom.

"I miss you both, you know," Pablo began. "We ate breakfast already—Budd, too. Lucky there's some left for you both," he awkwardly continued, as his eyes grew more pensive. "The fathers are waiting for you, you know. They're waiting."

"We know," Faith halfheartedly responded. "We know, Pablo."

"We are in this together, right?" Pablo questioned his sister. "Right? So let's go into the kitchen. Come on, you two, march!" They all nervously laughed out the door and into the hallway leading to the kitchenette. As they entered, Mrs. Martin warmly greeted them and immediately sat everyone down at the table, and began serving breakfast. They each drank the juice so quickly, that more was served, and then they devoured the toast and scrambled eggs. Eerily, no one spoke at all.

"What's wrong?" Gian began as he set his fork down. "It is only morning, the day is just beginning, so why so quiet?"

"We want you both to eat in peace," Reverend Martin responded. Gian's hunger quickly disappeared as he asked another next question. "Have you heard from…" he asked quietly, "From the Pope?"

"He hasn't called, if that's what you mean," came the answer.

"Wasn't the television on before?" Pablo questioned as he made his way toward the set. "That's why it is so quiet in here."

Reverend Martin tried his best to attract Pablo's attention as he continued toward the set, but to no avail, so he placed his foot out before him, and Pablo tripped over it, stumbling awkwardly to the floor below. Without missing a step, though, he picked himself up, and continued on his mission.

"Oh, I'm so sorry," Reverend Martin almost whispered.

"Don't fret, reverend, Pablo falls all the time," Faith joked.

"What?" Pablo questioned. "What did you just say? Oh, forget it, forget all of it." Distracted, he walked toward a chair in the corner of the room, and just sat down and sulked.

Faith and Gian finished as much as they could of breakfast, and thanked Mrs. Martin repeatedly for her hospitality. Budd reentered the room at that point with officer Simon.

"Hey, I'm glad to see that everyone is all right."

"Thanks to the both of you," Faith replied. "Thanks for staying last night. We appreciate it."

"Yeah, thanks, good buddy," Gian added.

"Don't worry yourselves about it," Budd replied. "A breakfast like this one was worth it." Everyone chuckled, and just as quickly the mood changed as Budd innocently continued. "So Gian, can you believe the Pope, huh buddy, saying mass today in an outdoor arena?"

"Oh, Budd, you must be mistaken," the good reverend quickly interrupted, gesturing him to be quiet.

"Oh, now I understand, boy do I," Pablo innocently spoke from his corner chair.

"Just turn on the TV, gents," Budd continued, completely oblivious of the reverend, "And see for yourselves."

Faith and Gian just looked at each other, too aware of the reality of it all to understand fully what everyone was trying to hide from them.

A male voice was heard first, and then everyone in the room could clearly see the news reporter on the screen. "This pope has repeatedly confounded all of us, and all precedents before him," he began describing the chaos behind him. "He has scheduled an outdoor mass, seemingly overnight, where he is supposed to make a very important announcement," turning to face the crowds waiting in line to enter. "As you can see, a white canopy has been erected already. Security forces are in place, and rain is expected—" With that, the set was turned off by Reverend Martin and a solemn silence took its place.

A silence ensued in which Gian reentered the world of his nightmare. He began to experience flashbacks; intense images flashed before his eyes. He could plainly see that dramatic white canopy all around. He could hear the fierce wind and rain. He could hear hundreds of voices chanting unintelligibly, but he couldn't respond. He was trapped in another reality, one all too real, all too overwhelming, and all too consuming. His heart pounded inside, as perspiration flowed from his face to his shirt below, and he began to tremble. He could not escape. His whole body began to shake, and he could barely hear Faith's voice.

"Gian, Gian, can you hear me?" she called out, her face fraught with worry as his body continued to tremble despite her desperate attempts to hold him in her arms. "Gian, please, come back to me, please," she sobbed as his body slowly responded to her pleas.

Once still in her arms, Gian could finally hear Faith's voice. He struggled to open his eyes to see her beautiful face, to stop her tears. He struggled to open them, and once opened, his eyes found hers, and her pleas ceased.

"Oh, thank you God," she exclaimed as she held him tightly in her arms, afraid to let go, afraid to move.

"I'm fine, Faith," Gian could barely speak, but he knew that he must reassure her that he was all right. "I'm fine," He finally spoke. Monsignor Lilli and Reverend Martin and Pablo all neared. Pablo grabbed hold of Faith's shoulder and she immediately stood. She leaned forward toward Pablo, and wrapped herself in her brother's arms.

"Gian, what happened?" His good friend Monsignor Lilli began in a fatherly tone. "Tell me, whatever it is, whatever just happened to you, please tell me, my son."

Everyone in the room turned to face him. All eyes were upon him in the silence, awaiting his response.

"Please tell us, Gian, please, for together we can handle the burden, we can help," Monsignor Lilli repeated.

"My boy," Reverend Martin began, "We are all here today because God wants us to be here with you; he wants us to help you, Gian. You must believe it, you must trust it."

"My brother," Pablo added in a mature voice, "Your family is here with you; we will always be here for you; you will never be alone again, never."

Gian still could not bring himself to tell them what he so vividly recalled from his nightmare. He wanted to keep them safe. He loved each of them too much to tell them.

"Gian," Faith began in a resilient tone, as she wiped away all signs of fear from her face and her voice as she continued. "I love you; everyone here loves you. Together we are stronger; together we can go forward. Together we can accomplish anything. You must believe in this; you must believe in us; you must trust in us."

Faith was right. Gian couldn't keep it to himself any longer.

"It was raining," he began quietly. "It was dark, so incredibly dark. I remember the howling winds. I was trapped in a storm. It was so hard to see." Gian closed his eyes in silence for a part of him still did not want to remember. Outside, a gentle rain began to fall.

"I remember hundreds of people, no—thousands, all around me. I begged them to allow me to pass. Some of them shouted at me, some grabbed me, and then I arrived under this huge white canopy. The pelting rain ceased, but the winds were tearing at our shelter and winning."

He paused again, afraid to continue, as he gazed out the kitchen window to witness the rainfall outside, and hit the pane with more force than before. He could not continue.

"Gian, please, my son," Monsignor Lilli begged. "We need to know, we need to help you. Please believe me when I tell you this. Please trust in me."

"I could hear shots," he continued reluctantly. "I could hear bullets being fired. Everyone gasped and then there was silence. An eerie silence, a cryptic silence before the panic began, before the truth was known. I gazed up upon the stage, and there upon it, high off the floor, was a banner, a large banner. It was white with a purple cross on it, and the word PEACE was above it in sky blue. I could not take my eyes off of it at first, for it contained such a simple message. I could hear voices below the symbol call out my name. Upon the stage I could see security men surrounding a figure on the ground. Some held weapons in their hands and peered nervously about the masses before them. Two of them were calling out to me. The crowd around me began to recognize me, and they too began to call my name. Amidst the pelting rain and the ravaging storm, after a hale of bullets had pierced the atmosphere, only my name was heard. Members of the crowd escorted me up to the stage, whereupon a security force surrounded me, and brought me slowly closer to the center of it all. 'He is asking for you,' one of the security men stated before making the sign of the cross. 'Who?' I asked him. The security force parted for me to see who was indeed requesting my presence, who was the target of that rage of bullets. As I approached, the security man responded, 'His Holiness, the Pope.' Upon a stretcher he laid, IV fluids were running in, and his body and head were bandaged, with stains of red upon them. He wore a neck brace above his ornate, splattered, purple and white attire, and his chest heaved up and down, more rapidly than it should. I fell to the floor and knelt down by his head. At first I could hear only the howls of the wind and the fierceness of the rain overhead. I could sense only darkness, feel only pain. It was as if all of the light in the world had faded, all the calm departed, the soul of our world seemed distant, for this simple man of peace, for this fragile man of hope, for this symbol of life and love and goodness and purity now lay there near me as his life flowed from him, and all of us present were witness to the tragedy."

Gian could not continue, as tears welled in his eyes, and he could feel Faith's gentle hand grasp his own, then he knew that he must.

"I was too late," he sobbed, "too late," No one present could answer. "It was so real, you all must believe me; this wasn't a dream. It was too real and that is all that I remember, nothing else. Oh my God almighty, that is all."

"Gian," Pablo's soothing innocence could be heard. "It is not too late; the Pope is alive. He is alive."

Gian turned toward Faith and within her eyes he could see his own. For the first time he knew that they connected on a different level than before. They did not need to speak, to sense each other's truth.

"We need to turn the television back on so that Gian can see that the Pope is all right," Budd plainly stated to the others.

"You're right, my son," Reverend Martin agreed. Everyone turned toward the set as Pablo turned it on, and all were relieved to see the male correspondent still talking calmly in front of the stage.

"Tens of thousands are gathered," he proclaimed, "in an unprecedented show of support for this religious leader and his power. A mass has begun behind me despite the ferocious weather. Security is tight as uniformed and plainclothes officers are present in large numbers. The world is watching this event unfold as I am joined by literally hundreds of cameramen and reporters." He paused. He seemed to be eliciting instructions from his director before announcing that he was turning to his colleague, Mary Luce, who was closer to the Pope.

"Speculation is high," the obviously weather-beaten young reporter began from inside the canopy as music played from the choir just behind her, "that the Pope will indeed announce a summit today involving almost every powerful religious leader in the world, a summit whose goal is reportedly one of unity of faith instead of division. A summit of hope, as it is called, by religious insiders, a summit of peace."

The music stopped, as did the news reporter's commentary, as the camera panned back to the podium, where a fragile Pope sat on an ornate chair upon a stage. His head bent down in prayer, it seemed, and deep in thought as those around him spoke in turn, recited responses from the crowd followed. The camera was focused on this fragile man of God, and the ravages of his long and pensive life were all too evident in the etchings of age upon his face.

What happened next took with it the very breath of everyone present in that small room, their concerted gazed fixed upon that small television screen. The camera panned back to reveal the full glory of this makeshift altar, and there, high above the participants, was a giant religious banner aflutter in the wind. It was white. It contained a large, purple cross and the word PEACE was evident. Gian turned toward his friends and each of them was motionless, almost frozen, as they stared at the picture before them, and it was then that he realized the truth. Everyone continued to face the television and watch as the Pope stood up in his purple and white robes, just as Gian had foreseen in his dreams.

Gian turned to face his family and friends in the room, and their faces reflected a blend of concern, fear, sadness, despair, and disbelief.

"My friends, my family," Gian began in a strong voice, as he turned to face each of his loved ones. "I love you all and trust you with my life, and you must love me enough, and trust me enough, to believe me when I tell you that I know that which I must do. I must trust in God to protect me and to guide me and keep me safe. We must act, and I need your help; please help me." He paused as he searched the room, and his soul, for answers. "Please help me to fulfill my dreams, so that my nightmare does not become reality."

Budd reentered the room at this point with Officer Simon, and all turned to face him, surprised, for no one had realized he left. Officer Simon spoke in a commanding voice, as if they were his troops and they were embarking on a wartime effort. "I will take you, Gian, in my police car to the mass, and within minutes we will arrive. I will protect you with the help of my comrades, so that you will always be safe."

"We must all leave," Budd interjected, "But only three of us can travel in the police car with you, Gian. The rest must come with me and follow in my car."

"I will go with you, Budd," Reverend Martin began. "Bishop Lilli will gain you entry into the stadium upon your arrival, and Faith and Pablo, well, you need to be together in this time of turmoil, in this test of faith."

They each hugged each other in silence, realizing how important it was for them to depart as quickly as possible. Gian kissed Faith, and arm in arm with Pablo they soon exited the building to the waiting police car, its lights already flashing. Monsignor Lilli sat up front, as the rest quickly climbed in the rear. Gian sat in the middle, protected by Faith on the one side and his brother Pablo on the other. They had all come so far as the sirens began their sad song, and they departed together that day. They had lived a lifetime in just a few days, and yet they were all still children there in the rear of that car, hands clasped for strength, so close to each other, like triplets in a womb.

A security team suddenly surrounded the car, as they neared the blockade around the perimeter of the event. Officer Simon quickly rolled down his window to confront several men surrounding the vehicle, some in full riot gear. He flashed his badge and began to yell, "We need to gain entry now!" he began. "I have Bishop Lilli here with me, and here is his ID. Please allow us entry."

"That is impossible at this point. Please exit this area immediately," came the reply.

"But you don't understand," Officer Simon continued. The rest of what he said Gian could not hear, for he knew what he must do, and so did Faith. She opened the rear door, and ran out, creating a commotion that instantly surrounded her with security forces. Gian shot out into the crowd from the rear seat of the car. A shot was fired, but he kept running.

"Hold your fire!" Officer Simon screamed in response. "Hold your fire! Stop! It's Gian! Gian from St. Gerard's church!"

"He is innocent, please don't shoot!" Bishop Lilli yelled out in fear.

A few moments later, a sharp tug on Gian's arm forced him to stop. He had been caught. He thought it was too late. He looked down as two hands grasped his arm so tight, that he could not remove them, but there beside him was an elderly, disheveled man whose eyes met his in fear and recognition. His face had seen the ravages of time, and upon it was etched an unkind tribute to old age. His clothes smelt of poverty as they clung to his skeletal frame. Gian could not take his eyes off of him.

"You, you," he began in an almost inaudibly frail voice amidst the chaos of weather in which they found themselves. "You are Gian," he paused, "Gian."

Gian could not believe that such a frail man could hold him there against his will, yet somehow he was his prisoner.

"Please," the old man continued in such a pitiful voice, "Please forgive me, Gian, for I abandoned my family oh so many years ago, and now look what I have become."

Gian could not move nor speak.

"Please forgive me, I beg you," he cried as his moist eyes met Gian's in the pouring rain, and all one could feel was sorrow.

"Gian, forgive me," he pleaded in an almost recognizable voice before mumbling, "Gian."

"I forgive you," Gian was finally able to reply. "God has forgiven you, and so do I. I forgive you, I do."

The old man let go of his arm in response, and lowered his head, as Gian continued upon his urgent journey.

"I am so proud of you, my son. I love you, Johnny boy."

With those words spoken, Gian stopped, and quickly turned to face the man whose voice he now recognized, the voice of his own father from a lifetime ago. No one else had ever called him Johnny boy but he, no one else, but the old man was gone. He searched the crowd for a sign of him, but he was not there. He screamed out, "I forgive you, father, I forgive you!" with such raw emotion that sorrow and pain and remembrance seemed to accent every syllable. Gian somehow knew that his father had heard him, and a part of him was healed in that moment. The little boy, who often wondered about his father and why he would have left him, was finally at peace.

Gian suddenly found himself very close to the front row, as he continued weaving through the crowd toward the stage. The rain was unrelenting overhead, and he could picture this now, this very moment, for he had been here before. Oh God, he thought. The moment was so familiar as he struggled closer to the altar, and then the shots began. And for a moment there was silence, before all within that canopy heard a gasp of breath. A rapid succession of gunfire began to destroy anyone and anything upon that podium, and the desperate screams arose from the crowd, as utter chaos ensued. Gian was only a couple of feet from the stairway to the altar, but he could not move in the crush of the frightened crowd. This time it was real.

He was too late, he thought, but suddenly police in SWAT gear surrounded him. One of them called out to him. "Gian, we are here to escort you to the Pope. Come quickly, for he is asking for you, and no one else."

The gunfire had ceased, and audible sobs filled the air amidst the terror. They began their ascent up the altar's steps, and there, surrounded by Special Forces, was a fallen hero. As the crowd parted for Gian to gain access, he could see this holy man lying on a stretcher, his head bandaged and bloodied, his garments torn. Oxygen was flowing from a cannula into his nose, and IV fluids were evident at his side. Gian ran to him with tears flowing down his face. The Pope's gentle eyes greeted Gian's, as he began to speak in words so familiar. "It is time my son for you to help me to see; it is time for you to help the world to see."

"But father," Gian began in a pleading voice, "I could not even save you."

"But you have, Gian," came the weakened reply. "I have gathered the world here today for you, my son. The whole world is watching and waiting for you. This is exactly how it had to be." With those words the pontiff closed his eyes as if to sleep, his respirations were labored, but his hand was still warm.

"Please, please someone help him!" Gian yelled.

"I am in God's hands now, my son, and so are you. Speak to His children now, Gian, for they are longing for you," the Pope managed to say before being taken away to safety.

Gian turned to face the crowd and as he approached the bullet-ridden podium, he could see only faces of fear, sheer panic, and total chaos. Security forces surrounded him but he asked them to leave, for he needed for the people to see him, to recognize him, to hear him call out to them. As Gian stood there, the masses quieted, and all eyes were indeed focused upon him. All cameras and mikes were centered on him. Monsignor Lilli and Faith and Pablo and Reverend Martin joined him there, as a chant of his name began feebly and then strengthened.

The crowd screamed out in horror as one of the Pope's own security forces pulled out his semiautomatic and aimed it at Gian's head. Shots were fired, and within seconds the assailant fell to the ground in a pool of blood. The crowd cheered as the man was carried away, and police and FBI agents quickly surrounded the altar. As Gian began to speak, the crowd quieted, and the force of the winds and pelting rain were all that could be heard.

"The Pope is alive," were the first words he spoke, and the worldwide audience cheered, some crossing themselves in tears, others audibly crying. During these precious few moments, Gian prayed for strength and guidance. He prayed for the courage to stand in a fallen hero's shoes, here upon this makeshift altar, and fulfill what he knew to be his destiny. He glanced toward Faith and her beautiful eyes met his, and together they knew they could face the world, always together. Monsignor Lilli grabbed hold of Gian's hand, and Faith followed, as the crowd hushed.

"He is here," Gian began again. "God is alive, and He is here with us today, for He is always here."

The uproar from the crowd concerned everyone on stage, for everyone was talking, some audibly crying, some screamed, and television news reporters addressed their respective audiences in English and other languages. A quiet chaos ensued.

"What is happening?" monsignor Lilli asked of his friend, Reverend Martin.

"A miracle, my brother," the reverend responded, "A miracle."

"But where is this miracle, my friend?" the monsignor inquired.

"This miracle is here with us, my good friend. We have been blessed by his many miracles already, and now the entire world is witness to him."

Gian began to search the crowd for answers, and he could plainly see the faces of each and every one of them. They made up the colors of the world, a rainbow of humanity. They seemed to encompass all of the ages of a lifetime. He could see the children beside the aged, the poor interspersed with the wealthy. He could see the sick and the disabled, the hopeful and the lost, and they could see him. In those moments the rain ceased, and the Sun appeared in all of its radiant glory and warmth. The atmosphere was painted an incredible blue, as if the angels themselves had worked on it. The sky appeared more beautiful than anyone had ever seen before, more brilliant and overwhelming. Through ripped orifices of the canopy above, and surrounded on all sides, the glory of nature was evident.

A television newswoman approached, standing just below the stage, as her cameraman panned up and around the stage. Others quickly followed. All on stage could plainly hear her address her television audience.

"We are here today to witness what has to be the most incredible, most important event of our lifetime. The entire world is watching and listening, I am told, from every radio and television screen and computer. A few moments ago, just a few simple words in English were heard throughout the world in almost every country in many different languages." The newswoman paused, as she seemed to choke back tears in order to continue. "The Sun is shining brightly, and reports from the world in the last few minutes confirm that the brilliance of the Sun or the moon in the sky above is unprecedented. The world seems aglow in the light of the heavens. There are no words to describe what is happening here, right now, except to say that this young man has the world's attention, and we are witnessing a miracle here, nothing short of a miracle."

"That is the miracle, Bishop Lilli," Reverend Martin continued to tell everyone gathered there on stage. "The miracle of faith, and hope, and life that Gian brings today to the world in God's name."

Gian stood there in the sunlight and his very presence seemed to change, it was as if someone else was there, someone the world had been waiting for.

Faith clasped his hand tighter as she spoke to him in her gentle tone. "I am here with you, Gian. Your friends are here, too, holding hands with you, and one by one the world will hold hands with you. This circle of strength begins with you, and you will never be alone again."

Gian gazed about at the loving faces of Reverend Martin, Monsignor Lilli, Pablo, and of course, Faith, and felt safe, renewed in spirit and hope, renewed by the love that surrounded him. In front of him an audience awaited, a worldwide audience, hypnotized by a man, a relatively simple man, who commanded their attention.

"I am but a simple messenger," He began in a commanding voice as he gazed out upon his brothers and sisters. "Look at me; I am just like you; I am one of you. I have seen your soul and it is pure. I have felt your pain and it is real. I have touched your heart and felt your love, and I have witnessed miracles and I believe!"

He paused and bowed his head before family, and God's family before him, as everyone began to pray, and some sang in the distance, before him, as many began to pray and sing in the silence.

"Strong messengers have come before me with simple messages of hope, of faith, of love. Their messages were pure of thought, so pure in spirit, so full of light." He paused as if saddened by these simple truths.

"Where is God?" an angry voice bellowed from the crowd, startling everyone.

"Why can't we listen to the simple truths, and believe that God is here? He is one of us; He is in each of us. He is all of us." Gian paused to reflect on the question so angrily asked, and the questioner, so lost.

"You must believe that God is alive, and that His presence is felt in every good…person here today.

He is in every good…soldier, who sacrifices his life for us."

He paused in reflection before continuing.

"He is here in every good…policeman, who protects us.

He is here in every good…fireman, who saves us.

He is here in every good…doctor, who heals us.

He is here in every good…religious leader, who guides us.

He is here in every good…political leader, who leads us.

He is here in every good…teacher, who instructs us.

And most importantly…

He is here in every good…mother, who loves us and nurtures us.

He is here in every good…father, who loves us, and guides us.

God is alive in everyone who performs his duties to the best of his abilities.

He is alive in every living creature on Earth.

He is alive in every innocent newborn."

"When I gaze into your eyes, I see a reflection of Him. He is alive in every smile, in every helping hand, in every healing word, in every heroic gesture, in every gift of charity, in every beautiful embrace."

"He is alive in all those that have finally seen the errors of their ways, and who work every day to rebuild their lives, once shattered by darkness, with His guidance, His love and forgiveness."

"Is this it?" the angry voice continued. "Is this all you have?" it taunted. "Is this it? All I hear are words; all I see is you. God is not here. He is nowhere."

A silence ensued at the end of the questions, and everyone gasped in disbelief as all witnessed their speaker close his eyes, as tears flowed down his pale cheeks.

Gradually, the brilliance of the Sun faded away. A cold darkness replaced the warm light, as children cried, a distant cry was heard in the harsh wind that replaced the quiet Sun. Audible sobs at first, and then prayers, replaced the tears of the innocent. A small star appeared above, at first so ordinary that on an average night, it would have been lost amongst the other stars. But tonight its light shone brighter with each passing moment, transilluminating the stage at first and then those present. The sky surrounding it was empty, devoid of life, save for its solitary presence. All eyes remained focused above, as one tiny light grew to offer those blinded by darkness, sight, a reminder to all those present that miracles do occur, but if one lives in darkness, if one's eyes are always closed, and one's ears don't listen, and one's heart is lost, a miracle can be lost, too. Many prayers were answered that night, for all could see the beauty of a simple star, a single star that embraced the world with hope, and kissed the Earth with life.

"In the darkness," Gian began again, "No one can see. In darkness lives fear. It is here that life is lost, and with it hope. So many live in darkness. So many cannot escape its power. Here in the darkness there is only death. We must all walk together toward the light. Some of us must carry the others at first, until they are finally able to walk alone."

As the Sun returned to the heavens, the tiny solitary star faded at its side, its power lost beside its neighbor, but all present would never forget its brilliance, when all seemed lost, and how one single solitary star illuminated a path within people's hearts, a path toward light, out of the darkness that had surrounded them.

"I am but a simple man, here before you. Look at me, a tiny solitary star; I am just like you. I am one of you."

Gian paused to gaze upon his brothers and sisters. He could feel hope reemerge and the love in humanity grow. For a moment, just a moment, the world was quiet, filled with the magic of life, and all were enjoying its beauty. For a moment there was true peace.

Gian then continued in a strengthened tone, "Can you see the end of the rainbow? Can you touch the colors of heaven? Can you hear the glory that is life everlasting? Can you experience the star of everlasting hope? Can you stand up and pray for the light that is peace? Pray for peace. Pray for life. Pray for hope. Just pray. Pray. Just believe. Believe." A sense of true peace ensued, the quiet calm of peace.

"Believe," Gian continued, "And you will always see the light. Trust, and you will always feel its warmth. Love, and you will see it grow. Pray and it will forgive your sins. If you believe, you will live forever."

Gian bowed his head to pray.

The next things he heard were the loud sounds of jet engines all about. Gian opened his eyes gradually to accommodate the light that flowed in through the small windows near his head. He realized then, fastened within a large seatbelt, that he was in some sort of jet, one that he did not recognize.

"I have a feeling that this is just the beginning of our journey," a familiar voice echoed nearby. Gian could hear all of the quiet voices of people that surrounded him, some whom he couldn't wait to see again. One of whom he couldn't wait to hold again.

"Welcome back, sleeping beauty!" Pablo exclaimed, as he was the first to see Gian struggle up out of his seat. Pablo hugged his brother hard, so hard that he helped to keep him erect, for Gian was still fatigued from his ordeal. Once Pablo let go, Faith approached from the rear of the plane, and Gian could not take his eyes off of her.

Reverend Martin interceded, "Welcome back, Gian," he tearfully whispered into his ear before he embraced him.

"Gian," Monsignor Lilli began, as Gian turned to face him, happy to see his good friend again, "You blacked out, and we had to carry you into the Pope's helicopter. The Pope wouldn't take off without you. Yes, Gian," seeing the concern on Gian's face he responded, "He is fine. All of his wounds were superficial, none were life threatening. And, Gian, here we all are on the Pope's private jet to your new home, the Vatican; you will be safe there my son." He embraced his friend like a father would his son after returning from war.

After Gian searched for Faith, and he found her angelic face, her loving eyes, he couldn't take his eyes off of her. The Sun's rays surrounded them as they slowly approached each other, and finally they kissed and then embraced within its warmth, as they traveled together into the daylight of another time.

"I want to see forever light in a sky that never darkens..." Gian began in a whisper.

Faith just held on tighter before tearily responding.

"Gian, hold on to me forever," she paused before continuing, "I cannot live without you, Gian."

"You'll never have to."

"You promised me forever, once."

"Forever, Faith, forever."

978-0-595-67008-6
0-595-67008-3

Printed in the United States
32438LVS00008B/10

9 780595 670086